CORONATION

Eileen Enwright Hodgetts

Eileen Enwright Hodgetts

This majority of characters in this novel are fictitious. Certain long-standing institutions, public figures and documented facts are mentioned, but the story itself is purely imaginary

Published by Emerge Publishing
ISBN: 978-1-7376070-4-5

The Hidden Jewels

No human eye had seen their birth. They had been formed before the coming of man, when all the world was new and life could not survive amid the crushing chaos of creation. Trapped in the cooling rocks of the newborn planet, they waited for the coming of the light that would reveal their beauty, and the hands that would shape and polish them into objects of wonder.

The stones, two sapphires, a ruby, and a diamond, had each traveled a long road to come at last to this place of ignominy, packed carelessly together in a crude container and hidden in the damp, wormy earth. They had in turn been spoils of war, gifts of love, and symbols of power, but for the moment, they were nothing, just stones packed away in a biscuit tin, their hiding place known only to one man.

CHAPTER ONE

February 12 1952
Redbridge Library
Surrey, England
Valerie Chaplin

Valerie Chaplin held her breath and shrank back into the shadows. She could hear the intruder's footsteps as he prowled among the stacks. He was currently in the sprawling adult fiction section of the library, but she doubted he was looking for some light bedtime reading. The library was closed. She had already locked the front door and extinguished the lights, and now the room was lit only by the twilight seeping in through the window in the children's section. She had been about to leave by the back door when she caught sight of a bulky shadow lurking beside the reference desk. She called out, of course.

"We're closed."

He moved, and she caught a quick glimpse of his face as he lunged toward her. He was a big man, pale-faced and unshaven. She had no time to read his expression, but his voice, a hissing whisper, told her all she needed to know.

"Valerie."

He spoke only her name, and yet he spoke with such menace that she bolted away from him, back into the labyrinth of shelves that she knew well and he knew not at all. She moved silently, but he blundered, and the noise of his blundering concealed her movement until she was able to retreat into the shadows in the far corner, where the shelves held the scatter of books by authors X, Y, and Z.

He called her name again. "Just a few questions, Valerie. Won't take long."

Did he have an accent? Was he German? No, that was her imagination. The war had been over for more than six years, and she knew as well as anyone else that not all villains were German and not all Germans were villains.

He spoke again. "Just tell me where to find him."

Definitely not German. In fact, he sounded like a Londoner. She almost spoke her question aloud. *Who do you want to find?*

She did not speak, but he told her anyway. "Come on, love, just tell me where to find Jeremy Paxton, and I'll leave you alone. There's no need for any of this."

Jeremy Paxton! She had not heard his name in eleven years. She had thought of him so often over the years, and always with a mixture of anger and regret and a fierce desire to know what had happened to him. Her body reacted to the name with a physical twinge of remembered pain. She fought down the desire to respond. *I don't know. No one knows. He's gone.*

She crept around the end of the fiction shelves, into the reference section, and slipped past the glass-fronted cabinets. The rear exit was just a short distance away now. He would hear her when she opened the back door, but she would be free to run from him. The old medieval town was laced with narrow alleys and lanes, and all she had to do was work her way into the center of town, where she would be among bright lights and Friday-evening shoppers.

"Valerie."

She froze. She had moved silently, but so had he, and now he was at the back door, and she could make out his movements. His arm was extended, his hand searching along the wall. Any moment now, he would encounter the light switch, and then it would be over. She would be caught like a moth in torchlight. What did he want with her? How did he know her name? She was not the librarian, only the clerk. Her name was not on the noticeboard outside. He had not come here to accost just any librarian; he had come for her and to ask about Jeremy.

Click!

The light blazed. She saw his dark eyes searching in the bright spaces between the stacks. She ducked behind a card catalog cabinet but not in time. His eyes had caught her movement. He took a step forward, but as he moved, she heard the sound of someone pounding on the back door.

He turned at once, taking his eyes from her and reaching into his pocket. Her heart seemed to rise into her throat. He had a weapon.

It was all over in a fraction of a second, with the muzzle flashes searing her eyes and the sharp double crack of pistol fire echoing in her ears. Her instincts, born of a lifetime of paranoid warnings from her father, sent her to the floor to roll into a fetal ball. She was a non-combatant; all she knew to do was to hide.

After a moment, she felt a hand on her shoulder. Once again someone spoke her name.

"Valerie, are you all right?"

She opened her eyes and looked up. The man towering over her had brown hair, brown eyes, and a neat brown mustache; even his suit was brown.

He extended a hand. "Can you stand?"

For a long moment, she was unable to move, or even reach out to grasp his hand. A lifetime of conditioning, of being told that sudden loud noises would be "the death of your father" had left her weak and trembling and still expecting to see her mother weeping and her father hiding behind the sofa. They were not there, of course. How could they be? She willed herself to sit upright. She was a woman of twenty eight , and she could not give in to the timid child who so often ruled her life and forced her to jump at every unexpected sound.

She reached up for the extended hand, but her inner child recoiled at the sight of blood dripping onto the exposed cuff of his shirt and pooling on the floor.

Her voice trembled. "You're wounded."

"It's nothing. Just a graze." His voice, with overtones of a private-school education, was dismissive and nonchalant.

He took a handkerchief from his pocket and wrapped it around his wrist, where it slowly turned red. He did not offer his hand again, and Valerie rose by herself and stood upright on wobbly legs.

The intruder was lying on his back in the second aisle of the nonfiction section. His eyes were wide and staring, and his chest, red with blood, did not rise and fall.

"He's dead," said the man with the bandaged hand. "Do you know who he was?"

"No."

"Are you quite sure?"

Valerie studied the still face and shook her head. There was nothing familiar about the shell of what had once been a man.

A gravelly London voice interrupted her thoughts. "Why was he here?"

The man who spoke still held a pistol in his hand. *Smoking gun*, Valerie thought irrelevantly, although the gun was not actually smoking. Did guns really smoke, or was it just a literary convention, like "being caught red-handed," or "what's good for the goose is good for the gander," or ...? She fought the urge to escape into the safety of rambling thoughts and anchored herself in the present moment. Why was the intruder here? That was the question, wasn't it? Why was he here? Why were these other men here, and how did they all know her name?

Her legs were no longer trembling, and her panic subsided, leaving room for her to act rationally. A man was dead on the floor of the library, and the police would have to be informed. She turned toward the front desk. "I'm going to call the police."

The man with the bloody hand caught hold of her shoulder. "No."

"You killed someone," Valerie replied, doing her best to break free.

His grip was tight and unbreakable. "It was kill or be killed."

"You can explain that to the police."

His grip tightened, and she felt the soft ooze of blood penetrating the thin fabric of her white blouse. "What do you think he would have done to you?" he asked.

"I don't know. I didn't get a chance to find out."

"He would have asked you the same questions we are about to ask you," her captor said, "but after you had answered him, he would have killed you."

"You don't know that."

"Yes, we do."

"But ..."

The man with the bleeding hand released her shoulder. "Go ahead. Call the police. I think you'll find that Smythe and I outrank anyone on duty at the Redbridge Police Station."

"Are you saying that you're police officers?"

"In a manner of speaking, yes, we are. I'm Alan Lestock, and the man with the gun is David Smythe, both seconded to the Metropolitan Police, and we'd like to talk to you and ask you a few questions."

"Why?"

"Perhaps we should sit down," Lestock suggested.

"I don't want to—"

"But I do," Lestock said.

"What he means," said Smythe, "is that he should sit down before he falls down on account of the fact that he's bleeding all over your nice clean blouse."

When they reached the head librarian's office, Lestock shrugged off his jacket and collapsed in a chair. Having ripped open Lestock's shirt sleeve, Smythe fished in his pocket and produced a large white handkerchief. He turned and winked at Valerie. "This is where you should tear a strip off your petticoat."

"Just take care of it," Lestock growled. "It's a scratch."

"Bit more than a scratch, but you won't die—unlike our friend over there, selecting a book to take to his grave."

Smythe proceeded to tear his handkerchief into strips and bandage the wound as Lestock spoke.

"Just to confirm," Lestock said, "you are Valerie Chaplin, who at one time resided at number twenty-nine Lambs Farm Road, Lower Redbridge."

"Before Herr Hitler demolished it," Smythe added.

"Yes," Valerie said, "that's who I am, and yes, our house was blown up." Her voice trembled as she fought the tears that always accompanied the memory. Her home had been destroyed in a ball of fire. Number twenty-nine Lambs Farm Road no longer existed. The loss of the house was a matter of record, but how could pen and ink record the horror of that moment?

Lestock seemed unaware of her distress as he continued speaking. "The bomb, in fact, failed to explode on impact, and you and your parents were evacuated. Is that correct?"

She could still see the terror on her father's face and feel her family's shame as the Civil Defence wardens strapped him to a gurney while the neighbors looked on.

Valerie glanced back at the dead body staring sightlessly at the ceiling and returned her gaze to Smythe, who was once again holding the pistol. "That all happened a long time ago," she said. "Why are you talking about it now, and why was that man here?"

"We'll come to that," Lestock said impatiently. "Let's just establish the facts. According to our records, a bomb-disposal squad was sent to your house to defuse the bomb under the command of Major Cardrew Hyde. They failed. Your house was blown up. Two men of the bomb squad were killed, and you wrote a letter of complaint to *The Times*—a letter they did not publish."

"It wasn't a letter of complaint," Valerie said. "I mean, I wasn't complaining about the explosion. I was complaining about the major's treatment of his squad."

"Non-combatants," Lestock said. "Conscientious objectors who would not handle a weapon."

Although Lestock's tone was neutral, Valerie felt a resurgence of the outrage that had driven her to write her so-called letter of complaint. "They were brave men who had the courage to stand up for what they believed; they weren't just human sacrifices."

The neighbors watched from a safe distance as the uniformed squad set up a barrier of sandbags. Valerie stood in the front garden of number forty-two, far enough away to escape the blast if anything went wrong, but close enough to see the men taking their shovels and sandbags from the back of their lorry and to hear their major's barked commands. The major was an old man with a ferocious white mustache. His tunic was adorned with medal ribbons, and he was armed with a swagger stick, which he used for pointing, hitting, gesticulating, and generally making his presence felt.

Ton Ferrers, fifteen years old and chafing at the bit to join the war, provided a running commentary. He had been deemed old enough to join the Home Guard, and now he presented himself as an authority figure for the neighbors who had been evacuated from their homes.

"Non-combatant squad," Tony said. "They're conchies. Too afraid to fight, so now they're digging up bombs. I bet they wish they hadn't registered as objectors. They'd be safer in the regular army."

Valerie had seen the bomb that had buried its nose into her mother's vegetable garden. She had edged past it during their traumatic evacuation and been close enough to read the numbers stenciled on its

12

casing.. She had done her civic duty and studied the bomb chart posted on the wall of the village hall. She knew this was a big one. If it blew, there would be very little left of her house or the houses on either side.

When the barrier of sandbags was in place, the major and most of the squad walked resolutely away, leaving only two men behind.

The major approached the gathered neighbors. "Won't be long now," he said encouragingly. He opened the gate and stepped into Mrs. Henderson's front garden. "Any chance of a cup of tea for me and the boys?"

Valerie heard Tony muttering under his breath. "What's the matter?" she asked.

"The officer is supposed to defuse the bomb," Tony said.

The major was old but certainly not deaf. He clapped a hand on Tony's shoulder. "Don't worry, sonny. They're conchies. They've made their choice. They'll take care of that bomb, one way or another."

The blood had soaked through Lestock's bandage and stained the arm of the chair he was sitting in. He seemed not to notice, or maybe not to care. His face, which may have been quite handsome in repose, was intent but not hostile.

"In accordance with wartime regulations, your letter was not published, and it was passed to the Security Service. Your complaint was deemed unpatriotic, and you were investigated."

"What do you mean?"

"You would not have been aware of it," Lestock said. "It was not an extensive investigation, just enough to know that you were a seventeen-year-old girl, known to be rather timid and reclusive but certainly not a security risk. Our investigators concluded that you had taken an interest in one of the men in the squad and maybe that was the reason for writing. You didn't want him exposed to any more danger. They did, however, continue to monitor and copy your correspondence until the end of the war."

"Wait a minute," Valerie said, dredging up the memory of her indignant seventeen-year-old self scratching out a furious letter. "Why would they investigate me? I didn't do anything, and I was not in any way involved with one of the squad. I wrote to register a serious complaint about the treatment of the conscientious objectors."

"Major Hyde's behavior was investigated," Lestock said. "He was an old-school officer. The officers in charge of the non-combatant units were all World War One veterans not fit enough to be sent to the front but still able to command. Unfortunately, they still commanded as they had in their war, sometimes treating the troops as cannon fodder. He should not have had command of a bomb-disposal unit—he didn't have the training or the temperament—but he was still needed, and he couldn't be relieved of duty. His company was given a new assignment, something where he was less likely to get people killed, but you know all about that, don't you?"

"How could I know that?"

"Through your friendship with Jeremy Paxton."

"I did not have a friendship with—"

"He wrote to you."

Valerie felt a shiver along her spine. What had happened? Why did anyone care about her relationship with Jeremy Paxton? How could any of this be happening? She felt violated by Lestock's words. She had written one angry letter, which *The Times* had not even published, and as a result, she had been under scrutiny. Her letters, those stupid lovesick scratchings, and Jeremy's equally embarrassing replies had been intercepted and studied, and somehow her stupidity from ten years ago had resulted in a man being shot to death in Redbridge Library. There was another possibility, of course. Maybe they had not stopped watching her when the war was over. Maybe she was still being watched. Maybe they knew about the other notes.

Lestock had described her as timid and reclusive. Well, she would not be timid and reclusive now in the face of this outrage. The best defense was a good offense, and she was offended. Apparently, modern Britain, where citizens felt free to express their opinions and vote according to their conscience, was really no better than the Soviet Union. How dare they spy on her? She was angry, really angry. She would write another letter to *The Times*. People needed to know about this.

She abruptly stopped her whirling thoughts and turned her anger on herself. She knew she would never write that letter. If she really meant what she said, she would be marching in the streets in any one of the rapidly growing protest movements, but she would never do that either. She would do nothing to draw attention to herself. She had secrets to keep.

Smythe broke the silence. "Can we just get on with this? Lestock's going to bleed to death if we don't get him stitched up, and we have to get this body out of here before morning."

"I am not going to bleed to death," Lestock said stiffly.

Smythe grunted. "That's a matter of opinion. You're messing up the upholstery, and questions will be asked."

Lestock nodded. "You're right. I'll make some phone calls."

"And what about her?" Smythe asked, indicating Valerie with a jerk of his head.

Lestock shook his head wearily, and when he looked at her, Valerie could see that the color had drained from his face. The bandage on his arm was now saturated with blood. "Miss Chaplin," he said, "do you know the man who broke in?"

"No."

"Do you know the whereabouts of Jeremy Michael Paxton, formerly of the British Non-Combatant Corps?"

"No."

Lestock staggered to his feet. "By the powers vested in me by the government of Her Majesty Queen Elizabeth II, I hereby charge you, under penalty of imprisonment, to speak to no one of what you have seen today."

"You can't do that," Valerie protested. "You don't have the authority. That's not even a legal charge."

Lestock swayed slightly as he spoke. "Under the emergency legislation for the protection of Her Majesty the queen and all matters pertaining to her coronation, I can lock you up and throw away the key, or I can simply ask you not to talk about what you've seen today. Which would you prefer?"

Valerie could not tear her eyes away from Lestock's challenging stare as she focused on his words. *The protection of Her Majesty the queen and all matters pertaining to her coronation.* What did he mean? There was not even a date for the coronation. The king had been dead for only a week; the new young queen had just flown home from Kenya. The king was still lying in state, awaiting his funeral. The heralds had blown their trumpets, and the words had been said—"The king is dead; long live the queen"—but surely it was too soon to talk of coronations. Throughout the country, flags were at half-mast; men wore mourning bands on their jacket sleeves, and all social events had been canceled.

The king's death had come as a surprise—he was only fifty-six years old—but apparently, someone had been prepared. Someone had already seconded these two men to protect the coronation, and somehow, protecting the coronation involved protecting Valerie, and asking questions about Jeremy Paxton.

"You realize that we are not here by coincidence," Lestock said. "Without us, you would be dead. I strongly suggest you do as I say."

Smythe's voice was a friendly whisper in her ear. "Just say thank you and promise not to spread tonight's events around, and then you can leave."

She turned to look at him, and he gave her a comforting smile. When she looked back at Lestock, his face was set in a grimace of pain, but his voice was steady and cold.

"Don't put us to the test. You've seen what we can do."

Valerie's anger at Lestock's harsh treatment had allowed her a brief period of defiance, but now it deserted her. All that was left was a memory of her own abject terror and a strong desire to go home, burrow into her bed, and pull the covers over her head. Tomorrow, in the cold light of day, she would think about what had happened tonight. Tomorrow she would think about Jeremy, but not now.

CHAPTER TWO

Southdown Hall
Dorking, Surrey
Major Cardrew Hyde

Major Hyde poured himself a snifter of cognac and raised it in a toast to the picture that hung above the fireplace in his study. King George V looked down upon him with slightly bulbous eyes and an expression of stern approval.

"The king, God bless him."

The tangle of hunting dogs drying out in front of the fire responded to their master's voice with an assortment of grunts and snorts. If their master wished to raise his glass to the old king who had been dead for sixteen years, that was no matter for them. They had done their day's work by retrieving a brace of rabbits and scaring up a covey of partridges.

Their eyes followed the major's tall, tweed-clad figure as he turned toward a console table bearing a plethora of framed photographs. The master had not yet sipped from his glass. Now he lifted the glass again, and his eyes settled on one small picture of a young man, almost lost among a sea of old sepia portraits but distinguished by its ornate gilt frame.

He spoke softly, a toast whispered under his breath.

"The king!"

This time he sipped from the glass and felt the warmth of the brandy warming his throat while he inhaled the mellow fumes that had been trapped in the bulb of the snifter. He studied the portrait of the uniformed young man with protruding blue eyes that matched the eyes of the bemedaled figure in the portrait above the fireplace—

the man who was his father.

"You have a weak Hanover chin," the major said. "You should grow a beard. People respect a strong chin."

A light tap on the door, followed by the creaking of the door hinge, caused the tangle of dogs to open their sleepy eyes and focus their attention on the man who was ushered into the major's presence. In the mixed pack of sight and scent hounds, a beagle lifted its head and scented fear from the newcomer. It was not the fear of a creature at bay, but it was definitely fear.

Sadheer Kumar, who had been with the major since his days in India, announced the new arrival, addressing the major in the long-gone language of subjugation.

"Sahib, this man is named Mr. Silliton, and he brings news of Vernon. Sahib."

Major Hyde dismissed Kumar with a wave of his hand and studied Silliton suspiciously. The beagle became more attentive as Silliton seemed to wither under Hyde's angry stare and the fear scent grew stronger.

"I don't want news of Vernon," Hyde barked. "I want Vernon himself. I told him to report personally. Who are you?"

Silliton was the kind of small man that Hyde despised. Hyde thought that there was nothing wrong with being short. He had commanded short men who could march all day on their strong, stubby legs, fight like demons, and drink like fish, but Silliton was quite obviously not one of those men. His narrow face was matched by narrow, hunched shoulders, and his hooded eyes darted around the room acquisitively, as if assessing the value of the many precious objects on display. Hyde had allowed his wife to decorate the reception rooms of Southdown Hall, but the study was his own domain. This room was for him alone, and this room reflected his life, from the cantonments at Agra to his billet in Verdun. They were mementos of the days when men had been men, and a man who would not fight was shot at dawn.

Silliton held his cap in his hands and twisted it in a nervous gesture as he spoke. "I'm Freddie Vernon's lookout," he said. "Or at least, I was."

London, Hyde thought. Vernon had recruited a Cockney sparrow as his lookout. Nothing wrong with that, but why send him here? Why not come himself? He knew there could only be one answer, but he wanted to hear it from this man's own lips.

"What happened?"

Silliton continued to twist his cap. Hyde was tempted to wrench it from his nervous grasp.

Finally Silliton cleared his throat. "We went there, to the library, and we waited for the head librarian to leave. Mr. Vernon had been observing for a couple of nights, and he knew that the woman, the one we wanted, always stayed late, like she didn't want to go home or something. That's what Mr. Vernon said. Anyway, he waited till she turned off the lights and locked the front door, and then we opened it again—leastways, I opened it." He looked up and grinned. "I'm good with locks."

"Get on with it, and wipe that grin off your face. This is no laughing matter."

"No, sir, of course not. So Mr. Vernon went in, and I kept cavey. He said it might take a while."

"It's not the British Library," Hyde said angrily. "It's just a little place. Why would he expect it to take any time at all?"

"Freddie Vernon's like that," Silliton said. "He likes to do a bit of stalking and give the fear time to build. He said it would make her more willing to talk." Silliton hesitated. "I think maybe he enjoys it."

"I don't give a damn what he enjoys. Just tell me what happened."

Silliton shrugged. "I don't rightly know. I was watching out front, so I suppose they came in the back."

"Who came in the back?"

"I don't know."

Hyde gritted his teeth and willed himself not to strike the idiot. Vernon was part of a family that did not take kindly to their friends and relatives taking a beating. He took a deep breath and spoke through clenched teeth. "Tell me what you do know."

"They had guns," Silliton said.

"I said no guns," Hyde growled.

"Mr. Vernon always has a gun," Silliton said, "but he don't often use it. I don't know if he used it this time, being as how I can't ask him—not anymore. It was the others, the blokes who came in by the back door. I didn't see them go in, but I saw them come out."

"Am I to assume that Freddie Vernon is dead?"

"As a doornail," Silliton confirmed. "It was a professional job."

Hyde was momentarily hopeful. If Vernon had been killed by professional thieves, things could still work out. He had no idea how they had found out, but true professionals would be open to negotiation. It would take money, but that could be obtained. Silliton's next words dashed his hopes.

"I stayed to watch, just to make sure. Snuck round the back, as I figured they would do nothing out in front on the street. They brought in a van, black and no writing, and took Vernon out. He weren't alive. Then they went in with cleaners."

"Cleaners?"

"Yeah, buckets, mops, that kind of thing. Mopping up the blood, I suppose. Don't know if Freddie did much bleeding, but there was a bloke with a bleeding arm all wrapped up. I reckon Mr. Vernon gave him one. If you ask me, I would say they was all government."

"Or police," Hyde said.

"No, not police—leastways not local police. A local police car drove by, and they had a few words, and the police car drove off and never came back."

"What about the girl, the one Vernon was supposed to bring to me?"

"I seen her," Silliton said. "Little blond bird, hair done up in a bun, good legs."

"I'm not interested in her legs. What happened to her? Where did she go?"

"I don't rightly know. Home, I suppose. She had a bit of blood on her, but I don't think she was wounded. She was crying a bit, but that don't mean nothing, what with young Freddie Vernon stalking her and him getting shot and the other man getting shot. She was a bit wobbly when she got on her bike."

"She rode a bicycle?" Hyde said in disbelief. "They didn't take her into custody?"

Silliton shook his head. "She rode away, all on her own. I didn't have no orders, and I didn't have no bike, so I didn't follow."

Hyde took another sip of brandy and savored the warmth in his stomach. All was not lost. The girl was still alive and unguarded. Apparently, special operatives had found out something about the girl, but they didn't know everything. If they knew everything, they wouldn't have sent her home. He felt in his pocket for a handful of change. "Buy yourself a beer, and tell your boss I'm going to need another man or two tomorrow."

When the little Cockney had departed, Hyde picked up the newspapers that had accumulated on his desk and sat by the fire to read the headlines.

GEORGE VI IS DEAD
PEACEFUL END IN HIS SLEEP
WORLD MOURNS WITH BRITAIN, A GREAT GENTLEMAN, A MODEST KING
ELIZABETH THE SECOND – GIRL OF 25 COMES TO THE THRONE

He opened the *Daily Mirror* and read the first few lines of the editorial, a paean of misplaced praise declaring that George VI had saved the monarchy after the abdication of his brother Edward VIII. He stopped reading. The world was full of fools who did not understand.

A full-page picture in the *Daily Herald* restored his good humor. The king was shown to be lying in state, with the Imperial State Crown resting atop his casket. Hyde shook his head. The thousands of mourners who would soon file past the casket would believe that the glittering crown was the symbol of the king's power, but he knew better. That crown was a deception, just as the dead king in the coffin had always been a deception. Even the pale young girl in the black dress who had been proclaimed queen was a deception, her accession flying in the face of the natural order of things. Deception would work for a dead king, but for a new king—he dismissed the thought of a new queen—there would be no deception.

He took another sip of brandy. He would have to make another long-distance phone call. He feared that his wife would read the phone bill and ask why he had made so many trunk calls, but he could not tell her the truth—she would never understand. She was a practical woman with no understanding of the mystique of monarchy, but when it was all over and the crown was where it belonged, she would know he had done the right thing.

Brethren Charity Home for Boys
Tunbridge Wells, Kent, England
Davie

"Are you going tonight?"

Colin shoved Davie to one side as he opened the dormitory window. "Don't tell anyone, or I'll—"

"Or you'll what?" Davie asked. Because of their difference in height and years, Davie had to tip his head back to look up at Colin, but he kept his face defiant. He wouldn't let his lower lip tremble. He wouldn't let Colin know how scared he was.

"You ain't gonna do nothing to me," Davie said.

Colin raised a hand as if to slap Davie out of the way, but Davie kept talking. "If you get away, you ain't coming back here to beat me up, and if you don't get away, you're going to Borstal, and you'll be in for years. There ain't no way you're coming back here to do anything to me, so just … just answer me."

Colin shoved Davie again. "Yeah, we're going tonight, so get out of my way."

On any other night, Davie would have been glad to get out of the way, but not tonight. Colin was leaving, and this was Davie's chance. He couldn't lose his courage now.

He kept his chin up and looked Colin in the eye. "I'm coming with you."

Colin laughed at the sheer absurdity of one of the little shrimpies thinking they could join him in his great escape. "No, you ain't. I'm not letting some gimpy little kid come with me."

"Leave him alone," Pete said as he pushed past Colin and looked out of the window.

Davie breathed a sigh of relief. Pete had never been cruel to him, or at least not as cruel as Colin. He hadn't told Pete any of the details, but he'd told him he had to escape. Pete's response had been to ruffle Davie's hair, a gesture Davie hated. *I'm not a little kid. I'm nearly eleven. I'm only three years younger than you.* When Davie repeated his request, scowling to show that he was serious, Pete said he could come if he wanted—if he thought he could keep up.

Now Pete opened the window and looked out, ignoring the blast of cold air that blew through the already chilly dormitory. He turned back to look at Colin. "If we're going, we're going now, and he's coming with us."

Beyond the window, the light of a halfmoon reflected feebly on the shards of glass topping the wall around the school. Davie, who was rarely taken on school outings, as he had trouble keeping up, was only vaguely aware of what lay beyond the wall, but even he knew that the main road was not far away, and somewhere at the end of the road lay the more or less mythical port of Dover, where the ferries departed for France.

"I'm not taking him," Colin said. "He ain't right in the head."

"Nothing wrong with my head," Davie said defiantly.

"Then you ain't right in the leg," Colin countered. "You'll hold us up. I ain't gonna spend time waiting for him."

"We won't," Pete promised. "He knows the score. He leaves with us now, and then he goes his own way."

"Goes his own way?" Colin mocked. "He ain't gonna go his own way. He's gonna drag along behind us, whining. I ain't carrying him."

"No one has to carry me," Davie said, "and I've got places to go. My ... someone's waiting for me." He had nearly said the word and given the game away, and he'd been warned not to do that.

"Shut up," Pete said. "Just blooming stop talking."

Davie clamped his mouth shut. Although they had been arguing in hushed whispers, there was always the danger that one of the other boys would wake up, and if that happened, everyone would be awake, and there would be no hope of keeping them all quiet.

Even Colin, the boy to be feared most in the whole dormitory, wouldn't be able to stop the whispers.

"Colin's making a break for it."

"Where you going, Col? You really think you can get to Dover?"

"How you gonna get on the ferry?"

If the talking rose even slightly above a whisper, Matron, who could hear a muttered curse word at fifty yards—"Wash your mouth out with soap!"—would be down on them like an avenging angel, and the opportunity would be gone. No one ever got more than one try at escaping.

Davie saw Colin and Pete gather up their coats and their small bundles of possessions. He hesitated, waiting for Pete to speak up for him, maybe offer to help him climb out the window, but Pete said nothing.

He heard the creak of bedsprings, and a shape moved in the darkness. One of the boys sat up and began to cough. Coughing would bring Matron down on them even faster than cursing. One more cough, and she'd be in the door with her bottle of Fennings' Fever Mixture, ready to dose everyone with the foul stuff.

Davie could feel a cough building up in his own chest. He was always the first to come down with a cough and the last to be cured, but he could not and would not cough now. When another boy began to cough, Davie knew he had no more time to waste.

He grabbed his bundle of possessions, shoved between Colin and Pete, and threw it out the window. Before either of the bigger boys could protest, he hauled himself up onto the window ledge. He didn't have the agility to turn on the ledge and lower himself down by the arms. The only thing he could do was jump, and so he did.

CHAPTER THREE

February 13, 1952
Churchgate Close
Redbridge, Surrey
Valerie Chaplin

Valerie slept fitfully, tossing and turning until dawn, when she climbed out of bed and dressed for work. She could not imagine how the library would be able to open, considering the amount of blood that had stained the carpet in the nonfiction section, but she was determined to show up on time and behave as if nothing had happened.

She wondered about the warning she had received from the man with the brown eyes and brown mustache. He had told her his name, Alan Lestock, but not his rank. He had been in plain clothes, but she was quite certain that he had a high rank. He said he had been seconded to the Metropolitan Police. *Seconded from where?* She didn't really need to know, as she had no plans to see him again. If she followed his instructions and said nothing, surely he would leave her alone.

She sat on her bed and tried not to look at the top drawer of her dresser. Lestock's instructions had been very clear: she was not to be involved. But surely what she did in her own bedroom was none of his business. She could look if she wanted.

She opened the dresser drawer and took out the cigar box that lay concealed beneath a layer of underwear. Her grandfather had always smoked a cigar at Christmas, and if it was one of his good days, her father would join him. The musty cigar smell that lingered in the red felt lining of the box reminded her of the days when the family lived at number twenty-nine Lambs Farm Road and war was not even on the horizon. War was something that had already happened and would not happen again. A normal life could still be lived, just so long as no one made any sudden loud noises around her father—not even a shriek of laughter.

She banished the memory of Christmas long past and untied the ribbon that bound the letters together. *Pathetic! You're pathetic. Why do you even keep them?*

She fingered the first letter, written on rough wartime paper.

Dear Miss Chaplin,
You were very kind to me …

She did not think she had been unusually kind. Burning debris from the explosion of her home had clogged the street, and the non-combatant squad had labored in vain to put out the fire and try to find their two missing squad members. The major had been no help at all, swatting at them with his swagger stick and calling them lazy conchies. Valerie had run two streets away, where the water main was still connected, and returned with a bucket of water for the sweating men to drink. The major had scoffed at them as they gulped down the cold water. *"Bloody cowards. Don't deserve your sympathy."*

Jeremy's letter had surprised her with its formality. He asked her permission to write occasionally; he had no one else to write to— at least, no other girl. His squad was no longer defusing bombs. They were somewhere outside London, but he was not allowed to say where, and they were digging shelters. They still had the same commanding officer, but at least he was no longer getting them killed.

The letter had come through the Red Cross, a welcome diversion from observing her mother's grief as the doctors explained that Ralph Chaplin would not be coming home again. They could do nothing for him. His mental condition—they labeled it shell shock— could no longer be controlled. They called their facility a hospital, but she knew it for what it was: it was an asylum.

Valerie returned the letter to its envelope and put it back in the box. The letters, tied up in a blue silk ribbon, had been her secret, but now everything had changed. She knew every word he had written, but so did someone else. Someone in a government office in

London had read his letters long before she had, and that same someone had read her replies, seeing formality turn to romance, and romance become frustrated yearning and dreaming. She blushed at the very idea that copies still existed. She wanted to close the lid of the cigar box and hide it away, along with the memory of Jeremy Paxton's freckled face and honest hazel eyes, but she could not banish him so easily. However painful the memory of their romance, she knew that he had written nothing in his letters and she had written nothing in her replies that would bring armed men into the library ten years later, so why had they come?

What about the other letters? The ones that were not in this box. Surely there was no connection. Those letters, in their sealed blue envelopes, were her secret and had not been seen by the censor. They had not come through the Royal Mail, and she alone had read them. *He has a deformed leg. He's paying the price of your sin. No one will want him.* She had burned the first one and then the second one. *He cries all the time.* Eventually, she had burned them all.

The sound of a light tap on her bedroom door brought her out of her reverie and back into the present. She managed to close the lid and thrust the box back into the drawer before her aunt Olivia opened the door and peeked cautiously into the room.

"Are you all right, dear?"

Aunt Olivia, her father's sister, was small and round, with a cherubic face crowned with white hair. She and Aunt Gladys were twins, and when one of them appeared without the other, Valerie felt that she was seeing a half person. She looked for Aunt Gladys, lingering behind her sister, but for once, Olivia was alone.

Olivia took a cautious step into the bedroom and repeated her question. "Are you all right, dear? You know we don't like to pry, but Gladys saw your blouse soaking in the sink, and …"

Her blouse! Her new white blouse, purchased last week at Allders. She had intended to rinse it out before her aunts were awake. Well, that hadn't happened, and now they knew about the blood. They were wonderfully innocent old ladies, but they had lived through the war and volunteered for the Red Cross; they knew blood when they saw it.

"There was an incident," Valerie said. "A sort of accident at the library. It's nothing to worry about. It's not my blood."

Olivia pursed her lips. "But it's someone's blood, dear. I hope no one was seriously hurt."

Seriously hurt? One man was dead! Valerie closed her eyes on the memory of sightless eyes staring up at the library ceiling and shook her head.

She parroted the words that Lestock had spoken. "Just a scratch, Auntie."

Olivia assessed her with cornflower-blue eyes that reminded Valerie of her father. They were the same blue eyes that Valerie saw in her own mirror, and they held the same level of innocent and willful naiveté—facing reality was not one of the strengths of the Chaplin family. Facing the reality of war had driven her father into a mental asylum. Last night reality had forced its way into the quiet of the library, and she had transported it here into the home of her aunts in the form of a bloodstained blouse soaking in the sink. Everything had changed.

Olivia patted her arm. "Gladys will wash your blouse; no need for you to take time out of your busy life."

"Really, Auntie, I'm not busy."

Olivia smiled. "Well, you should be. You're still young, dear. Whatever happened to that young man you were so keen on when you were in school? Your mother told us that he'd been writing to you. I'm sure it was very romantic to receive letters from a soldier."

Valerie saw a faraway look wash across her aunt's face and realized that long ago, in a different war, young Olivia Chaplin had received letters from a soldier.

"Jeremy," Olivia said.

Valerie was startled and guilty to hear his name.

Olivia smiled. "Your mother told us."

"Told you what?"

"Told us his name and said he was writing to you."

When Valerie fell silent, Olivia's pale, powdered face flushed in embarrassment. "Oh my dear, I am so sorry. How tactless of me. I know that things happen in wartime."

Valerie detected tears welling in the corners of her aunt's eyes as she patted Valerie's shoulder. "We'll say no more about him, but please, dear, don't waste the life you've been given. I'm afraid Gladys and I haven't set a good example for you. We have never been adventuresome, and your poor dear father finds the world just too much to bear, but you can't let that happen to you. You should talk to the new vicar. He's a very unusual man, but he has all kinds of ideas for social events in the parish. Perhaps you could help him, as you know so many people from the library. He's an interesting man. I think you would find his conversation quite stimulating."

Valerie had only glimpsed the new vicar at a distance, but even at a distance, his presence was not so much stimulating as unsettling. He had a lion's mane of white hair, which fell across his eyes, and a way of walking that was very close to marching. She was certain he had been in the army, not as a chaplain but as a soldier. The previous vicar had possessed a quiet, academic faith that imposed few requirements on his parishioners. This vicar had the fire of a zealot burning in his pale eyes and, according to his sermons so far, an apparent determination to overhaul every aspect of his parish's quiet Church of England life. She could not imagine holding any kind of conversation with him or joining in whatever innovative and unsettling activities he had planned.

"You still have time on your side," Olivia said, "and hiding away in the library is not—"

Olivia's emotional plea was interrupted by a loud knock at the front door. Olivia's eyes widened in surprise. "Oh my! Whoever can that be? I should go. Gladys is busy in the kitchen."

Valerie leaned over the banister to watch as Olivia hurried down the old, creaking staircase and collided with her sister in the hall. They mirrored each other's gestures in reaching up to pat their white hair into place, and in some choreography known only to twins, they managed to open the door, regard the figure on the doorstep, and step back in simultaneous surprise.

Valerie was equally surprised and found that she, too, had patted her hair into place. He stood on the doorstep, smartly dressed and smiling. The only sign of last night's mayhem was the bandage wrapping his left hand and, no doubt, the rest of his arm, currently concealed under a dark suit coat.

"Good morning, ladies. I'm here to see your niece." He extended his hand. "My card."

Olivia accepted the card, and she and Gladys studied it together.

"Oh my," Gladys whispered. "Police!"

Olivia patted her arm. "It's all right, dear. Valerie told me all about the accident."

Valerie observed a flicker of alarm on Lestock's face. Did he think she'd told them everything?

Olivia fixed her gaze on Lestock's bandaged hand. "Oh dear," she said. "It was *your* blood. We are not at all sure that we can remove the bloodstains from her new blouse. I hope that no one else was hurt."

"No one else," Lestock assured her gravely, "but we will need to obtain a witness statement. If I could speak with her ..."

As Gladys seemed to have been struck speechless by the arrival of the stranger, Olivia took control. "Let me show you into the parlor, and Valerie will come and talk to you. My sister will make tea. Please come in."

Lestock stepped into the hall. Olivia, stepping nervously past him, peered out at the street. "There's another man out there."

"There are several other men out there," Lestock said, "and that's why I need to speak to your niece."

Several other men! Valerie shivered, and for the first time, she feared for her aunts. She did not relish the idea of answering any more of Lestock's questions. He had read her letters to Jeremy, and she had nothing else to tell him. Of course, they would also have read his letters to her, so they would know how he had defended his position as a conscientious objector—not apologizing but letting her know what it had cost him to stand up for what he believed.

It's not an easy way out of fighting. I had to go in front of a magistrate for a hearing and have my name published in the newspaper. No one would employ me. I didn't have anywhere to live, and no one I knew would even speak to me. My parents disowned me. I'm not a coward. I'll do anything so long as I don't have to carry a gun and be responsible for killing. Thank God for the Non-Combatant Corps. They give us all the rotten jobs, but I don't mind.

Valerie responded to his honesty by writing about the misery of her home life, where everything revolved around her father's condition:

We can't even have dance music on the radio in case he gets excited.

His response to that remark had made her blush: *I'll dance with you anytime. What's your favorite dance tune?*

She did not say "Over the Rainbow," because it was not a dance tune and because a song that made her cry could hardly be a favorite. Judy Garland's melancholy words made her think of the impossibility of ever being in a place where her father's mind would be whole, and her mother would be her friend and not her watchdog. On a sudden whim, she cast caution to the winds and wrote "Someday My Prince Will Come."

Her response, her unspoken desire for Jeremy to be her prince, set the tone for the letters that followed, and soon Jeremy was putting words on paper that she longed to hear him say aloud.

She remembered how she had felt each time one of his letters arrived, how she would find herself smiling for no reason at all, even giggling with the girls at school, and she had never been a giggler. Jeremy's letters gave her a sense of belonging. Despite her problems at home, when she was at school, she could be like everyone else, because like all the girls she admired, she now had a boyfriend.

Even now she blushed at the thought of what she had written. It was one thing to know that an anonymous censor had been spying on their silly romantic dreams all those years ago, but it was something else to know that Lestock, who was waiting in the parlor, had also read every word.

The tea tray rattled as Gladys carried it precariously into the parlor. Valerie, halfway down the stairs, saw Lestock spring to his feet and guide the tray to a safe landing on the coffee table. As she passed her aunt in the doorway, Valerie heard her whisper. "He seems very nice."

"He's a policeman," Valerie whispered back. "He's here on business." *Don't get your hopes up, Auntie. He's not as nice as he seems. This is an act for your benefit.*

Lestock stayed on his feet and waited for Gladys to leave the room. When she had tiptoed away, he closed the door and sat down.

An uncomfortable silence settled over the room, broken only by the sound of tea being poured and Lestock stirring sugar into his teacup.

Valerie broke the silence. "How is your arm?"

Lestock gave her a wry smile. "It was more than a scratch, but it could have been worse. Seventeen stitches."

"I'm sorry."

His voice had a surprising amount of warmth. "It's not your fault."

Valerie ignored his friendly tone as last night's anger reemerged. "Really?" she asked scathingly. "I was under the impression that I had done something, or maybe failed to do something, that had caused this problem. Is it my fault that you couldn't find enough information by steaming open my correspondence and you had to come and see me for yourself?"

"We were not the only ones to come and see you," Lestock said calmly, "and not the only ones with weapons." He sipped his tea and set the cup down. "Wartime regulations permitted censorship of all correspondence. You were not the only girl to have her letters opened."

Valerie felt a blush rising in her cheeks. "They were just silly," she said.

Lestock shook his head. "They were ..."

She waited.

He sighed wearily. "I'm sorry," he said. "I know you would prefer to have kept them private."

Anger drove out her embarrassment. "Yes, I would. What gives you the right to invade my privacy?"

"All part of the job."

"And what exactly is that job?"

Lestock shifted uncomfortably. The parlor of the Chaplin sisters was more elegant than comfortable. The kitchen was furnished with shabby but cozy chairs, while the furniture in the parlor was spindly and not built for relaxation.

Valerie studied his face, finding that he was older than she had first thought. His brown hair was sprinkled with gray, and the worry lines on his forehead appeared to be permanent wrinkles. He returned her gaze with a steady, calculating look.

"Miss Chaplin—may I call you Valerie?"

"You might as well," she snapped. "You know so much about me."

He ignored the barb. "I'm a policeman, Valerie, and I'm on special secondment. I told you this last night, but I didn't tell you everything. I can see that you are offended by the fact that someone opened your correspondence—"

"No," she interrupted fiercely. "I understand wartime

censorship, and I am not offended by the censoring. I am offended that *you* are reading those letters now. The war is over, and they are none of your business."

"One war is over, but another is beginning," Lestock said quietly, "and your letters are still relevant. No one suspects you of being a security risk, but during the war, Jeremy Paxton's squad was assigned to some highly sensitive work."

"He said they were digging."

"They were. They were digging at Windsor Castle."

"Oh!" Valerie sat back in her chair. "Were they digging a bomb shelter for the royal family?"

"No, nothing like that. The cellars at Windsor were perfectly adequate bomb shelters, but because the squad was in such close proximity to the royal family, their correspondence was given extra attention."

"He didn't say anything, just that they were digging and they still had the same commanding officer."

"Yes, they were under the command of Major Hyde. He's the only person involved who is still definitely alive."

Valerie's heart turned somersaults. Even though Lestock was only voicing what she had long suspected, she had to ask the question. "Are you saying that Jeremy is dead?"

"We don't know. We've traced the other members of the squad and found that they were sent back to bomb disposal under a different officer. None of those non-combatants survived to the end of the war, although one regular army sergeant did. We are still looking for him, but we have no record of his death."

"They were all so young," Valerie said.

"That's the nature of soldiers," Lestock replied.

"But they weren't soldiers. They were non-combatants."

"In their own way, they were soldiers," Lestock said. "They wouldn't kill, but they risked their lives every day. I won't speak ill of them."

"Do you really think Jeremy is dead?"

His brown eyes met hers with a challenging expression. "What do you think?"

"He stopped writing to me," Valerie said, "but you know that already."

"And you're sure he never wrote to you again, or contacted

you in any way?"

She didn't want to lie, but she couldn't face the prospect of telling him what had happened. It was so much easier to say nothing, and she really had no information to give him. If the Metropolitan Police, with all their resources, couldn't find him, then obviously he couldn't be found. "I never heard from him again."

"One man is already dead," Lestock said with a note of warning in his voice.

"I know."

"This is serious business."

"Obviously."

Lestock sighed. "For your own safety, and for the safety of your aunts, I am going to take you into protective custody."

"No, you can't do that."

"I can and I will. Didn't you hear what your aunt said? There are men outside."

"Your men."

"Two of them are mine, but the other two are not. You are attracting a good deal of attention."

Valerie shivered. "Why? Why is anyone watching me?"

"I'm not in a position to share that information, but I can tell you that you're not safe here, and your aunts are not safe with you being here. The best thing you can do for them is to be seen to leave through the front door with me."

Valerie fought against the prospect of change. She was comfortable with Gladys and Olivia and their daily routine. Laundry on Monday, ironing on Tuesday, choir practice on Thursday, fish on Friday, church on Sunday, and a glass of sherry on special occasions. Once a month, they would visit her father in the asylum, and at Christmas and Easter, they would put flowers on her mother's grave. She was content. How could she leave?

"What will happen to my aunts?"

"I'll leave a couple of men on duty. They'll be safe, but you have to leave."

"Where will I go? Are you going to put me in prison?"

"No, of course not." He looked at her sternly. "Unless you're withholding information."

Valerie allowed the threat to hang in the air. He was just guessing. He could not possibly know the nature of the information she was withholding, and there was no need for him ever to know. The secrets contained in the other notes would not help him to find Jeremy, because those notes had come later, long after Jeremy had disappeared. They were her own personal nightmare and nothing to do with anyone else.

She forced herself to respond with a brittle inquiry. "So where will I go?"

"To a safe house."

"For how long?"

"Until we find what we're looking for."

"And what are you looking for?"

Lestock's chair protested as he leaned forward, his face bereft of all kindness, his eyes cold and hard. "A very great treasure," he said.

Southdown Hall
Dorking, Surrey
Major Cardrew Hyde

Personal courage had never been Major Hyde's strong point. He had always done a fine job of testing the courage of other men, especially those of lower rank, but he rarely put his own courage to the test. He had consumed a considerable amount of brandy before he finally found enough of that scarce resource to place a phone call.

Now, as the woman on the other end of the line began to raise her voice, he saw Kumar making a hasty exit. *Little rat*, he thought, *leaving a sinking ship*.

He returned his attention to the telephone. The ship was not sinking. He would not permit it to sink. He knew that the woman on the phone would not accept defeat, and neither would he.

The woman berated him in a rasping, querulous American voice. "Where have they taken her?"

"I don't know, but I'll find out."

She sounded dubious. "You haven't found out much so far."

Hyde straightened his spine and twitched his lip in a way that made the ends of his mustache quiver. That had always put the fear of God into the recruits, although it would have no effect on the woman on the phone. Still, it felt good to snap to attention and imagine that she was in the room, ready to be quelled by the ferocity of his demeanor. "May I remind you, madam, that this has come at very short notice."

The woman on the phone contradicted him without so much as an apology. "It has come at just the right time. Princess Elizabeth's youth will strengthen our case. The timing is not the problem; you are the problem."

"I beg your pardon!"

"When you first approached us, you led us to believe that you had far more than you actually have."

Hyde puffed indignantly. "I told you exactly what I had."

"You have nothing. You told us you could acquire the stones, but now you tell me that you cannot find them; you cannot find the man who has them; you cannot even question the girl who may know where that man is. It's not good enough, Major. I believe you have sold us a pack of lies. Our friends have advanced money to you, and my husband …"

He remained silent and allowed his mind to wander while the American woman told him how disappointed her husband was and how his many powerful friends were also disappointed, and how he, Major Hyde, was personally jeopardizing their plans for the future of Great Britain.

He did not need her to tell him all these things. What was she, after all? Just a jumped-up foreigner who had lured the heir to the throne into her trap and robbed him of the chance to become king. Of course, if their plan succeeded, Edward VIII would be restored to the throne, his abdication forgotten, and this annoying woman would, unfortunately, become queen, but she was not queen yet.

"I advised my husband against becoming involved with you. His claim is good enough without all this mumbo jumbo about magic stones and …"

His raging internal anger drowned out her voice. It was nothing, just the drip, drip, drip of her ghastly ignorance.

Mumbo jumbo! Magic stones! Even if he explained, she wouldn't understand. The stones in the crown meant nothing to her, but everything to Britain. The Black Prince's Ruby had been worn by kings of England since 1367. It had been on Henry V's helmet at Agincourt, but he doubted she'd even heard of Agincourt.

If she wanted proof of magic, she needed only to look at St.

Edward's Sapphire, which had been a Crown possession for over a thousand years and had been mystically bestowed on King Edward the Confessor by St. John the Evangelist himself. Hyde was not a religious man who relied on saints, but he was willing to believe that the sapphire had somehow been responsible for the miracles worked at Edward's tomb.

She'd probably appreciate the Cullinan Diamond, he thought. She'd at least understand the value of the largest diamond ever discovered. If she was not satisfied with the diamond, maybe she'd appreciate the Stuart Sapphire, because that belonged to a king who'd had his head chopped off. Yes, she'd like that, because she was an American, and they didn't like kings. How ironic to think that if he helped her husband to become king again, he would be helping this harpy to become a queen—or at least queen consort.

She was still talking and airing her grievances. "I blame everyone involved," she said.

Everyone except yourself, he thought. *It's your fault he gave up the throne in the first place.*

"The people around King George should have known how sick he was. He smoked ike a chimney; no one should be surprised that he died."

Hyde had never thought to attach the king's cigarette habit to the cancer that killed him. Everybody smoked. He couldn't imagine what would happen if they were told to stop.

She was still talking, still explaining, as if he, of all people, needed an explanation. "His death, coming so soon, has played into our hands," she said. "Obviously, Elizabeth is far too young and inexperienced. This is exactly the right time for us to put forth a better candidate for the throne, and my husband's supporters believe that possession of the jewels from the crown will send a very strong signal, but you, Major, have let us down. It has become increasingly obvious that we will have to involve other people, because you alone do not have the resources to do what needs to be done."

"I'm doing my best." Hyde could have bitten his tongue. Why had he said such a thing? He sounded weak.

"Your best is not good enough. According to you, Jeremy Paxton is our only lead, and if we are going to succeed, we are going to need professional help in our search for him."

Hyde found himself stuttering. "P-p-professional. I d-d-don't know what you mean." *Is she bringing in another crime family? She'll start a crime war.*

"Twenty-four hours ago, Scotland Yard received an anonymous tip and two names."

Hyde rubbed his eyes, as if clearing his vision would somehow clear the fog in his brain. *Scotland Yard! Police. What is she suggesting?*

She was still talking in his ear. "Hyde, did you hear me?"

Oh, yes, I heard you, but I need time to think. Why would you call Scotland Yard? We don't know if the police are on our side.

He ignored her while he put two and two together. Now he understood why Vernon's raid on the library had been such a spectacular failure and ended with gunfire. She could at least have told him what she'd done. She'd changed everything by giving Scotland Yard the two names they needed, Valerie Chaplin and Jeremy Paxton, and now the police knew who to look for. From now on, he'd be tripping over them wherever he went.

"All you have to do now is follow the police," she said. "They have the names, and they'll flush him out. When he shows himself, you can retrieve him."

"I'm not some blasted gundog."

Anger cleared his mind, sweeping away doubt and building his confidence. He would be damned if he'd let her take over the operation. He'd started this. He was the one who had discovered what was hidden at Windsor. He was the one who had told Paxton what to do, and he was the only person to know for certain what Paxton had stolen. She wouldn't know Paxton if she tripped over him. So, she'd brought in Scotland Yard. So what? He could handle this. Time was running short, and now he would have to go back to the beginning—a beginning that only he knew about.

Vernon had bungled his attempt on Valerie Chaplin, and now Scotland Yard had their eyes on her, but there were other ways to get this done and stay one step ahead of Scotland Yard. If he couldn't talk to Valerie, at least he could retrieve and read her letters. Scotland Yard wouldn't know about the letters. He'd been the only one to hear the stupid boy's mawkish confession of love and longing.

Windsor Castle was no more than a dark shape in the dark countryside. Blackout curtains draped every window of the castle and town—every window of the entire country. On this night, when clouds hid the moon and the stars, Hitler's bombers droned overhead across a pitch-black landscape with never a glint of light to guide them.

Paxton lit a cigarette, and Hyde, with the instinct of a man who had spent an entire war avoiding becoming a target, knocked the match from his hand. Tonight was not the real thing, just a recce, just a chance to finalize their plans. Hyde had no liking for his companion—damned conchie coward—but he couldn't show his contempt. Later, when it was all over, he would tell him what he thought of a man who would not pick up a gun, but for the moment, he was forced to listen.

Paxton was still rattling on about his girlfriend. He patted his pocket. "I've been writing to her, telling her how I feel. I have her letters here, and she has mine tied up in a ribbon; that's what she says."

Hyde bit back a response. "Real soldiers keep letters in their pockets as they face death. You're not a real soldier, and you're not going to die. You have no right to keep them in your pocket."

Hyde set aside his memory of that strange, dark night and concentrated on the future. He would go to Redbridge first thing in the morning, and he would go alone. He wasn't in his dotage. He could still climb a ladder and open a window, and he knew about soldiers' letters and the girls who kept them, most probably in a dressing table or even in a drawer with their scanties. He'd written a few letters himself in the long, long ago, building castles in the sky and making plans for an impossible future with a girl whose name he could no longer remember. Paxton would be no different, and if he had named a place where he and Valerie could share their dreams, Hyde would have a clue that was known to no one else.

The woman on the phone was still talking, dripping doubt in his ear. "Maybe he sold them to someone else, or maybe someone else took them from him."

"Sold what?" Hyde said distractedly, with his mind on the letters.

Her voice was a snarl. "The stones. The jewels. Pay attention."

When he failed to respond, she snarled again. "Maybe he's dead. Has that thought occurred to you?"

Hyde could not respond the way he wanted. *If he's dead, we'll never find them, and you'll never get what you want.* He could not think that, not even to himself, because what she wanted was also what he wanted. Why else would he put up with her?

"Even a dead man can be found," he said, hoping that he sounded enigmatic and not just absurd.

"Then find him."

He heard the phone disengage.

He chewed the ends of his mustache. There was no way around it. Before he spoke to her again, he would have to retrieve the letters.

CHAPTER FOUR

St. Ebba's Hospital
Ewell, Surrey
Valerie Chaplin

Valerie stared in disbelief at the large brick building. She had been lost in her own thoughts and had paid little attention as Lestock took the byroad that passed Epsom Downs Racecourse. It was not until he brought the big black Wolseley to a halt that she realized where they were. The sign at the gate told the world that this was St. Ebba's Hospital, but she knew it for what it was: an asylum for men and women so mentally disturbed by war that they had willingly committed themselves to be locked behind its high walls. This was where Ralph Chaplin had come to find peace from the demons of combat that had haunted him since before Valerie had been born.

"Why are we here?"

"To visit your father."

"Why?"

"I think he has information."

For a moment, she was merely confused. "Why do you need me with you?"

"Because you'll encourage him to speak."

Valerie shook her head. "I'm not going in there. It's not my visiting day. He won't understand, and he'll be upset."

"I need information, and if you won't give it to me—"

"I don't have any information," Valerie snapped, "and neither does he. I'm not going in. You said you'd take me to a safe house."

Lestock nodded. "I will … eventually, but first we're going to visit your father."

Valerie didn't know how to express her anger at the man sitting so smugly at her side. He had lied to her. His promise of safety meant nothing. She doubted that he even had a safe house. She set her mouth in a stubborn line and settled into her seat with her arms crossed. She glared at him, and he responded by turning off the engine and cutting off the flow of warm air from the heater.

She wished she could make him understand, but she doubted he was the kind of man who would listen to reason. If he wanted information about Valerie's life, he would not get it from her father. Ralph Chaplin was a mere shell of the man he had once been. Her mother's protection of her shell-shocked husband had been such that Valerie had hardly known him at all as she had grown up. Now she visited him only once a month, and always in the company of her aunts. They took grapes and magazines—nothing too stimulating— and talked only of events that would not upset him.

She found the visits tedious and doubted that Ralph himself derived any benefit from them. Whether they sat in the garden or in the dayroom, they were surrounded by white-coated attendants and her father's fellow patients. Some of the men looked at her with interest, but most of them seemed to be in a world of their own, eyes turned inward. Ralph rarely spoke.

Lestock interrupted her thoughts.

"Unless you want to freeze to death sitting in a cold car, we need to go inside. They're waiting for us, and I'm not leaving without seeing him."

Valerie finally found her voice. She lashed out at Lestock from within a well of anger that had been building for the past twenty-four hours. *Or maybe a lifetime.* "How dare you? I'm not going to let you drag my father into this. He's been through enough."

Lestock turned to face her, and his eyes were shadowed. "I know what he's been through."

"Then you know he mustn't be disturbed. If anything startles him, he—"

"He's back in the trenches, reliving the horror," Lestock said. "I know. It must have been very frightening for you as a child."

Valerie rejected the sympathy in his voice. "I wasn't frightened. How could I be frightened of my own father? We were just very careful. No loud noises." *Not even laughter, not even high spirits, definitely not tears or tantrums.* "We protected him, and I'm not going to let you hurt him."

"I have no intention of hurting him, but if you won't tell me what I need to know, I will have to ask him some questions."

"I won't tell you anything, because I don't know anything, and he doesn't know anything either. He's been in here for years. I won't let you do this."

"You won't be able to stop me," Lestock said, "so don't waste your time trying. We can sit out here in the car for as long as it takes, but eventually, you will have to get out." He surprised her with a rueful grin. "I'd love to turn the heater back on, but then we'd both get too comfortable, and this could go on forever."

She ignored the hint of camaraderie in his voice as she felt the unfamiliar prickle of angry, frustrated tears behind her eyes. She rarely cried. *"Don't upset your father."* She swiped a hand across her eyes and swiveled to face him. "Who do you think you are, and what gives you the right to treat me this way?"

"In answer to your first question," Lestock said, "I'm the man who took a bullet to save your life."

Dramatic but true. The bandage on his arm was proof.

"What about my other question?" Valerie asked. "What gives you the right to treat me like this? We're not living in a police state."

"And I am not a regular police officer." He gave her a considering look. "Believe it or not, Valerie, my silence has been an attempt to protect you, but I can see that you are not interested in that kind of protection."

He leaned forward and inserted the key in the car's ignition. "I'm going to turn on the heater and get comfortable, and then I'm going to tell you as much as I can. I can't tell you everything, but perhaps I can convince you that what's happening here is not just about you."

She bristled at his words. *Not just about you.* Of course it wasn't about her; it was about protecting someone who could not protect himself, and the only way to protect him was to remain silent.

"If you won't accept protection for yourself, will you at least help me protect our nation?"

His words startled her, and she blurted out an immediate angry response. "Protect our nation? You're talking nonsense just to get my attention."

He shook his head. "No. It's the truth, and I'm telling you

now because time is running out and you have left me no choice."

He turned the key in the ignition, and Valerie unfolded her arms as a wave of warm air passed across her feet and rose upward.

Lestock was still speaking. "I think you know that the king's death caught everyone, even the security services, by surprise."

"The king," Valerie repeated vaguely. Why was he talking about the king?

"Yes, the king. Let me speak."

All she could do was nod.

"The operation on the king's lungs was considered to be a success," Lestock said. "His doctors thought he was making a good recovery, and when he died, quite unexpectedly, in his sleep, certain important plans for the succession had not been completed. The country is now in a precarious position, and the succession is not as secure as you may have been led to believe." He paused and looked at her. "Do you understand?"

She shook her head. "No, I don't. Queen Elizabeth is his heir; everyone knows that."

"Not everyone accepts that."

"Well, I accept it. What does this have to do with me?"

"You'll see. Let me continue. There are, in fact, powerful people who do not think that Elizabeth should be the king's heir. They say that she is too young for the responsibility—she's only twenty-five. There are equally powerful people who think it likely that she, being young, will allow her husband to rule from behind the scenes, and they won't accept that possibility, because he's a foreign prince from a family of Nazi sympathizers. Then, of course, there are those who believe they have a better candidate for the position, and—"

Valerie could not help interrupting him. "A better candidate? Who are you talking about?"

"You don't need that information," Lestock replied brusquely.

Valerie was taken aback. No one in her small circle of acquaintances had ever said anything that suggested Princess Elizabeth was not the legitimate heir to the throne or was unsuitable to rule. She could not imagine what kind of people would be saying such things or how there could possibly be an alternative to Elizabeth.

"It is my task," Lestock said, "to find the leaders of these various movements and silence them."

Valerie shuddered. She had seen how Lestock and Smythe silenced people. Her heart was pounding at the memory but also at the idea that she was somehow involved in any of this high-flown intrigue. Her voice trembled, and she could hardly frame her question. "What does that have to do with me?"

"It has to do with Jeremy Paxton."

"No!" The fear was gone, replaced by a sudden sense of the absurd. For some reason, he was fooling her, taunting her with the memory of Jeremy Paxton. Why would Jeremy be involved in a plot to change the line of succession? He was a conscientious objector, not a traitor. "You're making this up."

Lestock indicated his bandaged hand. "I didn't make this up." His look was almost imploring. "You have to believe me. It is vital that we know Paxton's whereabouts."

"I don't know anything."

Lestock spread his hands. "In my experience, there are times when we don't realize what we know. I don't want to think that you are deliberately withholding information that is vital to the security of this country, and so I will assume that there is some seemingly insignificant piece of information that you have simply forgotten. Therefore, as I cannot speak to your mother, I am going to speak to your father and see if he remembers anything. I would like you to come in with me and put him at ease. That's all I ask. Come with me."

He turned off the ignition and forestalled Valerie's questions by opening the car door and stepping out. When Valerie, stunned into immobility by the idea that Jeremy Paxton was involved in a threat to national security, failed to move, he walked around and opened the passenger door. The expression on his face told her that his patience had worn thin, and if she did not move of her own accord, he was fully prepared to make her move.

"Your father will be different today," Lestock said. "He will not be medicated."

Valerie climbed out reluctantly. "He's never medicated."

Lestock shook his head. "He's *always* medicated. How do you think they control a ward of shell-shocked old soldiers from two wars whose minds are still in the trenches and for whom bombs are still exploding? They're all medicated, but today your father will be himself again."

"But my father doesn't even know Jeremy."

"Your father was there when the bomb exploded your house. He was there when you brought Paxton a drink of water. Your father was a silent watcher. Who can say what he saw then or later?"

Later? Valerie lowered her head to hide the rush of blood to her cheeks.

Lestock stopped at the office and flashed a badge in a leather wallet. The attendant, a muscular man in a white coat, acknowledged him with a salute. An old soldier, Valerie thought, someone who recognized Lestock's rank, whatever that might be.

"Second visitor today," the attendant said as he unlocked the interior gate.

Lestock jerked to attention. "What did you say?"

"He had a visitor early this morning."

"And you let him in?"

"Yes, sir. We were given no special orders about visitors."

"Who was it? What was the name?"

The attendant returned to his desk and consulted a ledger. "Hard to read, sir. Looks like Joseph or Johnson, definitely a J."

Lestock grabbed the book from the attendant's hands and studied it briefly before throwing it down on the desk. "It's an intentional scribble. For God's sake, man, don't you check the identity of visitors?"

The attendant scowled, no longer impressed by Lestock's rank but obviously annoyed by his display of temper. "We are not required to do that. The people here aren't a threat to society. They're all voluntary patients, and you, sir, gave no orders to prevent visitors or check papers."

Lestock pulled Valerie to his side and demanded that the attendant open the gate. When the way was clear, he pulled her into the long white-tiled corridor and gestured impatiently. "Which room?"

"Twelve, but I expect he's in the dayroom."

"I doubt it. Without his tranquilizers, he'll be exhibiting some symptoms."

Valerie resisted Lestock as he urged her forward. "You have no right to interfere with his medications. You're not a doctor, and this is dangerous." Fear of what her father might say or do made her waspish. "I should report you to … to … to whoever is in charge of you."

"You might try Sir Harold Scott," Lestock said. "He's commissioner of the Metropolitan Police, but I doubt he'll have time to deal with you, what with everything else he has on his plate. The king is lying in state. Crowds are pouring into London, and the state funeral is in two days' time. There is a coronation to be planned, and we have a problem with one of the crowns."

"One of the crowns?" Valerie asked. "How many are there."

"Two," said Lestock. "St. Edmunds crown is used for the ceremony. And then when the queen emerges from the abbey she will wear the Imperial State Crown. The same one that is currently on the king's coffin. That is the crown the people see."

"And which one has a problem?"

"The Imperial State Crown it's…"

Valerie saw his expression change as he realized that he had said too much. He stared down at her, his expression intense and his voice very close to a snarl. "For your own safety, forget that I said that."

He released her arm. "This is number twelve. Shall we go in?" He tried the handle. "Well, at least they haven't locked the door. That's a good sign."

Ralph Chaplin was sitting in an armchair beside his bed. His sparse hair was standing on end. His cheeks were flushed, and his eyes were unusually bright. His eyes had been bright like that when Valerie was a child. She remembered how they had been constantly moving, darting suspicious looks into every corner of the room. Her mother had kept the lights on all the time and never permitted any room to be dark. Valerie had slept with her light on. *"In case he starts wandering. He doesn't like the dark. Best not to frighten him."* She still slept with a light on.

"Valerie!" His smile was too bright as he sprang from his chair. "Oh, it's been so long."

Valerie shook her head. "I was here last month."

"But I wasn't," Ralph said. He smiled again. "I haven't really been here in years." He looked at Lestock and then extended his hand. "Are you the one I should thank for getting me off those damned pills?"

Lestock took the extended hand. "Alan Lestock, Metropolitan Police."

Ralph released Lestock's hand and gave an exaggerated, enthusiastic salute. "Thank you, sir."

He sat down abruptly, seeming to leak energy like a rapidly deflating balloon. "Two policemen in one day. I thought I answered all of his questions. I did my best. They didn't need to send another one."

"No," Lestock said, "they certainly didn't. I'm sorry about that. Well, at least I brought your daughter with me. That's a bonus for you."

Ralph looked at Valerie and then back at Lestock, and his sudden bright smile returned. "She's a beauty, isn't she? And smart too. She could have been anything she wanted, but I held her back. I was living in hell, and I pulled my family down with me."

Tears formed in the corners of his eyes, and he buried his face in his hands.

Valerie flung herself down beside her father's chair. "It's all right, Dad. It's not your fault."

"No!" He lifted his head, suddenly angry. "I blame your mother."

"Dad!"

"She should have let them lock me away. She thought if I could just have peace and quiet, I would be cured. I know what you did, tiptoeing around me, never making any loud noises, no laughing, no crying, not even when you were a baby. You weren't even allowed to have friends in the house."

"I had a friend. Mary was allowed to come into the house."

"Allowed to come in," Ralph parroted. "Do you hear what you're saying? One little girl was allowed to come into the house and see the crazy man in the corner. That's what I told the fellow who came this morning—the other policeman. He asked me about your friends, and so I told him."

Valerie heard Lestock's sharp intake of breath, but it was Valerie who asked the question. "What did you tell him, Dad?"

Ralph smiled. "I told him everything. I wasn't drugged in those days, and I knew what was going on. I knew who Mary was. Your mother approved of her, but I thought she was like a nasty little mouse—nothing to say to me but always muttering to herself. I didn't trust her."

Valerie couldn't say what she thought. *You didn't trust anyone.* She touched her father's hand. "She was just praying, Dad."

"Praying for what? Praying I wouldn't jump up and kill her?"

Valerie found it difficult to speak as memory overwhelmed her. "She was praying for you to be better," she said.

She had hated the days when Mary came to "play," and dreaded the idea that anyone at school would discover that she was friends with the dullest, mousiest, and most religious girl in her class. The worst part, worse than the social embarrassment of Mary being allowed in the front door, had been listening to Mary's fervent whispered attempts to cast out Ralph's demon.

Ralph looked at Lestock. "I told your colleague about the prayers and said she and her whole family were from some obscure Christian sect. I wasn't sure of the whole name, but it was Christian Universal Kingdom Conquerors or Brethren, or some such name, and they were always collecting money for orphans or missionaries." He rubbed his forehead in frustration. "I don't remember all of it, but they had a chapel in Redbridge, and I think they sent their members off to Africa before the war. Maybe they still do. He said that would be enough to help them find her, although I don't know why he'd want to."

"Did you tell him about anyone else?" Lestock asked. "Were there any other friends?" He looked directly at Valerie, but she would not meet his eyes.

"I feel so bad about how I was," Ralph said. He shook his head. "My wife thought she was doing the right thing for me, but it was hard on Valerie. She only had one other friend."

Valerie looked up in shock. She had not expected him to remember. "Did you tell him about her?"

"I certainly did." He looked up at Lestock. "That was a red-letter day. We had some fireworks that day."

Valerie turned to Lestock and tried to hide the pleading tone in her voice. "I'm sure you don't need to hear any more about this. It's not important." *It's nothing to do with kings and crowns and coronations.*

"I'd like to know what your father said to my colleague," Lestock said evenly. "It will save me making a phone call to him." He smiled at Ralph. "What did you tell him about your daughter's other friend."

"April Brady," Ralph said. "Redheaded girl. I'd seen her father in the pub a few times—not that I went to the pub very often, not in my condition." Ralph looked at Valerie and winked. "I'd sneak out every now and then. I was glad when April came to the house. She was just what you needed, a real firecracker, but what did you tell your mother? Did you say she was another quiet, churchgoing girl like Mary?"

Valerie could not resist defending her adolescent self. "I didn't invite April. I wanted to, but I didn't dare, and then she just came one day, without an invitation or anything. Mum couldn't turn her away on the doorstep, not with the neighbors looking, so she said we could go into my bedroom so long as we were quiet."

How could they be quiet? Valerie sometimes wondered if her mother had ever been young, if she had ever known what it was to be sixteen years old with war on the horizon and one last chance to grasp joy before it was taken away. One shriek of laughter had been enough to end the prospect of joy in the Chaplin house. When the whispers in Valerie's room had turned to giggles and then laughter, her mother had entered the room with all the righteous indignation of an avenging angel. It was all over in seconds, with April banished.

The ensuing fight, the only time Valerie had openly challenged her mother, had to be conducted in whispers while Ralph, shocked by the sudden laughter, crouched in a corner.

"Now look what you've done."

"I didn't invite her; she just came."

"Well, tell her not to come again."

"I'll tell her to be quiet next time."

"There won't be a next time."

"Mum ..."

"Why don't you invite Mary? Perhaps she could come to tea."

"I hate Mary."

The good thing about April's visit was that it brought about the end of Mary's visits. The house was quiet again, no visitors allowed, but Valerie was redeemed in the eyes of her school friends by disavowing any friendship with Mary. With Mary out of the way, Valerie finally had friends.

"Mr. Chaplin," Lestock said, "what do you know about Jeremy Paxton?"

Ralph nodded. "Ah yes, Jeremy Paxton. That's what the other

officer said. Missing-person case. He must be important to bring two of you over here to see a crazy fellow."

Valerie tried to interrupt. "You're not crazy, Dad. You—"

Lestock's voice cut through her protest. "What did you tell him, Mr. Chaplin?"

"Nothing," Ralph said. "I don't know anything. I said Jeremy was a nice young man, and I thought that Valerie had taken a shine to him, but that was all. Naturally, he asked me all about Valerie and if she'd ever said anything about him after the war, but I told him it came to nothing—a few letters, that was all."

Came to nothing! Valerie was suddenly grateful that Ralph had chosen to have himself locked away at St. Ebba's. Here in the tranquility of the hospital, he knew nothing of what had happened next.

She thought back on what her father had said so far. Both Lestock and the previous visitor now knew that Valerie had had a friend named Mary who was from a local Christian sect, but that information would get them nowhere—Mary had always said she was destined to go overseas as a missionary, and she'd probably left as soon as the war had ended. Unfortunately, they also knew about April Brady. There was a trail here that they could follow, but only if either one of them could find April, and only if April had read the note she'd delivered to Valerie at school, and only if April still remembered Valerie and Jeremy's silly plans. She consoled herself with the thought of the number of ifs that would have to be negotiated for any clue to emerge. Surely there were too many. Surely her secret was still safe.

Outside in the corridor, someone dropped a tray with a clatter that reverberated off the marble floor and the tiled walls. Ralph flung himself to the floor, clapped his hands over his ears, and curled into a ball. Turning from him to Lestock, Valerie saw that he had flattened himself against the wall, eyes wide and staring. Even as she watched, she could see him regaining control and dragging his mind back from whatever hell it had momentarily occupied.

Ralph, without his medications, was incapable of doing what Lestock had done. He was buried deep in illusion. She could not know what he was seeing, but she had read enough poetry and seen enough photographs to paint her own picture of a bleak landscape of skeletal trees and barbed wire, a hell of mud and death—and men, hollow-eyed and bloody, once again climbing the ladders, once again facing the explosions.

The door crashed open, and an orderly appeared with a syringe. Lestock pulled himself together and led Valerie from the room. Out in the corridor, Valerie could hear the cries and groans of her father's companions, the ones whose memories had not been medicated into submission.

CHAPTER FIVE

Churchgate Close
Redbridge, Surrey
Major Cardrew Hyde

Hyde kept his eyes peeled as he progressed slowly along Churchgate Close, the tree-lined street that led from the market house at the town center to the parish church. He had considered various disguises for his recce of the home of Gladys and Olivia Chaplin and concluded that the best answer would be a dog. Although he would have preferred something large and masculine, and preferably still in possession of its gonads, he knew that such a dog would do nothing to disguise his innate military aura. He needed something small and ridiculous, but nonetheless male. A male would stop at every tree, and Churchgate Close was lined with trees.

He had accordingly borrowed the gardener's grunting, toothless old pug. His explanation to the gardener had been simple: "If you want to keep your job, you'll lend me your dog."

During the journey to Redbridge, Roger—*Ridiculous name for a dog*—had been restrained in a box on the back seat of Hyde's Rover and had perfumed the car with evidence of its unhappiness and the probability that it was fed whale meat diet. By the time they reached their destination, Hyde was beginning to regret the whole idea of Roger and was wondering if it would be entirely immoral just to abandon the creature in the center of town. Fortunately, when he pulled into a parking space outside the parish church, Roger had redeemed himself by exiting the car and performing exactly as Hyde had anticipated, showing interest and enthusiasm for every tree on the ancient tree-lined street.

The Chaplin sisters lived in a small but picturesque house halfway along the street. Hyde approached from the opposite side of the street. He leaned on a cane and limped. He tried dragging one leg, but the gait proved painful for his gammy knee, and so Roger would have to suffice as an excuse for his extremely slow process. Whatever part of the whale Roger had eaten, along with the journey in the Rover, had upset Roger's stomach, and his intestinal distress was a more-than-sufficient reason to linger in the region of the Chaplin sisters' little dollhouse.

While Roger made a generous donation at the root of a plane tree, Hyde surveyed the street from beneath the shade of his tweed cap. Many years had passed since anyone had wanted to make use of his military skills, but they were still sharp, and what he discovered was worrying. The Chaplin sisters were definitely under police protection, with a uniformed copper standing conspicuously outside the front door. Hyde had his own men in place, of course, lurking in various shrubberies along the street. He refused to make eye contact with them. *Let's see if they can see past Roger's unfortunate behavior and recognize the man who is paying them.*

Unfortunately, it seemed that a third player had joined the game and was doing a decent job of appearing innocuous. Dressed in a boiler suit left over from the war, he was lifting drain covers, peering officiously into the darkness beneath, and then replacing them. If Roger had been a dog taking its walk at any kind of normal pace, Hyde would not have been able to observe that this man lifted the same covers many times over, and always in the vicinity of the Chaplin house.

Roger tugged at the leash, looking for new places on which to bestow his offerings, and Hyde considered his options. He had no qualms about robbing the old ladies. Some would say that it was not cricket, but Hyde had never been much of a cricketer, and he had always found it easy to sacrifice his few morals. The problem now was the presence of the policeman. He doubted he had a weapon, but he would definitely have a radio. And there was the other man, the inspector of drains. What would he do? What did he even want? *Ridiculous question.* They all wanted the same thing, didn't they? They wanted Jeremy Paxton.

Roger settled on a new tree just as Hyde saw the police

officer jerk to attention. The front door opened, and the Chaplin sisters emerged with their shopping bags. White-haired and round-bodied, they were not quite as alike as two peas in a pod. One was a little taller than the other, and their coats, although similar, were not identical. Apparently, even the twins had been forced to bow to wartime shortages and buy whatever coats they could obtain. They had settled on navy blue, but one wore tweed and the other wore a rather military gabardine. The hats, each with a feather, were identical. They nodded to the police officer, and to Hyde's relief, he fell into place behind them.

Hyde's spirits rose, and he jerked on Roger's leash. His two men would have no trouble with the faux drain inspector. All they had to do was …

He saw movement in the bushes that hid his men. So they planned to do battle in the street. He glanced up and down. No pedestrians in sight, no movement at any of the windows. Two against one, and he would help them if necessary. He could still perform a few moves, and he had his cane.

To his surprise, the men did not come out into the street. Instead of stepping forward, they stepped back. He grunted in frustration. *Idiots!* They were going to follow the sisters. He tried signaling to them, but they responded by fading away into the landscape of the surrounding houses. *Both of them! Cretins! Unmilitary nincompoops!* Since when did two watchers leave their posts at the same time? Now it was up to him. Well, that was the burden of command.

He held his breath, watching the faux drain inspector. He grinned as the man replaced a drain cover with a hasty clatter, tucked his flashlight into his pocket, and set off in the direction taken by the sisters.

Hyde pulled on Roger's leash, feeling a sudden affinity with the snuffling, diarrhetic dog as he experienced a worrying cramping below his own belt. It happened even to the bravest of men: sometimes the bowels turned to water before combat, but Roger wasn't to know that. The dog regarded him curiously. "Pull yourself together," Hyde commanded. "We're going in."

Churchgate Close
Redbridge, Surrey
Harry Mayfield
Formerly Sergeant, Royal Engineers

Harry Mayfield had already removed the drain cover outside the Chaplin sisters' house, and he hid a smile as he pretended to make a close inspection of the drain. He had spotted Major Hyde a few minutes ago. The old fool had not changed much in the past tenyears. He'd grown thinner, and he stooped a little, or perhaps the stooping was to assist the impression that he was paying attention to the dog and not to the watchers outside the house of the Chaplin sisters.

Mayfield assumed that Hyde was unaware that he was also watching—watching the police and watching the other men he had so far failed to identify. It occurred to him that maybe they were working for the major. Hyde was not the kind of man who would do his own dirty work. So maybe he was here to watch the watchers—wheels within wheels.

He had to hand it to the old coot: the dog was a clever touch. He could not imagine what the major had done to spur the number of deposits the dog was making, but it had worked. The major's progress along the street was convincingly slow, and the dog's behavior appeared completely unforced. *Of course it is unforced.* There were things you could get a dog to do, but that wasn't one of them.

Finding that his old commanding officer was here in person was an unexpected bonus. Word in the criminal underworld, which Mayfield very much wanted to join, was that Major Hyde had put out a contract on a woman named Chaplin. Mayfield was used to working on his own at the very bottom of the crime ladder, but finding out that Major Cardrew Hyde was involved in a contract changed everything. Now he had a chance to move from petty thievery to major crime and get a foot in the door with one of the London crime families. The Londoners didn't want to work with an outsider from Yorkshire, but they would change their minds when they discovered what Mayfield had to offer. No one except Mayfield knew what Hyde was really up to, and that knowledge was about to pay off.

He kept one eye on the Chaplin sisters as they set off down

the street with their police escort, and the other eye on the watchers. He smiled to himself as he saw Hyde attempting in vain to get his men to stay in place. They ignored him. In fact, Mayfield doubted they knew who he was. *Need to know and that sort of thing. The major always was too big for his boots.*

He settled the drain cover back into place with a deliberate display of haste and then walked away, following the sisters toward the center of town. Moments later, when he was out of sight of the major, he made an abrupt turn and slipped behind a clump of laurel bushes. He shed the boiler suit, stepped out onto the street, and walked boldly back toward the Chaplin house. He wouldn't need caution—the major would never recognize him. Hyde was not the kind of officer who made an attempt to get to know his men. When the major had spoken to him during their time at Windsor, it had only been to bark orders and wave his swagger stick.

"You there, Sergeant. Are you in charge of these men?"

"Yes, sir."

"Damned conchies, all of you."

"Not me, sir. Royal Engineers. Seconded to keep the conchies in line."

Possibly the major had glanced at him, but the huge hole they were digging was in semidarkness. A massive tarpaulin had been spread across the top so that no light would leak out and be visible to the Luftwaffe, and the diggers were lost in shadows.

"Get them digging. It's important work."

"What exactly are we—"

"None of your damned business."

Mayfield returned to supervising the conchies as they burrowed into the chalky soil surrounding the massive castle. The major returned to pacing impatiently and waving his swagger stick.

Mayfield did not think that the major would recognize him on the strength of that one brief encounter. Of course, there had been another encounter, one where Mayfield had made himself known, but on that occasion, Hyde had been preoccupied with the royal librarian, and he and Paxton had been nothing but nameless lower ranks. Mayfield enjoyed the thought of jogging the major's memory, a little at a time.

The dog—on close inspection, Mayfield saw that it was an

elderly pug—had been tied to the railing of the Chaplin sisters' garden gate. It regarded Mayfield hopefully as he approached.

Mayfield shook his head. As a Yorkshireman, he believed the only dog worth having was a whippet, and this fat little creature with round, puzzled eyes was no whippet. Ignoring the hopeful wagging of the dog's tail, and its pathetic little whine, he vaulted over the low stone wall beside the gate and strode toward the back of the house.

As he had expected, the major was doing a very poor job of housebreaking. He'd managed to find a stepladder, and he was teetering on the top step and attempting to lift a second-story sash window.

"Morning, Major."

Hyde turned and came very close to falling. He managed to recover his balance but not his dignity, and he stared down at Mayfield with panic in his faded blue eyes.

"It's not what it seems. I have authority. I'll speak to your chief constable."

Mayfield shook his head. "Don't bother. I'm not police. You won't remember me, but I remember you. Windsor Castle, 1940."

"I don't know what you're talking about."

Mayfield grinned as he began to mime. "We dig, dig, dig, dig, dig, dig, dig."

"Stop it! What do you think you're doing?"

Mayfield sang louder. "In our mine the whole day through."

"Stop it at once. The neighbors will hear you."

"You're the one they'll see," Mayfield said. "You're the one up the ladder. I'm just a concerned citizen serenading you with a song from Disney's *Snow White*. It's all about digging. It should bring back happy memories."

"You're a lunatic."

"No, I'm not a lunatic, and you are not a cat burglar. Come on down, and I'll show you how it's done."

Mayfield stood back, enjoying the moment. He'd seen Hyde's treatment of his company, and he'd heard rumors of what had happened when they had been assigned to bomb disposal. He couldn't understand why anyone wanted to be a conscientious objector when they could instead be given a gun and sent to kill people, but even the conchies didn't deserve to be killed off by the major's sheer incompetence.

58

Well, it was over now, and Mayfield's time with the Non-Combatant Corps was about to pay a handsome reward. Major Hyde was a man with money and influence, but he was a babe in the woods when it came to understanding the underworld. He would need a right-hand man, and Mayfield intended to be that man.

He resisted taking any more potshots at the old man and waited for him to creep back down the ladder. Once the major had both feet on terra firma, he confronted Mayfield with a fine display of pompous bluster. "I don't know who you think you are, or why you think you know me, but—"

Mayfield executed a perfect salute, standing straight and clicking his heels together in a way he had not done since he'd been issued his demob suit and sent home. "Sergeant Harry Mayfield, Royal Engineers, reporting for duty, Major Hyde, sir!"

"Do I know you?"

"Windsor," Mayfield said. "I was with your unit."

Hyde shrugged. "That was a long time ago. You can't expect me to remember every face."

Mayfield grinned. "Or every conversation," he said.

Hyde's face flushed angrily. "What are you talking about?"

"Something I overheard ... at Windsor."

Hyde's face was now bright red, and Mayfield wondered if he'd gone too far. He didn't want the old man dead, or at least not yet.

He turned his back on the major and studied the stones in the Chaplin sisters' rock garden. He selected one of the right weight, walked over to the back door, and smashed the glass.

When Hyde gasped, Mayfield smiled reassuringly. "All over in a couple of seconds, and the neighbors haven't heard a thing." He reached through the window and slid the old-fashioned bolt that held the door closed.

"There you are," he said. "What are we looking for?"

"I'm not going to tell you."

"All right, then. If you won't tell me, *I'll* tell *you*. I believe that we're looking for something that will lead us to the items we buried in a biscuit tin at Windsor."

Major Cardrew Hyde

Hyde stood back as the Yorkshireman moved quickly and efficiently through the house. He racked his brain, trying to recall seeing or speaking to this man during the long days and nights at Windsor Castle. He said he had been a sergeant in the Royal Engineers. He was probably telling the truth. Real soldiers had had to be brought back from the front lines to keep an eye on the damned conchies who were failing to respond to discipline.

Hyde knew that he had been nothing but window dressing with his medals and his outdated uniform and little more than a swagger stick to keep the men in line. He would not admit, even to himself, that his courage had failed him completely when he'd found himself in charge of a bomb-disposal unit, but he would not let that weigh on his conscience. Obviously, the men in Whitehall, who had been fighting the war from behind their desks, had felt that the conchies were expendable, and Hyde agreed. However, he didn't see himself as expendable. He wasn't about to indulge in any kind of *noblesse oblige*. Let the cowardly conchies take whatever was coming to them.

Windsor had been different: a nice, safe dig just outside the walls, where the tunnel of a medieval sally port provided a secret exit from the castle. The first information received—that they were digging drains—had been a blow to Hyde's dignity. All very well to send the conchies to dig drains, but he was Major Cardrew Hyde, DSO and Bar, and not a damned plumber.

It all changed on the day that he had observed the slight figure of the king, out of uniform but under close escort, staring down into the pit they had created. Since when did kings inspect drains? Something else had been afoot there. This had not been about toilets for the little princesses.

Mayfield interrupted his reverie. "We're done here."

"Did you find anything?"

Mayfield nodded. "Yes, I did, but no thanks to you," he said in his grating Yorkshire accent, "standing there woolgathering."

Hyde pulled himself together and returned insult for insult. "Housebreaking is your area of expertise and not mine. What have you found?"

Mayfield grinned and held up a cigar box. "Letters from Paxton."

Hyde hesitated. He would have to tread very carefully.

Obviously, this Yorkshire fellow knew something of what had happened at Windsor. Perhaps he knew what had happened to Paxton. Perhaps they'd talked.

"So you knew Paxton?"

Mayfield nodded. "Aye, I knew him. I knew all of them. They were good lads."

"They were cowardly conchies."

Mayfield shook his head. "No, they weren't cowards. They just didn't believe in killing."

"The country was at war. England expects every man to do his duty."

"Not now," Mayfield said impatiently. "I can't stand around here quoting Lord Nelson. We've already taken too long."

"But are you sure you found everything?"

"If you're asking me if I found a name and address for the current location of Jeremy Paxton, the answer is no. I found letters, and I plan to study them, but I'm not doing it here. You can stay here if you want."

"No, no, of course not. We'll go together. We can read them in my car."

Mayfield looked at him shrewdly. "Who says I'll give them to you?"

"But—"

The rattle of a key in the front door brought a rapid end to negotiations, with Mayfield shoving Hyde toward the back door.

"The broken window," Hyde protested. "The ladder."

"Too late now," Mayfield said.

It was only when they were out of the house and making the best exit they could by pushing through a tall privet hedge that Hyde thought of Roger the pug, still tied to the front gate. Well, it was too late to do anything about that now.

They fought their way through the flourishing landscape plantings of three backyards before they emerged onto the street and were able to observe the activity outside the Chaplin house.

One of the sisters held Roger's leash as they both stared down at him in puzzled alarm. "Where did he come from?"

"I can't imagine. Do you think he's been abandoned?"

"Maybe we should take him inside."

Roger tugged at the leash, pulling the chubby little twin in the direction of a stately oak tree.

"He wants to go walkies," she declared, leaning down and patting his head.

The other twin shook her head. "Not now," she said, mirroring her sister's action in patting the dog's head. "We'll take you inside and give you something to eat."

With one determined tug on the leash, Roger achieved his destination at the root of the oak tree. While the sisters gasped in horror, Hyde came to the conclusion that Roger would not be going inside the Chaplins' house just yet. He also concluded, with complete lack of guilt, that he would not be returning Roger to his owner anytime soon, if ever.

If you don't like it, you can find another damned job.

CHAPTER SIX

An Abandoned Barn in Kent
Davie

Davie surfaced from a deep sleep, and for a long, happy moment, he simply enjoyed the unusual warmth of his bed. Perhaps Matron had brought an extra blanket, not that anything like that had ever happened before. On second thought, maybe he was in sick bay. In sick bay, Matron would sometimes put a hot-water bottle in the bed, and definitely sick bay had extra blankets. He tried to snuggle into the blanket, but the blanket fought him, scratching his nose and eyes.

What the hell? He hoped he hadn't said that aloud. He knew the price for swearing, and *hell* was one of the words no one was allowed to use.

"Hell is not a place to be taken lightly. Hell is a real place, and it is where you misbegotten boys will end up if you don't mend your ways."

He could feel a cough beginning to claw its way out of his chest. So that was why he was here. He was sick again. Well, at least he wasn't forbidden to cough. He sat up in bed and was surprised to find that his bed was not a bed, just a deep pile of straw. Memory returned in a rush. He was out! He was over the wall! He was free! The cough fought its way to the surface, burning as it rose.

"Shut up! Stop coughing!"

He was fully awake now and staring into Colin's bloodshot eyes.

"Shut up before I shut you up."

To Davie's relief, Pete erupted from a pile of straw and defended him. "Leave him alone. He's not hurting anyone."

"Someone will hear us."

"There ain't no one around," Pete said. He stretched luxuriantly. "Jeez, I slept like a dead man."

Jeez—that was another forbidden word.

"Our savior did not sacrifice his life so that nasty little boys could take his name in vain."

Davie, suppressing another cough, started to take note of their surroundings. They were high up in the loft of an old barn, obviously disused. The straw that had kept them warm all night was tinged with green mold. The walls were at a perilous angle, and daylight streamed between the siding boards. Peering between the boards, he saw fields white with frost beneath a washed-out blue sky. The sun, pale and obviously without warmth, was well above the horizon. He didn't need a watch to tell him that he had slept later than he had ever been allowed to sleep before.

Pete stretched again and then rooted around in the straw until he found his pack. "We have to keep moving."

Colin shook his head. "We're fine right here."

"No, we're not. Think about it. If we can find this barn, so can someone else."

"No," Colin scoffed. "*You* think about it. Look at this place. There ain't a cow or a sheep in sight. It's abandoned. No one's coming in here."

"It's the first place they'll look."

"Who?"

"The police. They send police after us if we run away. By now someone will know we're gone, and we can't be the first people who've thought to sleep in here first night out. We have to move on, and we have to go where no one expect us to go."

Davie, watching the exchange of opinions, knew that Pete was right.

The law of the dormitory held that whoever was first to realize that the window was open would close it, and all and any inquiries would be met with blank faces.

"Don't know, Matron. Didn't see nothing."

They wouldn't have been missed last night, but that was last night, and this was morning—late morning. If there was any established escape route, the police would know about it. They hadn't stopped to think last night. Even Pete, who was most definitely smarter than Colin, had not been able to think past the need to find somewhere out of the cold wind, and the old barn had been an obvious refuge.

Davie, although he would not admit it, could not have gone on. Limping as fast as he could, he had fallen behind, and true to their word, they had not waited for him. He was fortunate that the glimmer of moonlight had shown him where they were headed.

"Come on," Pete said. "We have to find some food."

"Where we gonna do that?" Colin asked.

"Don't know," Pete said, "but there ain't none here, so we have to move."

Davie looked at Pete, slowly realizing that his hero didn't really have a plan. He had talked wildly about stowing away on a ferry to France, where he would live on sunshine and grapes, but Davie hadn't asked for details, because Davie had no intention of going to France. Davie had other plans.

Colin rummaged through the straw for his pack and moved to the top of the ladder. Last night the ladder had come close to defeating Davie. He still was not sure how he had managed to find the energy to climb up into the loft. Well, it was morning now, and going down wouldn't be a problem.

He spun around in a circle, looking for his pack. He didn't remember burying it in the straw, but he assumed that was what he'd done. *No! Oh no!* He remembered throwing the pack through the window and then leaping out behind it. He remembered the pain of landing and the relief that he'd been able to scramble to his feet and follow the other boys to the wall. Pete had helped. He'd told Davie to take off his coat and throw it over the glass shards, and then he'd boosted him up. There had been another rough landing on the other side, but once again his weak leg had withstood the challenge, and then they'd been off and running. He knew that they'd all wanted to whoop with joy, but they'd run silently. They'd run and run and run, Davie pumping his arms to keep up. Davie running without any added weight—empty-handed. Davie had not picked up his pack.

He had nothing, not even the note in the blue envelope.

Safe House
Dorking, Surrey
Valerie Chaplin

The house was a solid detached suburban villa on a quiet cul-de-sac.

"You'll be safe here," Lestock said as he carried her suitcase to the front door. He rang the bell and waited for the door to open. "I won't come inside. This is Mrs. Gordon. She's the caretaker. You're in good hands."

He departed immediately, leaving it to Mrs. Gordon to usher Valerie into the sitting room and pour tea from a Royal Doulton teapot into floral teacups.

Valerie took the teacup and studied her hostess, or guardian or jailer—she was not sure what description fit the bill exactly. Mrs. Gordon was a tall, dark-haired woman with a comfortable layer of middle-aged fat over her large frame, and a face whose unconventional disparate parts somehow combined to create an impression of unforgettable beauty. Her smile was warm and engaging, but behind the smile and the plumpness overlaying her bones, Valerie sensed an iron will that could not be broken and a rigid spine that would not bend to circumstances. If she was indeed Valerie's guardian, then Valerie would be safe. If, on the other hand, she was Valerie's jailer, then Valerie would not be leaving.

Mrs. Gordon spoke with a soft Scottish accent. "I don't live here, dear, but I'll stay here with you as long as necessary. I'll sleep on the ground floor, and you'll be sleeping upstairs. Anyone who wants you will have to get past me."

She responded to Valerie's dubious look by rolling back her sleeve to reveal a network of scars. "Parachuted into France," she said. "Things went wrong, and I didn't wait for rescue. Made my own way out. I can take care of myself, and I can take care of you."

"Oh, I wasn't doubting you. I just don't understand why anyone would want me so very badly. I don't know anything."

Mrs. Gordon shrugged. "I've seen any number of people come through here. Some people know exactly what they've done and why they're being hunted."

Valerie shuddered. *Hunted? Is that really the right word?*

Mrs. Gordon continued unperturbed. "We have others, of course, who don't know. Alan—that's Mr. Lestock—explained that you may not be taking your danger seriously. I must say that surprises me. By the look of you, you don't see a lot of killing in your everyday life."

"I'm a librarian."

"As I said, you don't see a lot of killing. I thought you'd be more shocked to have someone killed in your library."

"Oh, I'm shocked," Valerie protested, "but I still don't understand. Mr. Lestock won't tell me why everyone is looking for Jeremy."

"That's for your own protection, dear, although I think he's mistaken." A faraway look crept into Mrs. Gordon's eyes. "Not knowing doesn't stop people from asking, and sometimes a small offering of truth will be enough." She shook her head. "I'm sure there's no need for you to concern yourself with anything like that. If you can just make up your mind to bide here for a couple of days, Alan will get to the bottom of whatever this is, and he'll be back to collect you. When he has a job to do, he's like a dog with a bone: he never lets go. Try not to be offended by his manner. He has a tendency to forget that we are all human and not just cogs in a machine, but he'll get the job done."

"Have you known him long?"

"We were in France together, undercover. That's what changed him and made him what he is today. He's thoughtless, but he's not unkind."

Valerie, remembering his treatment of her father, disagreed. "I would say he's very unkind."

"We're all entitled to our own opinion," Mrs. Gordon said, with a note in her voice that suggested the discussion was over.

Valerie came to her own conclusion. *We were in France together. That's what changed him.* Valerie remembered his reaction to the dropped tray. She guessed his age to be somewhere around forty or forty-five—too young for the first war but just the right age for the second. She wondered what scars he was hiding and what had changed him from a man to a machine.

Mrs. Gordon rose abruptly. "Let me show you your room."

She picked up Valerie's suitcase as though it had no weight at all, and Valerie followed her along the hall and up a wide staircase to the second floor. She could not fail to notice the other woman's limp, but she said nothing. She had the feeling that any comment would be unwelcome. Mrs. Gordon did not embrace weakness.

She wondered what such a woman would make of the Chaplin family—the two spinster sisters who lived in the house where they had been born, Ralph, who had fallen apart in the trenches and could not be put back together, and Valerie, who had hidden herself in a library and refused to face the world. Would Mrs. Gordon be surprised to know that Valerie had once ventured far beyond the library, and that she had paid such a high price for that adventure that she had never gone adventuring again?

She turned to Mrs. Gordon as they entered the spacious bedroom. "Am I a prisoner?"

"Goodness, no!"

"What would you do if I tried to leave?"

"I would try to stop you."

"How?"

"By telling you not to be foolishly impatient. Whatever this is, it will blow over, and you'll be able to return to your normal life."

Why did that sound like something she didn't want to do? She eyed her suitcase. "I didn't bring my ration book."

Mrs. Gordon smiled. "We're on the government's ration book. We can feed you for a few days."

Valerie looked at the sun shining beyond the window. "Would I be allowed to go for a walk?"

Mrs. Gordon's face lost its overlay of geniality. "You're a mite too restless," she said. "Alan told me you'd be easy to get along with."

"Alan knows nothing about me," Valerie declared.

"He saved your life."

"He doesn't own it!"

She was surprised to find that the deep well of anger that had revealed itself in her father's hospital room was still full to the brim and threatening to spill over. *Keep a cool head. Don't do anything yet.*

CHAPTER SEVEN

Safe House
Dorking, Surrey
Valerie Chaplin

Mrs. Gordon's voice, not loud but still commanding, floated up the stairs. "Valerie, could I have a word, please?"

Valerie, staring out the bedroom window, took in the tone. Mrs. Gordon may well call herself a civilian, but she had once been an officer. The request was framed politely, but the "please" seemed to be an afterthought.

She looked at her watch. It was four thirty, and the short winter day was drawing to a close. The sun, a red ball with no warmth, was setting behind skeletal trees. The sunset was a mere ghost of what it could have been; even in the depths of winter, surely it could do better than this. It seemed to Valerie that the sun was mirroring her mood: bleak, hopeless, and unwilling to believe that things would ever be better.

"Valerie!"

Mrs. Gordon's voice now held a definite note of unapologetic command.

Valerie turned from the window and slumped down the stairs to the sitting room. To her surprise, she found that Mrs. Gordon was wearing a hat and coat, and they did not seem to be anything left over from war-time rationing. There was a touch of Paris about Mrs. Gordon's ensemble. Perhaps the coat was part of her wartime disguise. It did seem to fit a little snugly, as though to confirm that Mrs. Gordon had been putting on weight.

"Did you hear me?"

Valerie gathered her scattered thoughts. What did she care

what Mrs. Gordon was wearing or saying? She noticed that the other woman was carrying a battered canvas shopping bag that seemed totally incongruous.

"I'm going to the shops," Mrs. Gordon said.

Oh, that's why she has the bag. So what? It doesn't matter.

"Don't worry. I won't be long. The bus stop is on the corner, and it's just five minutes into town. I'll be back before you know it."

"You're leaving me alone?"

Mrs. Gordon patted her arm. "Just for a few minutes. No more than half an hour. I'm going to lock all the dead bolts so no one can get in."

"So I can't get out," Valerie said dully.

"You're not a prisoner."

"But I'm locked in."

"For your own protection, dear. I'm going to get some sausages for our tea, and then we can listen to the radio, although I'm afraid it will only be news bulletins and solemn music. We won't have anything else until after the king's funeral. Perhaps you'd like me to buy you a book to read, or a magazine. Is there anything special you fancy?"

Kindness did not sit comfortably on Mrs. Gordon's shoulders. Valerie had a sense that thoughtfulness was not her strong point. Perhaps it was being forced upon her. Perhaps it was Lestock who was suggesting sausages and books and magazines—anything to keep the prisoner quiet.

The librarian in Valerie could not resist the challenge. "*The Day of the Triffids.*"

Mrs. Gordon raised her eyebrows and repeated the title questioningly. "*The Day of the Triffids?* I've heard it's quite a violent book."

"Which is why my library won't buy it, and why I want you to buy it for me," Valerie said forcefully.

"You don't strike me as the violent type."

Valerie thought that Mrs. Gordon was probably violent enough for both of them, but she kept her opinion to herself. "*The Day of the Triffids,*" she repeated. "Or if you can't find that, I'll have *My Cousin Rachel,* or just a *Woman's Own.*"

Mrs. Gordon nodded, and Valerie thought it most likely that her jailer would return with a copy of *Woman's Own* and nothing else, which was a shame, because she really wanted to read *The Day of the Triffids*. Yes, it was a violent book, and she had not fought the library's censorship, but now everything had changed. Her newly discovered angry and outraged self wanted to read the book that the library had banned.

Mrs. Gordon seemed flustered by the request, to the extent that she started to pat her pockets and search through her handbag in an agitated fashion.

"If you're looking for your gloves, they're on the hall table," Valerie said.

Mrs. Gordon scooped up her gloves. "Thank you, dear. I must rush, or I'll miss the bus. Don't worry. I won't be gone long. You'll be quite safe, and if you hear anything, anything at all, ring nine-nine-nine. The police know about this house."

Valerie looked around. "Where's the phone. What room?"

Mrs. Gordon spoke over her shoulder as she let herself out of the front door. "In the sitting room, dear. Must go! Won't be long!"

Mrs. Gordon slammed the front door behind her, and Valerie stood in the suddenly silent front hall, waiting for the sound of the key turning the dead bolt from the outside—waiting and waiting.

She stepped into the small reception room adjoining the front hall. She could see Mrs. Gordon's figure retreating along the quiet street in the rapidly fading light. The streetlights had not yet flickered into life, but they would as soon as the last of the daylight faded. She studied Mrs. Gordon until her tall figure turned the corner at the end of the cul-de-sac. Something was not quite right, but she couldn't put her finger on what it was, and she did not have time to waste. The front door was not locked from the outside. She was not a prisoner.

For one brief moment, she considered remaining where she was. Mrs. Gordon would return with sausages, and maybe even a copy of John Wyndham's book. She could spend the evening reading the book and listening to music on the radio. She was safe here. Mrs. Gordon was made of steel, and Alan Lestock had already proved himself once by taking a bullet on her behalf.

No, that was overdramatic. Lestock had been shot, but despite his claims, she couldn't be sure the bullet had been intended for her. She could not take any comfort from the idea of his protection. He had a job to do, and he was doing it. He had put her here to keep her out of the way while he …

And there it was. He'd put her here while he tried to find April Brady, and if he could find her, then April would tell him what Valerie had told her. If she allowed that floodgate to open just a little, it would all come out. She couldn't allow that to happen. She would have to find April before he did.

She tried the front door, and it opened easily. The house was set in a substantial front garden, but there was no gate to bar her path. As she stood indecisively on the doorstep, the streetlights flickered to life, revealing a deserted street. She studied the shadows and found no sign of life. She should leave—now.

She looked up at the stairs. Her suitcase was up there on the bed, but carrying it would slow her down. She would need money for the bus fare, and she would need her coat. She had no need of anything else.

The bus stop was exactly where Mrs. Gordon had said it would be, standing in isolation with no bus shelter. The fact that it stood beside a streetlight was a mixed blessing. She felt vulnerable waiting alone, the only figure on the street and visible to anyone who cared to look. However, the streetlight allowed her to read the timetable displayed in a glass case. Perhaps more than one bus stopped here. Perhaps she would have to make a choice.

She checked her watch and ran her finger down the timetable. Only one bus, the 465, stopped here, and according to the timetable, its extensive, meandering journey would take her all the way to Kingston-upon-Thames, a place she had never visited. She didn't need to go so far. She traced the timetable again and decided that she would get off at Leatherhead.

And what will you do then?

I'll get off at the bus station, and there'll be other buses going to other places. No one will know where I've gone.

And where will you go?

To find April Brady. I know where she is.

You know where she was. She could have moved.

I have to try.

You'll be out all night, and the buses will stop running. Look for yourself. See how long it will take.

Once again Valerie ran her finger down the columns. She felt as though she were playing a children's game, tracing her finger through a maze that led to one blind alley after another. She would never get there this way. Riding the bus would never work. She would need a train. Train stations stayed open all night. Train stations had ladies' waiting rooms. She would go to the station.

She returned to the timetable. It seemed that the bus ran every hour, and its second stop would be the train station in Dorking. She checked her watch again, pleased to find that she would only have five minutes to wait. She stamped her feet and buried her hands deep in her pockets. No wonder Mrs. Gordon had wanted to take her gloves.

Mrs. Gordon—there was something about Mrs. Gordon. She had wanted her gloves, and she'd been impatient with herself as she hurried to catch the bus, the bus that came every hour and had not yet come. Valerie's plans suddenly fell apart. Had Mrs. Gordon really been in a hurry? Had she really been too flustered to lock the dead bolt? She was a woman who bore the scars of some unspeakable torment in France. She had rescued herself from the Nazis without waiting for assistance. She had worked undercover with Alan Lestock, a man who spoke of necessary killings. Mrs. Gordon would not forget to lock a door.

There was something else. Valerie racked her brain—something she had seen when Mrs. Gordon had walked away from the house in the twilight. She was going shopping, and she carried a shopping bag. That was what it was—the shopping bag had seemed to be full. Where would she put the sausages and the copy of *The Day of the Triffids*? She would not put them anywhere, because Mrs. Gordon was not going shopping.

The lights of the bus cut through the gathering dark. It pulled up next to the bus stop and presented its warm, brightly lit interior. It was a double-decker, with most of the downstairs seats filled. She only had to go two stops—no point in climbing the stairs. The conductor swung from the pole on the platform. "You coming, love?"

Valerie stepped up. She had done what they wanted her to do: she had left the house. Now she would do something they didn't want her to do.

Redbridge Police Station
Alan Lestock

Lestock looked up from the ledger he was studying. "Well?"

The young constable looked at him with a mixture of awe and resentment. Alan's warrant card looked in many ways similar to the one the constable himself carried, but it also bore markings that carried their own message.

Do whatever this man wants.
Don't ask questions.
Security of the realm.
Much more than a policeman.
Ignore the rumors of a shoot out at the library.

Lestock doubted that the constable himself had deciphered all these clues. Obviously, his superintendent had explained whatever needed to be explained, and Lestock had been left alone to occupy prime office space.

"I'm to tell you that the two old ladies are unharmed."

Lestock was relieved. The thought of a break-in at the home of the Chaplin sisters had troubled his conscience. The Chaplin twins were symbols of a vanished world, where innocence was still possible and kindness had not been forgotten. It was the world once inhabited by his parents, a world he had tried in vain to save.

He thought that removing Valerie Chaplin from the house would be all that was needed to keep the sisters safe, and he had salved his conscience by placing a constable on watch to provide reassurance. He had been certain that the shadowy figures who were so determined to find Jeremy Paxton would concentrate on Valerie, and so he had taken her into custody. Surely it was obvious to anyone that the sisters knew nothing—if they had known anything, he would have done more to secure their safety. Whoever was watching Valerie would know that, but it seemed they had begun to panic and make desperate moves that would draw unnecessary attention.

He ran a hand across his forehead. He had a simple assignment: find Jeremy Paxton if he was alive; if he was dead, find where he'd been before he'd died, and get there before anyone else. Lestock knew he was in a race, but he had not known that the field was so crowded.

He looked up and found that the constable had not moved.

"Did you want something, Constable?"

"There's a dog."

"A police dog?"

"No, sir. A pug."

Lestock summoned a mental picture: small dog, squashed face, wrinkled skin. The look on the constable's face told him that the younger man was not here to waste time talking about dogs. He had a point to make.

"What about this pug?"

"The thieves left it behind."

Lestock sat back in his chair. "Is it dead?"

"No, sir. They tied it to the front gate. It's fine, sir, except that it's ..."

"It's what?"

"We think it's been eating whale meat."

"What makes you think that?"

The constable waved his hands helplessly. "We examined the ... evidence."

Just for a moment, Lestock was actually happy. He had been peering into shadows for so long, and now something had emerged from the shadows and presented itself in daylight. Why on God's green earth would someone who was robbing the Chaplin sisters' house bring along a pug, let alone a pug with an upset stomach?

"Where is this creature now?"

"One of the sisters—I believe it's Miss Gladys—is concocting something to settle its stomach."

"The police vet can take care of that," Lestock said. "Have it sent over to the kennels."

"We tried, sir. The ladies will not part with it."

Lestock knew he could insist, but what was the point of upsetting the ladies? It didn't really matter where the dog was; it only mattered that it existed. It was a clue. The question was how such an unusual clue could be used.

The phone on his desk rang, and Lestock waved the constable away. Pug or no pug, this call was important.

He picked up the receiver. "Well?"

Smythe's voice was filled with admiration. "You wouldn't recognize her."

"Recognize who?"

"Mrs. Gordon. She's done herself up like a working man: cloth cap, overalls. You'd never think she was a woman. I was one bus stop back, waving my warrant card and holding the bus while she got ready. She got on the bus bold as brass and sat downstairs. Your Valerie never even suspected—"

"She's not my Valerie."

"She's your cat's-paw."

"I feel bad about that," Lestock admitted.

"Needs must when the devil drives," Smythe said.

"So where is she now?" Lestock asked.

"At the railway station."

"Has she bought a ticket?"

"Not yet. She bought a platform ticket and went into the ladies' waiting room. Mrs. Gordon doesn't have another change of clothes, so she's waiting outside. It's bloody freezing out there, but she doesn't seem to care."

"Mrs. Gordon is made of strong stuff."

"Yeah, I know." Smythe hesitated. "Have you found anything?"

Lestock looked down at the open ledger. "Not yet. It's like looking for a needle in a haystack."

"I don't know," Smythe said. "I think you have the right idea. If the girl was christened April, it must mean she was born in April. You wouldn't call her April if she was born in May, would you?"

"Well," Lestock said, "assuming that being at school with Valerie Chaplin puts her at roughly the same age, I've looked at registered births in the Redbridge area for April 1921, 1922, and 1923, and there's no April Brady."

"Irish," said Smythe.

"So what?"

"Not a local name. Not a Sussex name. She could have been born somewhere else."

"You're telling me something I already know, but I have to start somewhere."

"Census?"

"No census in 1941, and no copy here of 1931."

"Hold on," Smythe said. "Something's happening."

"What?"

"She's gone to the ticket office. Mrs. Gordon is on the move, right behind her. I don't think she suspects anything. I'll ring you back when I know where she's going."

CHAPTER EIGHT

Southdown Hall
Dorking, Surrey
Major Cardrew Hyde

He had no choice but to bring Mayfield home with him. In a moment of clarity, he realized that the former sergeant was exactly what he needed, and there was no point in trying to get rid of him. He'd found Hyde in flagrante delicto at the top of a ladder, so best to bring him aboard before he took that story to someone else.

He wondered if Mayfield would be expecting a monetary reward for whatever it was he knew. *He can't know much, and he couldn't have seen anything.* If he expected money, he was going to be disappointed. There was no money in this for anyone, just the satisfaction of doing the right thing, and maybe a place in the New Year Honors List. He drew himself erect as his mind played a personal heraldic trumpet blast. He would be a hero of the age. He would be one of the men of vision who had seen the country going along the wrong path and had taken drastic measures to prevent disaster.

The king's sudden death had turned most people into twittering idiots. Even before they'd planted His Majesty in the ground, the newspapers were calling Britons the New Elizabethans, and the talk was of nothing but the coronation of that girl. He supposed they were planning a crown for her husband as well. Why couldn't they see how wrong they were? Even Hattie, his own wife, was talking of the need to purchase souvenirs and wondering if she would have to host a celebratory tea party.

Where others saw celebration, Hyde saw a once-in-a-lifetime

opportunity. He could only imagine what was happening in the back rooms of Buckingham Palace and Windsor Castle, where finding the jewels from the crown had become an urgent necessity. Those men, the ones who fawned on the Princess Elizabeth, had no idea where to look, but he did.

He entered his study and glanced up at the clock on the mantelshelf. The thought of the American's imminent phone call caused a cold sweat to break out on his forehead. He had made a rash promise that had not yet come true, but he would have to tell her something.

Mayfield was ensconced in a leather wing chair beside the study fire. He had scattered the envelopes around on the floor and held the letters themselves in his hands.

"Well?" Hyde asked.

Mayfield shook his head. "I don't see anything. It starts off very formal, 'Dear Miss Chaplin' and so on, but it doesn't take them long to get down to business. It's silly stuff, really, him being her prince and her being the love of his life. I'm not surprised. I know what he was like. I had him under my command."

"He was under my command," Hyde insisted. "You were all under my command."

The tone of Mayfield's Yorkshire voice was as dismissive as only a Yorkshireman could be. "Under your command? You did a lot of shouting but not a lot of commanding. I don't know who was pulling the strings, but it wasn't you. They were fooling you as much as they were fooling all of us. All you did was wave your silly little swagger stick and tell us to dig deeper."

Hyde knew that the stick had been a mistake, but he could hardly have carried a sword, and he had to have something in his hands to keep them steady. The doctors called it palsy, and they also called it incurable. The stick had been with him since his days in India, long before he needed it to control the tremors. Times had changed, and apparently, men now resented traditional symbols of authority.

It would get worse if the girl was allowed to be in charge. If the men resented the authority of battle-hardened officers—he included himself in that description—why would they kowtow to a girl in a silly hat and a flowery dress? Every member of the armed forces would be required to swear an oath of loyalty to her, but he could not imagine that happening. He was retired, but he'd never resigned his commission; they could call him back at any time, but he would be damned if he'd swear fealty to some chit of a girl, or worse yet, her husband. *Damned foreigner!*

"Major."

"What?"

"Are you listening to me?"

He turned angrily. "Yes, I'm listening, but if you intend to defend those blasted conchies, I'll have you thrown out of here."

Mayfield shook his head. "I wouldn't do that if I were you. You don't want me telling anyone what I know."

"You can't prove anything."

"You left a clue."

Hyde hesitated. Urgency had made him careless of late. "What clue?"

Sergeant Mayfield was laughing. "You left the dog behind."

The dog! Hyde could only feel relief as he dismissed the whole idea of Roger as a clue. The dog couldn't talk. He'd been glad not to have it in the car all the way back to Southdown Hall.

Mayfield sat back in his chair and spoke with studied nonchalance. "I wonder what they have on top of the coffin."

Hyde looked away, unable to speak or even catch his breath. *He knows! The damned man knows!* How had he found out? He must have seen something while they were digging. Security had been tight, but the men weren't blind. They had to have been asking themselves why they were digging such a large chamber, and of course, they would have seen the king when he came to inspect their progress. There was one more thing flickering at the very edge of his memory. He turned again to look at Mayfield and remembered sending a runner to fetch a screwdriver. Was this the same man?

Mayfield grinned. "What are they using for stones in the crown?" he asked.

Hyde's heart sank. Mayfield wasn't guessing; he *knew*. The crown jewelers had worked wonders with gilt and paste, and the mock stones in the Imperial State Crown would serve their purpose for the funeral procession, but they would never suffice for the coronation.

Hyde thought of himself as a practical, down-to-earth man, but his blood came from ancestors who had walked the hills and downs of southern England before the country had even been united. His people predated the Normans and had given homage to the kings of Wessex and the saintly Edward the Confessor, whose sapphire must once again sit atop the crown. History must not be denied. The stones must be found. Fakery would work for a funeral but not for a coronation. The stones must be in the crown when the monarch emerged from the abbey to ride through London in the gold state coach.

He glanced up at the clock. What was he going to do when the phone rang? He would have to say something. If he didn't give them the information, they would look elsewhere, and before long the whole world would know what was about to happen. At this moment, everything was low-key and mostly under control, but the American woman was impatient and likely to blow everything up if she didn't get her own way.

Mayfield was sitting back in the chair, laughing now. "You've got a face like a wet weekend," he said. "You want to know how I found out, don't you?"

"I don't know what you're talking about."

"Yes, you do. We're talking about Jeremy Paxton taking the jewels from the crown."

Hyde spoke before he could stop himself. "How did you …?"

"How did I find out?"

"No. How did you know they were …?" Hyde could not bring himself to finish the question.

Mayfield grinned. "How did I know they were being hidden from Hitler? It didn't take a genius to work out that that was not an everyday hole we were digging. We all saw the king making his inspection. Very kind of him to come and look at the sweating workers, but not what you'd expect, not with a war on. And then, of course, there was you, and your friend in the dark suit."

Hyde drew in a sharp breath. He was right. This was the man with the screwdriver. He'd permitted himself one moment of indiscretion in greeting an old friend, and this was the result. Deep, dark, blasphemous words he had not used since he had sent men to climb out of trenches sprang to mind, tasing foul and bitter in his mouth. Although the indiscretion was not his own, he had taken advantage of it.

They had almost been at the end of their workday when it had happened.

Frederick Morhouse had changed over the years, but Hyde recognized him when he saw him at Windsor. They had been boys together at Marlborough College, and they'd met up again in Flanders in 1915, where Morhouse had distinguished himself by winning a number of medals. There was something ironic about seeing him now, twenty-five years later, when they were once again overseeing earthworks. Hyde had no idea why his unit had been set to digging, and he doubted if Morhouse knew. Last he'd heard, Morhouse was an assistant royal librarian, with no responsibility for digging holes.

Morhouse wore a formal suit and a worried frown and carried a Bath Oliver biscuit tin under his arm. He was pleased enough to see a schoolmate but seemed abstracted, and he wasted little time on small talk.

"I need a tool. Would one of your men happen to have a screwdriver?"

"They're a bunch of damned incompetent conchies," Hyde said, letting Morhouse know that he was not proud of his current assignment. "They won't carry a weapon."

Morhouse was agitated. "I don't need a weapon, just a screwdriver. No one told me I would have to do this. It's sacrilege, Hyde. Sacrilege!"

"You ordered me to find a screwdriver," Mayfield said.

Now Hyde remembered. He'd clicked his fingers, and no doubt he'd waved his swagger stick. Mayfield came back with Paxton, a screwdriver, and curiosity disguised as offers to help.

"You dismissed us," Mayfield said, "but you know how it is: sometimes a man's curiosity gets the better of him. I hung around. I heard you talking. Your friend didn't know how to keep his mouth shut, did he? What was it? Did he want to impress an old school chum?"

No, he was terrified. He was an educated man with medals for bravery, but the idea of touching the jewels had overwhelmed him. It had overwhelmed both of them.

Hyde could still see Morhouse's pale face.

"I'm to pry the stones out and hide them separately. Pry them out! What with?

There should be a jeweler here to do this, but there's no time."

When Morhouse took the screwdriver and walked away, Hyde waited a moment and then quietly followed, keeping his distance and quietly observing.

Mayfield's voice cut into Hyde's memory. "You watched him, and I watched you." He laughed. "A biscuit tin. A bloody biscuit tin!"

The phone rang before Hyde could respond. He'd given Kumar instructions not to disturb him, and he supposed that the Indian had gone to bed. He knew full well that the damned phone would not stop ringing until he answered it. That was the way she was. That was the way they all were.

He picked up the receiver, and she didn't even wait for a greeting. "The duke is on his way. He's coming to the funeral. Will you be ready?"

Little Clamping, Kent
Davie

Davie wished he had his pack, but there would be no point in going back for it. By now someone would have found it and read the note. He hadn't yet met his father, but already he had disobeyed him. His father's instructions had been very clear: *Tell no one and come alone.*

Despite everything, the relentless cold, the cough that would not be quieted, and the shame he felt in failing the first task his father had given him, Davie was comforted by the very thought of having a father. He knew, biologically speaking, that every child had a father and a mother; he just wasn't sure how he had managed to lose them both.

Matron was happy to supply an answer: "Your mother was a harlot, and your father was a fornicator. They threw you away."

Some of the older boys had been known to argue with Matron's version of their parentage. They remembered a life that was different, although not necessarily happy, but the younger boys remembered nothing. Davie had no memory of any place other than the charity home. His weak leg was additional proof that what Matron said was true: the sin of his mother was written in the weakness of his body.

They had walked all afternoon, Pete and Colin striding confidently, Davie hurrying behind them and trying not to cough.

Strangely enough, despite the chill wind, he was not cold, and in fact, he was sweating beneath his heavy coat, while Pete and Colin complained that they were freezing.

Winter sunset came early, casting long shadows across the stubbled hayfields but revealing the lights of a village just a short distance ahead. A village meant a road, and a road meant a signpost. Davie thought that his father would not have given him an impossible distance to walk. If he wanted Davie to meet him in Redbridge, then Redbridge must be somewhere close. He hoped he was right, because he didn't think his legs would carry him many more miles. Pete and Colin complained that they were hungry, but Davie couldn't think about food. It was always this way. When the coughing started, appetite went away.

They stopped on the outskirts of the village. Clouds had come in during the afternoon, and tonight the moon was nowhere to be seen. Fortunately, the village was well lit. Light shone from streetlamps, cottages, and the windows of the village pub. A light even hung over the pub sign, proclaiming it to be the Duke's Head and showing a haughty man within an extravagantly curled wig. Davie's somewhat sketchy education did not extend far beyond learning the rudiments of British history and didn't cover fashion, hairstyles, or any dukes except the Grand Old Duke of York, who had marched people up a hill and marched them down again and had become the subject of a nursery rhyme.

Davie hung back and watched as Pete and Colin crept up to the warm glow of the pub windows and peeked inside. He saw them turn away and creep around to the back of the building and wondered for a desperate moment if they were about to desert him. If they did that, where would he sleep? He looked up and down the street, seeing only closed doors. He knew, because Colin had been complaining, that this night was as cold as the night before, but he was experiencing waves of heat followed by moments of chill, and his knees were beginning to tremble. He wondered how long it would take him to go back to the barn, where he could at least lie down in the straw.

Pete reappeared around the corner of the pub and beckoned to him. Davie followed him back around the building and saw Colin squatting beside a window set low to the ground and protected by iron bars.

"In you go, shrimp."

"In where?"

"In through the window. Time to earn your keep. You're skinny enough to get through there."

Davie squatted down and looked through the bars at the dimly lit cellar below. "What's in there?"

"Food," said Pete succinctly. "There's not much, but I can see some packets of crisps and a few jars of pickled eggs. It's better than nothing."

Davie was not hungry, but he was thirsty, and the dim bulb in the cellar sparked a telltale reflection on the bottles stacked up against the walls. He eyed the bars and then eased himself out of his heavy coat. It would be a tight fit, but he thought he could do it.

He wriggled through the bars, feetfirst, and made the short drop down to the sawdust strewn cellar floor. When he began a cautious investigation of the shelves, Colin hissed at him impatiently.

"Get on with it before someone comes. We're not waiting for you if you get caught."

Davie did not need another warning. Although he did not know what would happen to him if he was found and returned to the charity home, he wasn't interested in finding out. Older boys who tried to get away were sent to Borstal, which he believed to be some kind of junior version of jail. He didn't know what happened to boys like himself. He was too young for Borstal, but they couldn't send him home—he had no home. He made a mental correction. He had never had a home so far, but he was going to have one in the future, because now he knew he had a father. All he had to do was reach him in Redbridge.

He felt a cough building in his chest and retreated to a corner to muffle the sound in the crook of his elbow. As soon as he had brought the cough under control, he returned to scouting the shelves. He worked as quickly as he could, passing jars of pickled eggs through the bars, followed by bags of potato chips, a handful of chocolate bars, and some dark, unlabeled bottles that he held up for Colin and Pete to inspect.

"Don't got time to taste them," Colin said. "Just pass them up."

As he watched his companions stuffing their packs with his booty, it occurred to Davie that he could not climb out of the cellar on his own. If he stood on a box and stretched his arms up, someone would still have to pull him. He saw Pete and then Colin close and buckle their packs. He called to them until they turned to look at him.

"You have to help me."

"Who says we do?" Colin asked.

Pete pushed Colin aside. "I say we do. He pulled his weight this time."

"Yeah," said Colin, "but what about next time?"

"We'll see."

CHAPTER NINE

Redbridge Railway Station
Redbridge, Surrey
Valerie Chaplin

Valerie didn't know when she'd last felt so tired, or so cold. Despite everything, her frozen fingers, her growling stomach, the gritty feeling behind her eyes, she felt just a little proud of herself. She'd done it! She'd fooled them, and she'd found her way home.

She warmed herself with the thought that they had learned nothing from their elaborate charade. Did Lestock think she was an idiot? *Probably.* He'd only seen her at her worst. When she wasn't being cowardly, she was being shrewish. What about Mrs. Gordon? Did she think she could fool her by chatting about sausages and novels?

She assumed that she was being followed, although she had not been aware of anyone. It didn't matter. She was not leading them to April; she was simply leading them home. If they were following, she hoped that they were even colder than she was. She'd had a chance to warm herself by the coal fire in the ladies' waiting room at Dorking, but she'd been alone in the room. Her watcher, presumably Mrs. Gordon in disguise, had not been in there with her.

The train clattered to a halt at Redbridge station, and Valerie stepped down onto the platform. This was the last train of the night. It had not originated in London, and it would not continue to the coast. It was a local train for late-night stragglers running from nowhere to nowhere, with a route as convoluted as that of a morning milk train. Looking back along the train, she saw a couple of drunks, a man in workman's clothes, and a mother with a small, complaining child. Valerie sympathized with the child's tired wails as he or she—bundled in a coat and scarf, so it was impossible to know the sex—was taken in hand and made to walk out into the cold night.

Valerie hoped that none of these people were Lestock's operatives. She hoped that he'd given up on her. She was sure that his people had watched her at the ticket office and found she'd purchased a ticket home. If that was the case, there would be no point in following her.

She was surprised by the thought that Lestock would be disappointed in her and that she didn't want him to be disappointed. He'd done nothing to endear himself to her, except to save her life, so why should she care what he thought? She imagined that he had expected better of her. He had thought that somehow she would conquer the bus system and make her way to April's house. Perhaps she should take that as a compliment. He hadn't thought she would give up so easily. Well, he'd been wrong. The night was cold; the timetable was complicated; and she had no idea if April still lived at her old address. Instead of doing what he'd expected, she'd done what she thought best, or maybe she had only done what was easiest—as usual.

Now she was in a hurry to get home. For a woman walking alone, the safest route would be to walk out of the front of the station and follow the main road to the center of town, but she balked at the idea of staying out in the cold any longer than necessary. She couldn't imagine that even a robber or a rapist would be out on such a night, and she was desperate to crawl under the covers of her own bed. She took a shortcut from the back of the station and headed down a narrow pedestrian underpass that her mother had always warned her against. *"Rats and dustbins, dear. Not a place for a nice girl to walk."* Her mother had never been more specific about what might happen to a nice girl, but tonight Valerie didn't care. She wasn't a girl anymore, and it was possible that she was really no longer nice; she was cold and she was angry.

The shortcut brought her safely out into the heart of the medieval town. The shops were closed, but the pubs were open. Their lights promised warmth inside, and it seemed that the drinkers intended to stay inside. The streets were deserted.

She did not hear the footsteps behind her until she had passed the King's Head, the last of the pubs, and was beyond the lights of the town center. Churchgate Close stretched ahead of her, with only occasional pools of light from the widely spaced lampposts, and far ahead the bulk of the church spire rose up to pierce the curtain of stars that hung over the old town. The church itself was dark, with no light showing at the windows. She should have been at choir practice tonight, but now it was over. Even the sopranos, who usually stood outside the gate, chattering and speculating about the marital status and no doubt checkered history of the new vicar, had gone home, and the churchyard was deserted.

She told herself that the footsteps behind her were not those of a stranger but just the footsteps of someone Lestock had sent to follow her. She'd been wrong about him giving up on her; he still wanted to know where she was going. Perhaps he was following her himself. She hoped he was as cold as she was.

She had to look, just a glance. She turned her head slightly and looked quickly from the corner of her eye. She glimpsed a man, taller and thinner than Lestock. She refused to be afraid and told herself that Mrs. Gordon was following her disguised as a man. She was tall enough to appear masculine, and she was no doubt a master of disguise. The man's coat and hat could have been in her shopping bag, and that would explain why it had looked so full when Mrs. Gordon had not yet been shopping.

The thought of Mrs. Gordon reassured her. *"Anyone who wants you will have to get past me."* Valerie was nearly home now, and she could relax. Having convinced herself once that Lestock's operatives were not following her, she now welcomed the opposite idea. Mrs. Gordon was following her, and she had nothing to fear.

Now she could see lights shining from her aunts' house, and a car was parked beneath the streetlamp outside. She made out the distinctive shape of a Wolseley. *Lestock!* He was here, already waiting for her. She steeled herself to face him. She wasn't going back to his safe house, not now and not ever. If he tried to arrest her, she'd scream bloody murder until all the neighbors came out to see what was going on, and let him try explaining his special powers to them. She had done nothing wrong.

The footsteps were closer now. Why didn't Mrs. Gordon just stop her right here? Did she really want to follow her all the way home and make a dreadful scene? Something was wrong with the picture Valerie was painting for herself.

She listened to the relentless tread of the follower's feet, hearing the same steady rhythm that she had picked up as she had left the town center. *Steady rhythm.* Mrs. Gordon didn't walk with a steady rhythm. Mrs. Gordon limped.

She hesitated. Her heart was pounding, and more than anything, she wanted to run. She was so close to home; all she had to do was cover the last hundred yards and fling herself in through the front door. She remembered the hoarse whisper of the man in the library, but this couldn't be him. He was dead, killed in a sudden explosion of pistol fire.

She wasn't sure who had fired first, but she knew one thing: the man who had whispered her name was not the only man to have been hit. Lestock had dripped blood from the wound in his arm. Anyone in that library could have been hit. Once the guns came out, anything could happen. What would happen now if someone started firing? If her aunts came out to see what was happening, would they be met by a hail of bullets?

The man in the library was dead, but obviously, there were others, or Lestock wouldn't have taken her to a safe house. If one man had a weapon, surely they all had weapons.

If she ran now, she would be leading her stalker directly into the house where the two people she loved most in the world were, no doubt, pouring tea for Lestock. He didn't know she was being followed. He wouldn't be ready. She couldn't go home, but what else was she to do? *Damn it!* She never swore, not even in her own mind, but this word, mild as it was, helped. *Damn it, I'm a librarian, not a spy! Leave me alone! Damn it, damn it, damn it!*

She looked ahead to the dark shape of the parish church. The new vicar had stubbornly insisted that the church doors should never be locked. If people wanted to pray in the middle of the night, then they should come. There had been fire in his eyes when he had made his declaration from the pulpit. *"Neither God nor the devil will ever rest, and neither will I."*

She was sure the stalker would not know the vicar's stance on unlocked doors, and she had a good chance of taking him by surprise. If she ran as she had never run before, she could reach the church before he caught up with her. Once inside, she would have an advantage. She knew every inch of the church, from the vestry to the altar. It had originally been a square-towered Norman building, but generations of worshippers had felt compelled to make their own marks on the building, including side chapels, balconies, ornate nooks and crannies, and a Victorian belfry with a towering spire. He wouldn't find her amid the jumbled architecture ... unless he located the light switches.

No time to think of that. Just run.

Southdown Hall
Dorking, Surrey
Harry Mayfield

When Major Hyde picked up the phone and listened to the caller, his face went immediately from red to white. Mayfield saw that he was swaying precariously, but the telephone cord, stretched to its limit, prevented him from reaching a chair.

In normal circumstances, Mayfield would have let the old man fall. He had no love for the officer class, and no respect for Major Cardrew Hyde. He wondered what stories Hyde had told to win his medals. No doubt he'd taken the credit for someone else's bravery. Mayfield knew a coward when he saw one, and he'd definitely seen a coward on the day Hyde had allowed his untrained men to defuse the bomb at Lambs Farm Road. Thank God he'd been taken off bomb duty before he'd killed the entire company.

Because he was very interested in knowing who was at the other end of the telephone line, he carried a chair across the room, took hold of the major's shoulder, and pushed him down into the seat. Now he was close enough to pick up some of the words being hurled at Hyde from the telephone. The speaker was a woman with a grating voice, and she was angry.

"Meetings ... high level ... duke will ..."

Hyde interrupted. "I can do that. I've spoken to—"

"No names ... phone!"

"But I thought you'd want to know—"

"You ... in person ... security ... watched every minute."

"How am I to talk to him?"

"Not personally ... name ... later."

"What about you? Will you be there?"

The woman on the other end of the line laughed derisively. "Never allow ... pariah."

She had an accent and a damned annoying voice. Mayfield thought she could be American, but if so, she had made some effort to change. Of course, he was only hearing snatches of conversation, but they were very interesting snatches.

The woman was becoming agitated. Her voice was loud enough now that he could hear every word. She seemed to have thrown caution to the winds.

"If you don't have the jewels, there is no point in us doing anything. Do you have them, Major?"

"I'm very close. We have several good leads."

"Leads will not make a crown. For the good of your country, Major, you have to find those stones. You lost them; you find them."

Hyde protested into the receiver, but Mayfield could hear the loud beeping of a call that had ended. When the beeping turned to a dial tone, he removed the instrument from Hyde's grip and restored silence to the room.

Mayfield broke the silence and was surprised by his own words. "The Duke of Windsor?"

Hyde would not meet his eyes. "None of your business."

Mayfield was still stunned, but his mind was working. "The Duke of Windsor," he repeated, but this time it was not a question. "Are you telling me that King Edward VIII wants his old job back?"

"I'm not telling you anything."

"He gave it up," Mayfield said, surprised by the memory of how disappointed he'd been at the time. "Ten months on the job, and he couldn't take the strain."

"That wasn't the reason," Hyde said.

Mayfield dragged his mind back to the shock of the abdication speech. "'I have found it impossible to carry the heavy burden of responsibility, blah, blah, blah, without the help and support of the woman I love,'" he parroted. "We all heard him. Selfish little bastard saw war on the horizon, and he didn't have the bottle for the job, so he gave up and gave the throne to his brother."

"I will not allow such disrespect in my house," Hyde said.

Mayfield laughed, remembering the disrespect he'd heard in the pub as the uncrowned king blamed his abdication on the fact that the church would not allow him to have a twice-divorced American woman as his queen. There was not a man in the pub that night who could see why their king would give up his throne for the sake of a woman as hard-faced and androgynous as Wallis Simpson. Helen of Troy was not a name that sprang to mind.

Mayfield ignored Hyde's protest. He couldn't imagine why Hyde would involve himself in something so absurd as an attempt for Edward to regain the throne. "King George did a bang-up job," he insisted. "We won the war while Edward hid himself in the Bahamas. Georgie Boy gets all the credit."

"If Edward had been king, we wouldn't have had a war," Hyde said.

Mayfield's day had been full of surprises, but this was the greatest surprise of all. "Wouldn't have had a war?" he repeated.

"Edward was willing to talk to Hitler. We could have come to an arrangement."

Mayfield took a step back and gave himself time to absorb the shock of Hyde's words. He knew himself to be a down-to-earth, ordinary man, a Yorkshireman to his boots and not given to flights of imagination. He could not now get his mind around the idea of a world where the war had never happened. Would it be a world where Hitler had just walked into Britain with the permission of King Edward VIII, or would it be a world where Britain, and even America, stood back and let Hitler have Europe so long as he didn't set foot in Britain?

His head hurt with thinking, and so he abandoned thought in favor of the current moment and the current benefit, but Hyde was not ready to move on and talk pounds and shillings.

"We can't have that girl as queen," Hyde said, leaning forward in the chair and fully alert. His pallor had been replaced with feverish red cheeks. "It will all work out for the best. Edward is fifty-seven, and he has no children ..."

"No surprise there," Mayfield said.

"So," Hyde continued, "if he lives to be seventy-five, that gives us eighteen years of a good king on the throne, and by that time, maybe the girl—"

"You mean Queen Elizabeth?"

"I mean Princess Elizabeth."

Mayfield chose to stay silent. Arithmetic was not his strong point, and Hyde's manipulation of dates and possibilities was rapidly approaching fantasy. What Mayfield really wanted to know was how he could benefit from this far-fetched plot.

"By the time Edward dies, Princess Elizabeth will be in a better position to be queen, and her son will be twenty-one, almost old enough to be king himself. We're not suggesting a radical change of inheritance, just a delay."

Mayfield shrugged and was about to inform Hyde of his lack of interest in anything but money when Hyde rose majestically to his feet and clapped him on the shoulder.

"All we need is the jewels," he declared.

Mayfield nodded. At last they had returned to the most important subject: the biscuit tin that contained the four greatest of the Imperial State Crown's jewels.

"They will give us the power," Hyde declared. "We will have the true crown and the true king, and we'll see what the people make of that. If Parliament is with us—"

"Are they?"

"Some of them are, and a great many of the aristocracy."

"If that's the case, why do you need the jewels?"

Hyde took a step back. "Good God, man, have you no soul? Think of their history. Think of the blood spilled for their sake. Think of the heads that have been crowned. How can we have a coronation without them?"

Mayfield knew the answer to that question. *Easy!* No one was going to get close enough to the crown to discover the stones were fake

So far as Mayfield was concerned, the jewels were just money in a different form. If he ever got his hands on them, they'd soon be reduced to chips and slivers, and women all over the world would be wearing engagement rings with stones cut from the Crown Jewels.

The major turned to the fireplace and studied the portrait of the old king George V. He spoke without turning his head. "I took Paxton into my confidence. He was a simple lad who thought the world could be all goodness and light if we'd just throw away our guns and beat our swords into plowshares. It all came together: me being in charge of your squad, Morhouse turning up looking for a screwdriver. I could see it for what it was: it was God's plan."

Mayfield interrupted before Hyde could disappear down another rabbit hole of fancy arithmetic and mysticism. "And so you told Jeremy Paxton to take the jewels for you."

Hyde was silent for a long moment, and Mayfield could see

that the major was finally calming down and putting two and two together. "You knew? All the time, you knew?"

Mayfield shrugged. "I knew you were going to. That's why I'm here. He told me what you planned."

He wasn't surprised that it had taken the major such a long time to see the full picture and understand Mayfield's role. From the moment they had left the Chaplin house together, Mayfield had been aware that the major was acting frantically and irrationally. Hyde was so wrapped up in his fantasy of stopping the coronation of Elizabeth II and under so much pressure from voices on the phone that he had not paused to remember that he had recently found Mayfield preparing to break into Valerie Chaplin's house, or to ask himself why.

Mayfield settled back into a comfortable chair and watched the major's face as understanding continued to dawn.

"Paxton had his own plans," Mayfield said, "and he didn't like your orders. When you looked at him, all you saw was one of your damned conchies, but Paxton wasn't some shivering coward you could push around. Yes, he was a conchie, a conscientious objector, but he wasn't a traitor, and he wasn't ever going to give you those stones."

"I'm no traitor," Hyde blustered. "I've told you—"

"You've told me what you're doing now but not what you were doing then. When you took the jewels, the war was still on. The king was not dead. There were no questions about Princess Elizabeth. You had something else in mind, didn't you? You were already a traitor."

"And what about you?" Hyde snapped. "What did you have in mind?"

"Money," Mayfield said. "I planned on making a good deal of money, although I didn't tell Paxton. I advised him to go through with it, and we'd decide later what to do."

"So he turned on you as well," Hyde said with a note of satisfaction, "turned on both of us, just took off in the dark, damned deserter."

"Why didn't you stop him?"

"It was dark and he was fast. I wasn't ready for him. I've always supposed that he told his girlfriend what he planned." He jerked his head toward the pile of papers on the floor. "I had hoped

95

that her letters would give us a clue as to where Paxton is now."

"So did I," Mayfield said. He decided to set a few of his cards on the table. "You have people working for you and access to records. Do you know for sure that Paxton is still alive?"

"No."

"So you've no record of him after we all left Windsor?"

Hyde scowled. "None. I told you, he's a deserter. In my day, he would have been shot at dawn, but we don't do that now. We don't even look for the damned cowards."

"Does he have parents?"

"I'm not a damned fool," Hyde snapped. "Of course I've looked for his parents. They're dead. Luftwaffe dropped a bomb on their house."

"So that leaves Valerie Chaplin," Mayfield said, "and the possibility that she had other ways of communicating with him. Have you tried asking her?"

"I tried. I sent someone to fetch her and bring her here."

"And what happened?"

"The Met has seconded a squad from the Security Service, under a man named Lestock. There was gunfire. My man died."

Mayfield made a quick assessment of the new situation. He should have expected gunfire, but not from Hyde. Considering the size of the fortune involved, perhaps Mayfield, too, should be armed.

"When you say that you sent a man," he asked, "who did you send, and who is going to be upset about him being dead?"

"I sent professionals," Hyde said huffily, "and the guns were their choice, not mine. I don't want the girl hurt."

"So you've called them off?" Mayfield asked.

"Of course."

In the years since he'd been demobbed, Mayfield had spent most of his time in various minor illegal activities, but always with the hope of moving up the ladder into something big. This was bigger than he would ever have expected, but it was also a lot more dangerous. Hyde may think he'd called off his troops, but that was because Hyde was a fool. In Mayfield's experience, the kind of criminals that carried guns were members of tight-knit families, and those families didn't take kindly to fathers, brothers, and uncles being shot dead. Hyde could dismiss them if he wanted to, but Mayfield doubted they had gone away.

CHAPTER TEN

Churchgate Close, Redbridge
Valerie Chapman

Valerie ran in through the side door of the church. She forced herself not to slam it behind her, but to close it slowly and quietly. She had expected the church to be dark but the sanctuary lamp above the altar pierced the darkness sending a wash of red light across the marble floor and into the choir stalls. Her heart pounded and her breath came in ragged gasps. It was years since she had run so far and so fast. now her knees felt weak. She wanted to sit but sitting wasn't an option. She had to be somewhere completely dark and hidden before her stalker found the light switches. If he had a brain in his head, he would look in the entry beside the carved oak doors. The array of switches would be easy to locate. If he had a flashlight, so much the better for him. He was just moments behind her.

The front doors crashed open and the dim light of the starry night cut through the gloom offering a sense of size and space. She saw his shadow in the vaulted doorway. He left the door open and the darkness retreated as starlight entered.

She tried to slow her breathing. Her gasps were so loud that he wouldn't even need a light to find her. She dropped to her knees. She had to find somewhere that the light would not reach; a room with a door. The church had not been designed with doors. The vestry had a door but she couldn't go that way without passing him. She could crawl along the line of pews, crawl and crawl, row after row, but eventually he would find the light and then he would find her. The sacristy behind the altar had a door but to reach it she would have to pass through the light of the sanctuary lamp.

The tower had a door but she hesitated to use it. Going up into the tower would be the height of foolishness. Everything she had ever read from the Hunchback of Notre Dame to Enid Blyton and the adventures of her Famous Five, advised against fugitives climbing towers, but she had no choice. No light would spill in through the door if she opened it because there was no outside window until the stairs reached the first landing. She had climbed the stairs before and she would crawl up them now on her hands and knees even in the pitch dark. She could be at the first landing before he found the door and opened it, and there was always a chance that he would not even find this door.

If she had the chance she could continue on past the first landing although she was not a bellringer and she didn't know what she would find higher up. She knew only that somewhere in the heights above the church's massive bells hung on a framework of wheels and axles accessible only by ladders. She had never ventured beyond the circular chamber where the bell ropes with their red and white sallies hung neatly. She had a memory of cupboards lining the walls that could possibly provide a hiding place. She hoped not to go any higher into the nightmare maze of the belfry.

She crawled to the end of the row of pews. To open the tower door she would have to come closer to her pursuer. He was moving into the church now but he had not brought a flashlight and so far he had not found the light switches. He took another step forward into the gloom passing the electrical panel without realizing. She would have a few more moments.

He was feeling his way along the wall, his hand searching for the switches. He would not go far before he realized he was in the wrong place and he would backtrack. She had only moments. She reached the tower door and found the heavy iron latch. She hesitated. What if the door squeaked or groaned?

Don't go up! Only silly girls in white dresses run up towers and nobody is coming to rescue you from the roof. You're not stupid. Don't go up!

He was still moving forward not bothering to muffle his footsteps. He knew she was stupid and intimidated. *Everyone knew she was stupid and intimidated.* He stepped toward the altar a menacing figure in the wash of red light from the sanctuary lamp. Valerie yanked on the door. It groaned as it opened and she saw him turn.

She took a deep breath. *Don't go up!*

Churchgate Close, Redbridge
Alan Lestock

Lestock was already awash in Typhoo tea and Miss Olivia Chaplin had departed to put more water in the pot. He could hear Miss Gladys in the kitchen as she prepared some kind of potion for the dyspeptic pug, and he caught occasional whiffs of whale meat effluvia followed by a chiding tone from Miss Gladys.

He looked toward the front door and asked himself what in the hell had happened to Valerie. Smythe had seen her board the train and Mrs. Gordon - he never called her Jane - had been right behind her. Now Mrs. Gordon, still dressed in a man's overcoat, was pacing the floor in the Chaplin sisters' small living room and neither of them knew what had happened to Valerie.

"She gave me the slip at the station."

"Did she know you were following?"

"I don't think she cared. It was obvious where she was going; she didn't make any attempt to hide it."

"So why would she try to throw you off the scent now?"

"I don't know, Alan. Maybe she didn't. It would have made more sense for you just to pick her up at the station without all this cloak and dagger nonsense."

"I wanted to see what she'd do."

"She's a real person, Alan; not some experiment. Bad enough that you used her as bait and had her waiting at a bus stop in the cold, you could at least have done the right thing for her when it was obvious that the only thing she would do is to go home."

"I thought she'd have more initiative and she'd lead us to April Brady."

"Has it occurred to you that she wasn't fooled and she had no intention of leading you anywhere? She has her own secrets to keep."

"Paxton?"

Mrs. Gordon shot him a meaningful glance. "No, the other secret; the one she doesn't know that we know."

Lestock tried to follow her reasoning. "If she doesn't know

that we know, she won't be worried."

Mrs. Gordon responded with a harsh glare. "You're the coldest damned fish I've ever met."

The insult hurt more than Lestock had expected and he made an attempt to defend himself. "I don't have time for feelings. I have a job to do. I can only focus on one thing at time."

Mrs. Gordon gave him a look that was almost sympathetic. "That was always your problem, Alan."

He shook his head. "I do what I have to do. We all know the risks"

"She doesn't. She's an innocent bystander."

Miss Olivia poked her head around the door and looked at him anxiously. "My sister was taking the dog outside to … you know … and she thinks something is happening up at the church."

Lestock stiffened as an instinct that been his since birth took hold. "What do you mean by something?"

"The lights are on and the lights are never on this late on a Thursday night. Choir practice was over a long time ago. I don't know quite what you're both looking for, but I know you're waiting for Valerie and I wondered … well …."

"Is the church locked?"

"No, never. Our new vicar has very strong opinions about that."

Lestock looked at Mrs. Gordon. "It could be just a coincidence."

Lestock had said nothing explicit to the Chapman sisters, but they had known all evening that something was wrong. Why else would Lestock be camped out at their sitting room? He had told them earlier that Valerie was in a safe house, but that was before someone broke their window, ransacked their house, and left a dog tied to their front gate.

Miss Olivia pursed her lips and looked at him with disapproval. "You are a policeman, aren't you?"

"In a manner of speaking."

"Well, I believe a crime is being committed at the church. For all I know there could be devil worshippers in there. Our new vicar is convinced that they are all around us."

Lestock shook his head. "I doubt that."

"And so do I," Miss Olivia said acerbically. "I think it is far more likely this had something to do with our poor Valerie and the reason why you have been sitting here all evening. I really think it's time you told us what is going on,"

Mrs. Gordon laid a hand on Miss Olivia's shoulder. "I'll go and see."

Lestock shook his head. "No, not both of us at once. We shouldn't leave the ladies alone."

Miss Olivia stood up straight and looked him in the eye. "Gladys and I are quite accustomed to looking after ourselves."

Mrs. Gordon smiled. She had the gift of rising above any situation and offering sudden comforting warmth; a gift that never been given to Lestock. "I'll stay here," she said. "Mr. Lestock will manage very well without me."

Miss Olivia was only slightly mollified. "I hope he doesn't find it necessary to shoot anyone else." She gave Lestock a glance of sudden piercing intelligence. "Dead men tell no tales so I hope you don't kill this one."

He left the house by the front door. He checked his pocket for his Browning and felt the throb in his arm from his last bout of gunfire. He could see that the church at the end of the street was not exactly ablaze with lights but it certainly was not dark. Dim orange light showed in the stained-glass windows another brighter light beamed from the open doorway onto a gravel path.

As he ran the length of the street, Lestock was aware of lights coming alive in houses on either side of him. The inhabitants of Churchgate Close were taking notice, well aware that the church lights should not be on at this time of night. Dogs barked, windows opened, men shouted. The back of Lestock's neck prickled. Many of those men now leaning from their upstairs windows had once been soldiers. A number of them would have brought home their service weapon; a number more would have brought home a German souvenir.

He ran the gauntlet of the awakening street and hurled himself through the open church door. No point in being secretive; the whole street was watching.

"Valerie!"

His voice echoed around the high vaulted interior of the church. As he waited for a response he made his way along the central aisle, glancing from left to right along the lines of pews hoping to find a crouching figure. He could not imagine what kind of blind panic had brought her into the church but he tried to make his voice reassuring.

"Valerie, it's Lestock. It's Alan."

Why had he said that? Using his Christian name didn't make him any less intimidating or turn him into a friend.

"Valerie?"

He saw an open door and, approaching with caution, looked inside. He drew his weapon and studied the stone steps that spiraled out of sight beneath the light of a single light bulb. Obviously the steps would lead upward to the bells but would Valerie really go up there? Would she be that stupid? She didn't strike him as stupid; on the contrary she gave the impression of quiet intelligence. She did, however, seem rather naïve. Running away by climbing a tower from which there was no escape would be a naïve thing to do. A man's voice drifted down to him from high above. He sounded ferociously angry.

Stepping as quietly as possible, Lestock advanced up the stone steps and emerged into the tower's well lit, orderly, and unoccupied ringing chamber where bell ropes snaked down through openings in the wooden ceiling. A smaller wooden staircase led upward from the chamber and the sounds from overhead were now easier to hear.

The only voice he could hear belonged to the angry man. Although he could not make out every word he could recognize "Satan" and "blasphemer". One particularly virulent string of words was accompanied by the sound of more than one set of feet pounding and scuffling on the wooden ceiling but still he heard no female voice. If she was here she was keeping quiet, or perhaps she was being kept quiet.

He crossed the ringing chamber and eased his way up the wooden stairs. This time he emerged into the open vault of the bell chamber. A chill wind whistled in through the unglazed windows and starlight from outside picked out the white of the bell ropes hanging down among a labyrinth of heavy timbers and ladders. The massive bells themselves were silent and unmoving but they radiated their own menace. It would take just one tug on the ropes in the ringing chamber to move the wheels and set the bells swinging on their axles and if the bells moved no one on the ladders would be safe.

The angry man shouted again. "Blasphemer, devil worshipper!"

The voice was strong and filled with righteous indignation but the only response was a sudden shiver of one of the bells as a shadowy figure ran lightly across one of the trusses.

"Oh no you don't!"

Now there were two figures in movement in the gloom but they both appeared to be men. *Where was Valerie?* Lestock was appalled at the idea of her being somewhere among the bells, tied to a beam, bound, gagged. If that had happened, it would be his fault. He had set this whole thing in motion. Smythe was right. He had used her as his cats-paw hoping that she would lead him to Paxton. He'd played with her life and this was the result.

He sighted up into the maze above and called out a warning. "Armed police. Stay where you are."

The response to his warning was a sudden frenzy of movement as a man ran nimbly from one set of ladders to another, and shimmied down toward him shouting as he came. "You have him red-handed. He won't get away this time."

The man landed with a thump on the floor beside him and Lestock took in the effect of a black shirt and a splash of white collar. The vicar!

"A woman?" Lestock gasped. "Is there a woman up there."

The vicar shook his head and his long white hair caught the light. "No, there's no woman. Just him. Bloody satanist."

"You know who he is?"

"Not yet, but I will."

Before Lestock could respond, the man above them -- possibly a satanist but Lestock thought that was not the case -- fired a weapon and a bullet zinged past the vicar's ear. The vicar responded with a soldier's oath and an attempt to grab Lestock's pistol.

While Lestock fought him off, the man above fired again. This time the shot was wild and the bell tower reverberated as the missile struck one of the bells causing it to shudder and give off a faint echo of the sound it was capable of making.

Lestock shoved the vicar down to the floor. "Stay down."

"Not bloody likely."

Another shot from above missed Lestock by inches. The man with the gun was moving quickly now. Lestock took aim at his fleeting shadow, fired a single shot and heard a pained grunt.

He shouted another warning. "Armed police. Give yourself up. Bring the girl."

The vicar was back on his feet. "What girl? There's no girl."

"There's a girl," Lestock said.

"There's no girl. Just shoot the bastard."

"I've winged him. I don't need to shoot him.," Lestock insisted. *Dead men tell no tales.*

Another wild shot from above struck a more than glancing blow at one of the bells. The whole great weight trembled and suddenly the vicar was tugging at Lestock's sleeve. "I'm not waiting here for the bastard to shoot me. I'll go down and get the bells going. He won't stay long once they start moving."

"There's a girl," Lestock protested.

"There's no girl," the vicar insisted. "She left."

"What?"

"Valerie Chaplin left. I saw her running through the graveyard. Don't know what she was doing in here."

Lestock made a grab for the vicar's arm, but the vicar was already in motion. "I'll shake him loose for you. Get down the stairs or I'll shake you loose as well."

Before Lestock could stop him, the vicar hurled himself down the stairs leaving Lestock alone to peer up into the rafters where nothing moved.

After a moment the vicar's head reappeared at the top of the stairs, bobbing up like a Jack in the Box. "I'm warning you," he said and disappeared again.

Despite the gloom of the tower, Lestock could see the white of the bell ropes and he saw that one of them was beginning to move. One of the bells began to swing. The rope moved again, more vigorously this time, the bell swung in an arc and the clapper moved creating a tentative sound. The rope moved again and the great wheel controlling the bell began to spin on its axle. The clapper struck again and the voice of the bell echoed through the chamber and pounded against Lestock's ears.

He took one last look up into the rafters but any activity from the man above was masked by the added movement of another rope and another wheel. He could not leave, not yet, but he could not remain standing among the bells. He retreated halfway down the steps to the ringing chamber where he was in a position to watch the rafters without being thrown off his feet.

He glanced over his shoulder. The vicar was controlling two adjacent bell ropes, pulling down and releasing in easy, practiced movements. Two bells were now swinging, two wheels were now moving, and the rafters creaked and moved with every swing of the heavy bells while the sound battered at his ears. He imagined that anyone on Churchgate Close who had not yet been awakened was now fully alert and police cars would be on their way.

He could only hope that the vicar was telling the truth and Valerie was not up among the rafters. He wanted to speak and ask him once again. "Are you quite sure?" but speech was impossible.

He thought he detected movement above and beyond the movement of the bells. He saw a muzzle flash from a position high above the bell wheels. He sighted with the Browning and fired. He knew better than to waste bullets on an unseen target but he needed to keep the man moving and there he was; a shadow moving among the rafters.

The heavy bells that had been hanging downward were now swinging easily on their axles coming closer to completing a circle. They swung higher with each pull of the rope until they stood almost upright on the beam before plunging downward. Another muzzle flash brought momentary brightness to the belfry and Lestock saw the moving shadow again. He was attempting to cross a rafter between the bells. Lestock held back. He had his target but if he fired the man would fall with every chance he would not survive.

The ringing had to stop. They had him trapped, the street was probably crawling with reinforcements. It was over. Lestock turned and made an attempt to get the vicar's attention. Sweat was pouring down the clergyman's face and he flicked his head to keep his long white hair from falling across his forehead. His eyes gleamed fanatically as he danced between the bell ropes adding a third bell to his efforts. Lestock descended the steps. He didn't wish to take his eyes off his quarry but the vicar was lost in a world of his own impervious to Lestock's shouts. He had to resort to grasping hold of the ropes himself to get the vicar's attention.

The vicar lost the rhythm of his ringing and the sound of bells became ragged and discordant. At last, he ceased his frantic activity and took a deep breath. He stared at Lestock with slowly focusing eyes.

"Did we get him?"

"You probably killed him," Lestock said grimly. He climbed the steps and peered cautiously intro the bell chamber. The bells were still trembling on their axles but the wheels no longer moved.

The vicar joined him on the steps. "Well?"

Lestock turned and shook the vicar's hand. "We got him."

The vicar smiled triumphantly. "I told you I'd shake him loose."

Lestock looked at the sorry figure of Valerie's assailant who lay in a crumpled but still breathing heap on the floor of the bell chamber. He looked back at the vicar. "Has anyone told you that you're a madman?"

The vicar grinned. "All the time."

Village of Little Clamping
Davie

Davie had never seen a drunken person before but he had listened to some of the older boys reminiscing about what they had experienced. He didn't think he was drunk; he'd only had a few mouthfuls of the stolen liquor, but he was pretty certain that Colin and Pete were very, very drunk.

They had carried their pilfered supplies out of the village and run until they came to a crumbling bomb-damaged cottage. Colin offered up a few swear words when he discovered the roof had collapsed completely and the walls were so precarious that they did not dare enter. Davie imagined that Matron would need a whole bar of soap to wash those words away - not that Colin was ever going to give her a chance.

Pete, scouting around the back of the cottage, found an unlocked coal shed and a pile of empty coal sacks. The stone building offered shelter but no warmth, and the coal sacks provided very little in the way of comfort but it was all they had and Pete and Colin were anxious to eat the potato crisps and the pickled eggs. They were even more anxious to open the unlabeled brown bottles.

They sat on the coal sacks and used the faint spill of light from the slowly emerging moon to divide the food among them.

Colin opened one of the bottles and took a long sniff. "It ain't beer."

"Cider?" Pete asked.

Colin shook his head. "Something stronger." He took a long drink from bottle and his eyes widened. "Blimey!"

"Blimey what?" Pete asked.

Colin coughed but held onto the bottle.

"What?" Pete asked.

"Get your own bottle," Colin said belligerently. He took another swig from the bottle and this time he grinned. "Blimey," he said again.

Davie, whose throat was so sore he could hardly swallow held out his hand. If Colin liked the stuff so much, maybe it would help soothe his throat, maybe even stop the persistent coughing. "Can I have some?"

Colin ignored him but Pete held out a bottle. "Try it."

Davie took a mouthful and almost gagged at the taste. He forced himself to swallow and felt the liquid sliding past the burning pain in his throat and down into his stomach where it continued to burn and send waves of warmth throughout his body.

In the short run from the pub to the church Davie's fevered warmth had given way to shivering cold but now he was warm again and tired. He opened a packet of crisps and ate a handful, washing them down with a swallow of the foul but warming liquid.

Colin opened another bottle and Pete eyed him warily. "Take it easy mate, that's strong stuff."

Colin leaned back against a pile of coal and hugged the bottle to his chest. "Don't tell me what to do."

Davie scooted away, putting distance between himself and Colin. He'd seen this before. Words like that were fighting words and he didn't want to be in the middle when the two big boys started in on each other. He was relieved when Pete took a swig from his own bottle. The liquor, Davie assumed it was whiskey or brandy, he had never tasted either so he didn't know the difference, seemed to have a calming effect on his companions. Pete ignored Colin's taunt and settled down to drink his way down the bottle while Davie took one more swallow trying to recreate the initial feeling of warmth.

Pete and Colin were laughing now, all thoughts of fighting forgotten. To Davie, their voices sounded muffled and seemed to come from far away. They were reciting all the swear words they knew, some of which Davie had never heard before. If Matron came storming into the coal cellar now, she wouldn't know how to punish them for all the sins they were committing - drunkenness, swearing, stealing, covering themselves in coal dust - even Matron did not have enough soap or a strong enough cane to take care of such ungodliness. They would probably just go straight to hell; wouldn't even have to die first.

No, that didn't make any sense - you'd have to die, that was one of the rules. Davie's head was swimming and he couldn't be bothered to sort out the religious problem he'd just created. He thought he should sleep but when he tried to lie down, Colin tripped over him and cursed him angrily.

Davie who knew how to keep out of trouble, clutched a coal sack and crawled away from the danger of Colin's feet into a dark corner where he curled into a ball, safe and invisible. He told himself that tomorrow he would leave the other boys behind. Tomorrow he would find out how to get to Redbridge. It was taking longer than he expected. He hoped his father would wait for him.

CHAPTER ELEVEN

February 14, 1952
Office of Sir Walter Perrin
Scotland Yard
Alan Lestock

If Lestock had been easily intimidated, he would have been intimidated by the expression on the special commissioner's face, the size of the special commissioner's desk, and the fact that the only paper marring its pristine surface was the single sheet on which he, Lestock, had reported his extraordinary lack of progress.

"I have been on the phone with the superintendent of police in Redbridge," Perrin said. "He would like your explanation for church bells ringing in the dead of night. They have already obliged us by covering up the fact that someone was shot dead in their library, but what do you expect them to say about this?"

"I suggest you blame it on Russian spies," Lestock said.

"I already did that. He is not satisfied."

Lestock was too tired to be tactful. "Do you want me to satisfy the local police, or do you want me to get the job done?"

"I would like you to do both," Perrin said, "but I realize that is not possible."

He picked up Lestock's one-page report, studied its few words, and then set it down again. "What about the fellow in the bell tower? Will he recover?"

"He'll be out of action for a while. He broke a few bones and he's in surgery. Won't be able to answer questions for another couple of hours."

Perrin nodded. "Any idea who he is?"

"I talked to him in the ambulance," Lestock said, "before they gave him the morphine. He didn't have much to say for himself. He's obviously a Londoner, but I don't think he knows much, just obeying orders."

Perrin shivered. "I hate that phrase."

"We all do."

Silence descended on the office, and the special commissioner squinted at Lestock's report as though careful study might produce additional words or insights. Finally he shook his head. "Don't suppose you know much about London gangs," he said gloomily.

"No, sir. Most of my work has been out of the country."

Perrin nodded. "I'll find someone to interview this fellow of yours when he comes round. There are some boys in the Met who know their stuff. Leave him to us, and if he tells us anything, we'll let you know, but I suspect that he's a low-level operator."

He gave Lestock a look of grudging encouragement. "At least you didn't kill this one, but you should never have let him go into surgery. You probably could have got more out of him if you'd left him in pain."

Lestock could not hide his expression of disgust. "Sir!"

"I know, I know. It's not cricket and it smacks of torture, but let me tell you where we stand. We're out of time. The Duke of Windsor arrives here tomorrow, and trouble has already started with rumblings in the ranks, if you know what I mean. People who've kept very quiet until now are starting to say what they think."

"Does that include the prime minister?" Lestock asked.

"I think you should leave Churchill out of this," Perrin said.

Lestock, still irritated at being scolded for *not* torturing a suspect, was not willing to leave the prime minister out of this. "He may be prime minister now, but in 1936, when he was a backbencher, he was opposed to the king's abdication. He thought Edward should be allowed to marry Mrs. Simpson. Fortunately, no one listened to him then. What is he saying now?"

"I would hope that he's saying 'God save the queen' and

nothing else," Perrin said. "In 1936 none of us knew what Hitler was going to do, and I can't blame Churchill for trying to avoid an abdication crisis, but once it was done, he made the best of it, like all of us. It was Churchill who refused Edward a military role and sent him to govern the Bahamas for the duration of the war. He didn't trust him then, and he doesn't trust him now, and that's all we need to know.

"When I refer to rumblings in the ranks, I am referring mainly to a cadre of aristocrats who do not approve of the new queen's husband, politicians who are out of power, and military gentlemen who no longer have command. I wish we did not need to take any of them seriously, but it seems that we will have to."

"And these people really believe that the stones in the crown will make a difference?" Lestock asked.

"Presumably so," Perrin replied. "The fact that they were stolen during the darkest days of the war leads me to believe that there was always a plan, but the king's sudden death has made them reckless and precipitated a crisis. The royal jewelers have done their best, but if anyone finds out what's on top of the king's coffin ..."

"No one will get close enough."

"I wish I could believe that," Perrin said, "but all it would take is one sharp-eyed pallbearer with a grudge."

He flicked Lestock's report with an angry finger. "What else do you know about this Chaplin woman? Why is she the center of so much attention? Have you confirmed that she was Paxton's girlfriend at the time the jewels went missing?"

Lestock nodded. "It seems probable."

Perrin shook his head. "Probable?" he repeated. "Is that all you can say?"

Lestock contained his rising anger as best he could, speaking through gritted teeth. "I am following that lead, sir, because it is the only one you've given me. My investigations, for which I have had less than forty-eight hours, have led me to conclude that the letters she wrote to Paxton were followed by meetings arranged through a third party."

Perrin consulted the paper. "April Brady?"

"Yes."

Perrin's look was far from friendly. "And that's all you have, an old friend who may have arranged a meeting?"

"It's not much, but if I can locate April, and she knows about this secret meeting place, it may lead us to—"

The special commissioner interrupted him with sudden, fierce frustration. "To what? Lead you to what? Lead you to some rural lovers' lane where they went when they were teenagers? I was told you were brilliant. Well, this isn't brilliant. Someone else is already onto this Chaplin woman, and instead of killing their operatives off or sending them into surgery, perhaps you should consider keeping them alive and awake and ready to answer questions."

Lestock took a deep breath and bit back his anger. He and the special commissioner were strangers who were forced to trust each other. Perrin was shooting arrows at Lestock because he had no other target. He did not seriously expect Lestock to withhold medical treatment from an injured suspect—the memory of torture was too recent for either of them not to recognize it for what it was.

The problem was that Lestock had been brought in at the last minute and presented with an anonymous tip and a rapidly assembled case that was no more than a house of cards, or maybe a pile of fairy dust. The special commissioner knew this, and yet still he wanted to shift the blame. If it were not for the fact that the monarchy itself was at stake, Lestock would have walked away. He didn't have to do this. He could take early retirement.

"Sir," he said, "may I remind you that the theft of the jewels has been known since 1945, when the chamber was reopened. You have had seven years and I have had two days and only the very vaguest of leads."

"The anonymous tip is the best thing we have. We are lucky to have that much."

"The tip is the name of a member of a non-combatant squad who worked at Windsor. Your officers have already informed me that the squad's former commanding officer is very unlikely to be responsible."

Perrin nodded. "Major Hyde was a senile old duffer even then, and quite incapable of forming a plan."

"But," said Lestock, "the fact that Jeremy Paxton is the only other member of the squad whose death has not been recorded does not mean that he took the jewels. The fact that he can't be found doesn't make him guilty. It might just mean that he is also dead."

Perrin scowled. "Two people, both armed, tracking Valerie

Chaplin—that's no coincidence. I'm not interested in your opinion; I'm interested in finding Paxton, and I'm hoping he's alive, because if he's dead, we have nothing, absolutely bloody nothing, and we'll be out of time."

He sat back in his chair and adopted a conciliatory expression. "We haven't been sitting on our hands for the past seven years, but we have had to work quietly in order not to raise any alarms. We've had gem experts throughout the world looking for traces of the jewels. We know their mineral composition. If someone has been cutting them up, we'd know about it. They haven't come on the market. They're still intact. If the king had not died …"

He raised his hands in a defeated gesture. "We don't have any more time, Lestock." He rubbed a hand across his forehead. "Why won't the Chaplin woman talk? She's seen a man shot dead; she's been chased through the streets of Redbridge; she's seen you take a bullet. You'd think she would be begging to tell you what she knows."

"So maybe that means she knows nothing," Lestock said.

"You don't believe that."

Lestock nodded his head. "You're right, sir. She knows something, but if I can't tell her why …"

Perrin's response was explosive. "You've told her enough already. You were not authorized to tell her that the line of succession was threatened."

"I had to tell her something. On the surface, she's quite shy and retiring—a typical librarian, I suppose—but underneath that quiet exterior, she's stubborn as a mule. She won't talk unless she knows what's at stake."

"And now you've told her what's at stake."

"I've said nothing about the jewels." No need to admit that he had almost let that slip.

Perrin shook his head vigorously. "I should hope not. You are not to breathe another word. You can't tell some gossipy librarian that everything she's seeing in the newspapers, every picture of the crown on the coffin, and everything on television is faked. You can't tell anyone that we've lost the Crown Jewels."

"All right," Lestock said with strained patience. "If we can't approach it from that end, what about looking at this another way? Who gave us the tip? Who put us onto Jeremy Paxton, and why do we believe them?"

Perrin rose from his chair and walked to the window. He stood for a long time with his eyes fixed on the skyline of London and the ragged gaps where the Luftwaffe had torn holes in the fabric of the city.

"We traced the number."

"And?"

"A call box."

"In London?"

"No, a call box in Paris."

Lestock's brain turned tired, half-hearted cartwheels. France, the home of the Duke and Duchess of Windsor—Perrin wasn't just guessing; he had real information.

Perrin turned back from the window. "Now you know why we're taking this tip seriously."

"So," said Lestock, "someone in France, where—"

"Leave it at that," Perrin said. "Don't jump to conclusions."

"How in the hell do you expect me to arrive at a result if I'm not permitted to make two and two equal four?" Lestock asked.

"So long as it's not four and a half," Perrin said.

Lestock shrugged impatiently, having already arrived at his own conclusion as to who would be phoning from France. If Perrin wanted to play a game, let him play, but Lestock was under no illusions.

"I would imagine that this person in France, who is notorious for living beyond his or her means, knows the name of the person he or she needs to find, but does not have the resources for a professional search," he said. "Therefore, he or she would like us to use our resources and drive the quarry out into the open."

Perrin nodded. "That's what I think. You should expect to be followed."

"But who came up with Paxton's name?" Lestock asked. "And why should we believe them?"

Perrin's tone was savage. "We don't have time for second-guessing. We have to go with what we've got. You, Lestock, have to go with what *you've* got, and it seems the only thing you have is Valerie Chaplin. What can you do to get her to talk?"

Lestock closed his eyes and pictured Valerie Chaplin's face. When she was not angry, and she was frequently angry, she had a look of wounded innocence. He knew he was about to wound her again, but the special commissioner was right—they were out of time. He would have to use what he had.

CHAPTER TWELVE

Churchgate Close
Redbridge, Surrey
The Reverend Martin McAlhany
Vicar of Redbridge Parish Church

McAlhany smoothed back a lock of his prematurely white hair and attempted to compose himself. Last night's activities had created a buzz in his brain, and he knew he would need to have it under control before he spoke to the Chaplin sisters.

His knock on the front door was answered by both of the sisters, each dressed in a tweed skirt and cardigan and each wearing an apron. Their greeting was a duet as they finished each other's sentences.

"Good afternoon, vicar. We are—"

"—so glad you came. Are you all right after—"

"—last night's disturbance? We thought you—"

"—were so very brave."

McAlhany brushed aside their compliments. He had not been brave; he had been reckless and out of control, but they weren't to know that.

"I've come to see your niece. Is she at home?"

"She's in the parlor. I'll tell her you're here. Would you—"

"—care for some tea?"

McAlhany shook his head. "No need to go to the trouble."

To his relief, the sisters now managed to separate their functions, and their conversation became less distracting.

"No trouble at all," said the taller one. "Olivia will show you

116

in, and I will prepare tea."

Olivia nodded. "Thank you, Gladys."

In the cozy, unthreatening peace of the Chaplin house, McAlhany was finally able to calm his emotions and concentrate on his function as vicar. Although they seemed to act as one, he felt it was important to tell the two ladies apart. The taller one was Miss Gladys; the other one was Miss Olivia. Despite the worry eating at the back of his mind, he felt he should at least keep that straight.

Miss Gladys opened the kitchen door, and a fat little dog bounded out and greeted him with several snuffling barks and an emission of foul air from its nether quarters. Miss Gladys flung up her hands in horror, caught the dog by the collar, and returned it to the kitchen.

Meantime, Miss Olivia opened the parlor door, and McAlhany saw Valerie sitting by the fire. She was a pale figure in a white blouse, with her blond hair hanging in loose curls. Last night, with his brain still buzzing with excitement and police cars and ambulances lined up along the street, he had gone into the graveyard to look for the woman he had seen fleeing from the church. He had found Valerie crouching behind a gravestone, shivering with cold, or perhaps terror. Last night he had asked no questions, but today he really wanted answers.

She rose to her feet, and he noted that she was not tall. *Not tall but very well made.* Well, that was an inappropriate thought for a man of the cloth at a time of crisis.

"Vicar," she said.

"Oh, please, call me Martin."

She gave him a weak smile. "Very well, Martin. Thank you for bringing me home. It was ..."

What? he wondered. What was it? What had happened last night? Surely it was his business to find out. He had to be aware of what was happening in his parish and know if there would ever be a reoccurrence of what had happened last night. *Forewarned is forearmed.*

Last night he had come close to losing control—no, that was a lie. He had not merely come close to losing control; for a few minutes, he had actually *lost* control. He had been so determined to shake loose whoever was running amok in the belfry that he had abandoned common sense. Thank God he had not killed anyone! Thank God the police officer had forced him to release the bell ropes and stand down.

He had sworn that he would never give in to his condition, but last night had been too close for comfort.

The diagnosis of his condition, given in the office of an army psychiatrist, had come as a relief. He was not mad. He had a recognized psychiatric disorder.

"Captain McAlhany," the psychiatrist said, "after a careful study of your record, I can tell you that although you are undisciplined and unpredictable, the army considers you to be a fine soldier and an outstanding officer. Reading the reports of your obviously heroic actions in combat has been quite illuminating, and I can see why you have been referred to me."

McAlhany, who did not know why he had been referred, prepared himself for an argument, but the psychiatrist was not willing to be interrupted.

"Let me finish, Captain. You need to hear what I have to say, because you should be prepared for what will happen next. Your skills were invaluable during the war, and the army is no doubt going to reward you with a number of medals, but your career as a soldier is at an end."

The psychiatrist held up a hand before McAlhany could speak. "I must warn you, Captain, that unless you can get yourself under control, civilian life will not be so kind and will probably reward you with jail time. However, I believe I can help you, if you will let me."

"Help me how?"

"I can give you a diagnosis and a way to keep yourself out of trouble."

"I don't need a diagnosis. What the hell are you talking about?"

"Your behavior, heroic as it may be, is due to a condition that has only just come to my attention. It is not yet recognized by the British Medical Association but I am confident that the condition exists and should be recognized."

"And what is this condition? What's it called?"

"I believe it will come to be known as Intermittent explosive anger disorder. To put it simply, once your anger is triggered by any number of often random circumstances, you are unable to control what happens next, and you react explosively, without any thought for the consequences to yourself or others."

Shocked to his core, McAlhany remained silent as the psychiatrist sat back in his seat and studied McAlhany's reaction to his words.

"Well, Captain, does this reaction sound familiar to you? Do you, in fact, know why you do what you do?"

McAlhany shook his head. "Not always."

"Are you able to stop yourself?"

McAlhany squirmed under the psychiatrist's steady gaze and finally gave him an honest answer. "No."

"While you are acting on this uncontrollable impulse, do you feel pain?"

"No, not at the time."

"There are certain drugs that I can prescribe," the psychiatrist said. "They will keep you steady." He moved his hand in a smoothing gesture. "They'll iron out the highs and lows in your moods, keep you calm."

"How calm?"

The psychiatrist seemed reluctant to answer.

"How calm?" McAlhany asked again, feeling something beginning to build in him and recognizing that he could be on the point of losing control.

"Maybe too calm," the psychiatrist said.

McAlhany drew in a deep breath and waited for the impulse to pass. "So what else can you do?"

"I can do nothing. You must do it yourself. Find a therapist and find a way to put an end to the explosions".

Six years had passed since that life-altering conversation, six years in which he had slowly learned to recognize and control his impulses. They had been good years, calm and quiet, but last night he had welcomed the return of that familiar buzz, and even now, he was still clinging to its memory.

He brushed his hair from his eyes, a hard-learned calming gesture, and looked away from Valerie as the door opened and Miss Olivia bustled in with a tea tray. She was followed closely by Miss Gladys, who interrupted the dispensing of tea to make an apology.

"We're so sorry about the dog."

McAlhany was at a momentary loss, and then he remembered the dog's unfortunate effluvium. He smiled reassuringly. "I don't see any need for an apology. What has the poor creature done apart from filling the air with a perfume rare?"

Miss Gladys's cheeks flushed at his oblique reference. "Someone has been feeding him whale meat," she said, "with unfortunate results. I have prepared a potion of beef broth and arrowroot. He's already a lot better than he was."

"He's not ours," Miss Olivia explained. "We fear he has been stolen."

"By the same person who broke into our house," Miss Gladys said. "We discovered the poor creature tied to the gate when we came home and found we'd been robbed."

"Not robbed," said Miss Olivia. "Nothing was taken, but the window was broken."

"The police want to take him," Miss Gladys said, "to find his owner, but we think we can do better on our own. We have employed the services of Ranulph Witherspoon from number eighteen."

"Such a pretentious name," Miss Olivia said, "but he's a very nice little boy, and he belongs to the Dog Spotters Society and the National Canine Defence League, and he has promised that he and his friends will find the owner. Pugs are quite rare."

McAlhany nodded agreeably, as if he, too, thought that Ranulph Witherspoon and his dog spotters would be far more effective than the police. For the moment, he set aside the discovery that the Chaplin sisters had experienced a break-in. No doubt the robbery where nothing was taken and the chase in the graveyard were related, but he would approach the subject with his newfound and hard-won patience.

He was glad when the two sisters completed their hostess duties and slipped out of the room, leaving him alone with Valerie.

He stirred sugar into his tea and broached the subject of last night's disturbance. "That was very quick thinking on your part, Valerie, to slip out into the churchyard and leave whoever he was to climb around up in the rafters. I must say that police fellow was also a very quick thinker, great presence of mind." He allowed his hair to fall across his forehead and shadow his eyes as he looked down at the floor and hid his expression. "I have been known to act impetuously," he said. "I don't aways think things through, and I was glad that the officer stopped me."

"Stopped you from what?" Valerie asked.

He was still looking at the floor and wondering why he felt such a need to confess to her. "I darned near killed the fellow. I got it into my head that he was a satanist. I suppose the whole neighborhood heard me shouting. He wasn't a satanist, was he?"

"No, he wasn't."

"I thought not."

McAlhany flicked his hair out of his eyes. If he wanted honesty, he would have to offer honesty. "I'm afraid I have a tendency to become obsessed. Sometimes I don't listen to reason. It served me well in the war, and ..."

"What did you do in the war?"

He looked away from her. "I killed people, mostly Germans. In fact, I killed so many that they gave me a medal. The thing is ..." He fell silent for a moment. "The thing is," he repeated, "I didn't have to kill so many. Like I said, once I get started, I can't stop."

Churchgate Close
Redbridge, Surrey
Valerie Chaplin

She wondered if the years of warfare had left any undamaged men behind. The vicar was partly mad and obsessed with satanists. Lestock was a cold fish. And Jeremy ... well, Jeremy had wanted no part in the war, and so the war had come to him.

Aunt Olivia interrupted her thoughts by ushering Alan Lestock into the room. She sprang to her feet. She didn't want to see him, or answer any more of his questions. She thought of using McAlhany as an excuse for not speaking, but the vicar had already risen and was pumping Lestock's arm with what she now recognized as an overeager handshake. Was that perhaps another thing that he did to excess? Lestock was grimacing, and she remembered that his arm was bandaged and his wound had not had time to heal. It had not even been forty-eight hours. So much had happened in such a short time.

Lestock broke free of McAlhany's handshake and nodded to Valerie. "I need to talk to you alone, if I may."

No, she didn't want to be alone with him. She would not risk him talking her into something else. She wasn't going back to the safe house; she wasn't going to allow him to use her father again; and she wasn't going to tell him where April Brady lived.

"You can talk to me in front of the vicar," she said.

Lestock eyed McAlhany, and Valerie recalled that Lestock was one of the few people who knew that the vicar had not been defending the church from satanists but only from his own fevered imagination. It was too late now to recall her words, and she could only repeat her intention.

"I won't talk to you alone. I want the vicar here."

"Should I also call in your aunts?"

Valerie was tempted to declare that she did indeed want her aunts present—she wanted everyone present so that Lestock had no chance to play any more of his cold, calculating games with her emotions.

"You may not want them to hear what I have to say," Lestock warned. He raised his eyebrows and waited. When Valerie failed to reply, he closed the parlor door, leaving Gladys and Olivia in the kitchen with the dog. McAlhany remained looking curious but suddenly professional, with his hands folded together and the fire in his eyes reduced to a smolder.

Lestock stood in front of the closed door, as if to ensure that they would not be disturbed. He looked at McAlhany impatiently. "I don't have time to explain, but I have to advise you that in remaining here now, you are agreeing to be bound by the Official Secrets Act of 1939 and also by current emergency legislation for the protection of Her Majesty the queen and all matters pertaining to her coronation."

McAlhany took a step backward, obviously shocked. When he looked at her, Valerie felt the full force of his unexpected outrage. "Miss Chaplin," he asked, "what are you involved in?"

"Nothing. I'm not involved in anything."

She was surprised when Lestock spoke up in her defense. "As Miss Chaplin's spiritual adviser, you may stay here and listen," he said stiffly, "but I shall ask you not to interfere or to comment. Valerie has unwittingly and very unwillingly become involved in a matter that impinges on the safety of the queen and her accession to the throne. Unfortunately, she has also put herself, her aunts, and law enforcement officers in serious danger. She is in possession of information that I need. So far she has been unwilling to tell me what she knows, but—"

Valerie was pleased when McAlhany interrupted. "I don't understand. I'm sure that Valerie would never knowingly endanger anyone's life."

Valerie could feel the vicar's eyes on her. She refused to look at him, but his words echoed in her head. *Valerie would never knowingly endanger anyone's life.* That was exactly what she had done, and she knew that she would have to grapple with that fact for the rest of her life.

"Vicar," Lestock said coldly, "I asked you not to speak. If you cannot restrain yourself, I will have you removed from the room. Do you understand?"

"Yes, but ..."

"Do you understand?"

McAlhany nodded.

Lestock turned back to Valerie. She could not read the expression on his face, but she sensed a sadness behind his words. "Valerie, I have to do something I don't want to do, but you've left me no alternative."

"Are you going to lock me up again?"

"Not if I can help it, but really, it's up to you. I don't have any choices left." From the way he spoke, she was now quite certain he was feeling not only sadness but a genuine reluctance to speak. He gestured to an armchair. "I think you should sit down."

She shook her head. She didn't like the way he was blocking her escape route through the parlor door, and she was not going to sit. Although McAlhany sighed audibly, she refused to look at him.

"Valerie," Lestock said, "you think that your secret is safe, but it's not."

Valerie felt a cold shiver along her spine. Yes, she had a secret, but she had spoken to no one. He could not possibly know.

"In April 1941," Lestock said, "a baby was born in Littlehampton, at the Convent of the Sacred Heart. As was the way with all babies born at the convent, the original registration of birth was not made available to the public, and just a few days later, a new certificate was issued, a certificate of adoption. You did not give the baby boy a name, but—"

When Valerie spoke, her voice seemed to come from very far away as her words struggled to free themselves from the thick curtain of silence that had held them at bay for so long. "They wouldn't let me name him."

"Can I call him Ralph?"

"It's not up to you; it's up to his new parents."

She closed her eyes. She was not aware that she was swaying or that her knees were about to buckle until McAlhany sprang forward and wrapped his arms around her. She should have felt smothered and threatened by his embrace, but his arms were comforting in a strictly professional sense. He was, after all, the vicar.

Lestock's voice sounded infinitely sad. "Your silence won't keep him safe. If we could find him, so can they."

Valerie knew that she should tell Lestock about the notes. She should say that someone had already found him, but telling him about the notes would mean acknowledging the possibility that they contained the truth, something she had never done. *It's just someone being spiteful. They don't know anything. He's happy. The nuns promised.*

"I didn't want to take it this far," Lestock said, "but your refusal to speak has left me no choice. The only way now for you to keep him secure is to tell us what you know and let us bring this to an end before anyone else has an opportunity to find him. You are the only connection we have to Paxton. We can't find a trace of him, but if you tell us where you went to meet him, at least we will have a starting point."

He looked at her coldly, as though defying her to be outraged. "I assume you did actually meet him, because I assume Paxton is the father of your child."

Valerie could not even bring herself to bridle at the implication. Her defenses had crumpled, and all that she could do was to cling to the vicar for support and confess. "Yes, I met him, and yes, he's the father of my child."

"And where did you meet him?"

"I took a bus," Valerie said, "to a place called Minstead. It's just a little village in the New Forest."

"I went to Minstead when I was a boy," the vicar said. "Went camping with the Boy Scouts."

Lestock's glared at him and McAlhany murmured an apology. "Sorry, I just thought it might be helpful."

"Well it isn't," Lestock snapped.

"He wasn't living in Minstead," Valerie said. "Minstead was as far as the bus went, but he wasn't in the village. We had to walk deep into the forest where there is a collection of huts. Jeremy said he'd gone to the forest at the beginning of the war to look for work. Before the Non-Combatant Corps was formed, he couldn't find work anywhere. When people saw he wasn't in uniform, they called him a coward. His family wouldn't have him, and neither would anyone else, but he heard that the charcoal burners in the New Forest would take anyone who could do the work and so he went looking for them."

"That's true," Lestock said. "Charcoal was desperately needed to make filters for gas masks. The charcoal burners have always been clannish and secretive—they've been in the forest since prehistoric times, and they have their own laws and their own secret settlements—but even they were persuaded to join in the war effort. I wonder how he found out about them. Did he have any family connections with them?"

"No," Valerie said. "His family disowned him when he registered as a conscientious objector. They just threw him out."

Lestock nodded as though she'd given him information he already possessed. Obvious, really—he would have checked with Jeremy's family and found out that they wanted nothing to do with him.

"His message to me came out of the blue," Valerie said. "I'd gone a week or so without a letter, and then he sent a message through April."

"How did he know about her?" Lestock asked.

Valerie had never considered that question. How *did* Jeremy know about April? She knew now that he'd not been far away at Windsor. Maybe he had actually been watching her and waiting for an opportunity to speak to her and discovered she was friends with April.

"He said he had something to confess, and he wanted me to hear it from his own lips so that I would not believe lies." She released herself from the vicar's steadying arm. "Do you mind if I sit down? I have to think before I speak."

She sank onto a chair and opened the floodgates of memory. She hoped that Lestock would leave her alone with her thoughts for a moment. Before everything turned sour, and before the vicar gave her a lecture on loose morals, she wanted to recapture the heady anticipation of her journey into the New Forest.

April had shaken her head in disbelief. "It'll take you all day to get to Minstead. Why do you have to go so far to find a few bushes or a hayrick to hide behind?"

April made everything sound sordid, but Valerie knew she was wrong about Jeremy. What Valerie had with Jeremy was special. They were Tristan and Isolde, Romeo and Juliet—lovers for the ages. Naming the deep and ancient forest for their tryst was not akin to looking for a hiding place behind a bush or a hayrick. On the contrary, it was a sure sign that Jeremy understood how magical their meeting would be.

It had taken every ounce of courage and cunning she possessed to sneak away from her parents and make the journey on unfamiliar trains and buses that adhered to no specific timetable. The new wartime restrictions were tightening their hold on every aspect of life, and buses ran as and when they could.

Ten years later Valerie could contemplate her actions and wondered that she had been able to complete the journey at all, carried forward only on the strength of a fairy tale she had chosen to believe. She knew better now: dreams do not come true; princes have flaws; poetry is just words made to rhyme; and acts of love have consequences.

July 1942
Minstead, New Forest
Valerie Chaplin

The weather was warm, even for July, and she was hot and tired by the time she reached the tiny village of Minstead, in the heart of the New Forest—a forest that had not been new even when William the Conqueror annexed it in 1066.

She climbed down from the bus and took stock of her surroundings. The air was tinged with the scent of smoldering fire, as though something in the forest had been burning for a long time. The village, a small patch of civilization in an uninhabited world of forest and heath, consisted of a collection of redbrick cottages surrounding a drought-stricken village green, where a herd of wild ponies cropped at what was left of the grass.

Two small groups of people had assembled at the bus stop, standing far apart and eyeing each other warily. One group consisted of women with shopping baskets and small children. The other group consisted of men who had the smudged faces of coal miners, and soot-blackened sacks were piled at their feet. Three men in uniform hovered at the edge of the group with kit bags at their feet, giving Valerie the impression that they were soldiers returning on leave.

As she stood nonplussed by her surroundings and wondering what to do next, she heard the soldiers jeering.

"Bloody coward."

"You'll get yours."

"Shot at dawn. That's what you'll get."

The men with the sacks returned the jeers with insults of their own, delivered in such strong and distinctive accents that the words were impossible to understand, although the meaning was clear. While insults flew back and forth, a soot-smudged man separated from the group, and Valerie recognized Jeremy Paxton's hazel eyes peering out from his blackened face.

"Don't be afraid," he said. "It's me they want, but my friends will look after me."

Valerie was too shocked to form words. She had come so far with such high hopes, and this was not the greeting she'd expected. She had been ready to leap into her lover's arms, but she found her lover covered in soot and surrounded by jeering enemies.

Jeremy eyed her anxiously. "It's all right, really. There's nothing to be afraid of."

Valerie looked from one group to another. The soldiers she understood, but the other men, the ones with sacks, were a mystery. "Who are these people?"

"Charcoal burners from deep in the forest. They took me in at the beginning of the war, when I had nowhere to go. We'll be safe with them. They follow the forest law. They don't care what I've done, so long as I don't break their laws, and they won't give me up if anyone comes looking for me."

When Valerie hesitated, Jeremy put his arm around her waist. The soldiers jeered, and Valerie drew back. He was so dirty! She knew that his hand at her waist was making smudges on her dress—smudges she would have to explain to her mother.

"This way," Jeremy said, pointing toward the beginning of a narrow forest trail.

She looked behind her at his companions.

"They'll come later," Jeremy said, "when they've loaded the charcoal on the bus. We'll be alone for a while."

Alone! It was what she had dreamed of, but not like this, with him tugging her deeper and deeper into the dim green light of the forest. They moved so fast that she couldn't summon enough breath to ask questions, and so she stumbled forward in silence until they reached a clearing where high-piled heaps of turf emitted choking smoke.

"Don't worry," he said. "This is just where we make the charcoal. My hut is down here, where there's no smoke."

They went even deeper into the forest, until they came to a small stream running between high banks. He jumped down into the stream and stooped to rinse his hands before he caught her around the waist and lifted her across the water.

She was touched by his gesture, and the flame of her love, which had been wavering, burst into new heat at his touch. She clung to his hand as he led her at last to a small hut made of woven willow and topped with grass thatch.

He paused in the doorway. "I'm sorry about the dirt on my hands and my face. It'll be all right now that those soldiers are leaving, but I can't afford to let them recognize me or know my unit."

"Why?"

"Please, just sit down and let me explain."

She looked into the dim interior of the hut and saw only a straw mattress laid directly on the swept-earth floor. So that was his bed—he was inviting her to sit on his bed. One part of her thought that was a very unwise move, but another part admitted that the bed came as no surprise. A bed was what she had expected, even hoped for. They had so little time; the whole world was at war. How else could they express their love?

She sat on the straw mattress, and he hovered in the doorway.

"I've deserted."

She couldn't hide her shock, and she couldn't totally smother the thought that desertion of a non-combatant would hardly count as desertion. He wasn't a fighting soldier, and his absence would make no difference.

Anyone could dig latrines. What did he have to desert?

She could only think of one question to ask aloud. "Why?"

"I was given an order I couldn't obey."

"Did they want you to fight?"

"No, worse than that."

"What?"

"To steal."

"And did you?"

"In a manner of speaking."

"What did you steal?"

"I can't tell you, not until I've decided what to do with it."

"With what?"

He shrugged. "I can't tell you."

Valerie shifted uneasily and wondered what kind of forest-dwelling creatures had taken up residence in the mattress. This was not going as she had expected. "If you can't tell me, why am I here?"

"So you'll know that I'm not guilty. Whatever you hear about me, you have to believe that I acted for the best. I couldn't let them do it."

Valerie was rapidly growing impatient, not to mention itchy. She had come to meet her Prince Charming, but her prince was appearing more and more like an unfathomable stranger who spoke in riddles. As for deserting, wasn't that an act of cowardice? Her father hadn't deserted, even when staying had cost him his sanity.

She imagined returning to Redbridge and having to tell April that nothing had happened and he had only wanted to confess some misplaced guilt, as though she were his teacher, not his girlfriend.

A horrible thought crossed her mind. Was Jeremy having second thoughts about her? Now that he was seeing her for the second time, was she less attractive than he remembered? In his letters, he'd told her she was beautiful, but maybe she wasn't.

That was it! She'd come all this way to see him, and he was putting her off with strange riddles about stealing and deserting, because he just didn't fancy her after all.

She felt tears of humiliation building up behind her eyelids and swiped at them as they slipped out to trickle down her cheeks. He was beside her immediately with an arm around her.

"What's the matter?"

"You think I'm ugly."

"No, no. You're beautiful."

"Then why are you just standing there talking?"

"Because I'm a fool," he said thickly, pushing her down onto the straw mattress.

Churchgate Close
Redbridge, Surrey
Valerie Chaplin

Valerie's flood of memory ended abruptly, returning her to her aunts' parlor and Lestock's impassive gaze. She tried to flee from the present, but her mind had nowhere to go. She had no more memories of Jeremy. She had never seen him again.

She looked from Lestock to the vicar, who was watching her equally impassively. He was a vicar, and no doubt he'd heard far too many confessions from foolish girls who did not think "it would happen to them."

"As you've already guessed," she said defiantly, "I had a baby out of wedlock."

"And where is the baby now?" McAlhany asked.

"I don't know," Valerie said. She jerked her head toward Lestock. "Maybe he knows."

"I don't, but I can find out, if that's what you want."

Yes, I want to know if he's happy.

No, I don't want to remember what I did.

What will I do if the notes are true?

When Valerie failed to answer, McAlhany smoothly changed the subject. "Why are you invoking the Official Secrets Act?" he asked. His face was calm, and he showed no sign of anything other than curiosity.

Valerie looked at Lestock, who spread his hands in a gesture that seemed to say, "Tell him whatever you like."

She wondered what would happen to McAlhany if she did tell him everything. Would he be taken away and locked in a safe house, or even a prison? She realized that she didn't know everything. All she really knew was that Lestock was convinced that an attempt would be made to replace Queen Elizabeth with another member of the Royal Family and that somehow Jeremy Paxton was involved—Jeremy, who she had not seen since that day in the New Forest when he had spoken in riddles.

For a reason she could not articulate, she thought that she could trust McAlhany. He had trusted her with the confession of his mental instability, even the confession that he felt unworthy of the medals he'd won, and so she should be willing to trust him. First, however, she had to deal with Lestock's question, which crowded out all other questions—did she want to know the truth about her son? It was a question she could not answer.

"Valerie!" Lestock's voice broke through her thoughts. "I'm sorry, but I have to tell you something else."

Valerie buried her head in her hands. "I don't want to know anything else."

"This has nothing to do with your son," Lestock said, "but whether you like it or not, it increases the likelihood that you are in danger, and if you choose to give the vicar any additional information, he will also be in danger. He is your spiritual adviser; I leave that decision to you."

Valerie kept her head buried in her hands, too emotionally exhausted to make any decision. Should she tell the vicar everything? She didn't know. Should she ask to be told her son's name? She didn't know. Would this nightmare ever end? She didn't know.

After a brief pause, Lestock continued in a businesslike tone. "When we talked to your father, he told us you had two friends. April Brady and a girl called Mary."

Valerie lifted her head. "She wasn't really my friend. I didn't trust her with any information."

Lestock continued as though Valerie had not spoken. "We have not found April Brady, but we know where Mary Carpenter is, or at least, we know where she was."

"She went to be a missionary."

"No. I'm afraid that Mary lost her interest in doing the Lord's work in foreign lands," Lestock said. "She's been living in Kent and working as a nurse's aide. We sent officers to her house this morning, and, strangely and worryingly, they were in time to see her leave home in the company of two members of the Vernon crime family. Unfortunately, the officers were not under orders to follow her, and so they did not."

Valerie could see Lestock's frustration. She assumed that he expected better of people under his command. She felt an unreasonable need to apologize for behavior that had nothing to do with her.

"I'm sorry."

"So am I. We believe that Mary could tell us a great deal. The man we killed in Redbridge Library, the man who was looking for Jeremy Paxton, was a member of the Vernon family, and we are assuming that the man who went to talk to your father was also a member of the Vernon family. That's how they obtained Mary's name, and we believe that they now have Mary."

Valerie shivered involuntarily as she realized how many tendrils still bound her to the memory of Jeremy Paxton. Now Mary was involved, but why?

"I'm sorry she's in trouble," Valerie said at last, "but she can't tell them anything about me. I haven't spoken to her in years."

"Are you sure about that?"

"Of course."

It was not possible for Mary to know anything. When Valerie abandoned their enforced friendship, the other girls took that as a reason to also abandon any attempt at friendship with Mary. Left to eat lunch alone, wander the playground alone, and spend her lunch hours in prayer, Mary had grown increasingly pious and isolated with each day that passed, and no one at school had anything to do with her.

"Does anyone else know about your child?" Lestock asked.

Valerie folded her arms, wrapping herself in the comfort of her own embrace. She could not bring herself to say the truth. *Someone knows. Someone has been writing me vile notes on blue paper.*

Her milk had dried up as the lay sister had promised, and her body had returned to its normal shape. Jeremy Paxton disappeared as though he had never existed. Her father had committed himself to the asylum. Her mother had died. And still the notes came fluttering through the letter box.

He cries all the time.

No one loves him.

He's always in trouble.

You should be ashamed of yourself.

She looked at Lestock and shook her head. The notes were

filled with lies, and she had burned them. He was nearly eleven years old now And she had no right to even hold him in her memory. He was another woman's child, and she would not intrude on his future by allowing Lestock to use him as a bargaining tool. She had nothing left to say.

CHAPTER THIRTEEN

February 15 1952
Southdown Hall
Dorking, Surrey
Major Cardrew Hyde

"Sahib."

Hyde looked up from his scrambled eggs and observed Kumar standing nervously in the doorway of the breakfast room.

"What?"

"The gardener is looking for Roger."

For a moment, Hyde was truly nonplussed. "Who the devil is Roger?"

"He says it is his dog, sahib."

Oh yes, the smelly pug. Where was it? He'd taken it to Redbridge with him, and … Now he remembered. He could hardly be blamed for forgetting. The pug was a minor detail in a very interesting day, and its loss was a small price to pay for having acquired the services of Harry Mayfield. He looked across the table at Mayfield, who was wolfing down sausages with messy enthusiasm. The man had no manners, but his usefulness promised to far outweigh his lack of civility.

"Sahib," Kumar said, "the dog."

"Tell him to forget about it. I did him a favor. It was an obnoxious little thing."

Kumar appeared to be stricken by grief. "It is dead?"

Hyde shrugged. "Probably not. I expect someone took it in."

"The gardener would like it back."

"Well, he's not getting it back."

"But, sahib—"

Hyde threw down his napkin in disgust. "Oh, for goodness' sake! Just tell the memsahib to give him a couple of pounds. Two should do it. It was old and almost dead, anyway."

Hyde attempted to shoo Kumar away with hand gestures, but Kumar stood his ground. "There are men," he said.

"Asking about the dog?"

"No, sahib. There are men asking about certain dead and injured members of their family. They are not happy."

Hyde was momentarily perplexed, but Mayfield set down his fork and pushed back his chair.

"About time too," he said.

"What? What do you mean?"

"I wondered when they'd turn up here." Mayfield's Yorkshire voice held a hint of "I told you so."

"Who?"

"The crime family you employed to make Valerie Chaplin talk."

Hyde's memory slid back to a few days ago, when Silliton, the Cockney lookout, had stood in the study, twisting his cap and announcing the failure of the raid at the Redbridge Library.

"Am I to assume that Freddie Vernon is dead?"

"As a doornail."

Hyde's scrambled eggs threatened to make a return journey up his throat, and he took a deep breath to calm himself.

"I told them their services were no longer required. They botched the job. It's not my fault they lost one of their men. I said no guns," he protested.

Mayfield shrugged. "Men like them always have guns."

Hyde choked back another attempt by his scrambled eggs to climb back out of his stomach. "Do you know these people?"

Mayfield shrugged. "Maybe." His voice took on a boastful tone. "I know most of the crime families in London. What name?"

"The Vernon family."

Hyde could not help noticing that Mayfield's face had suddenly lost its color. He shook his head in disbelief. "You tried to dismiss Lennie Vernon's family?"

"I told them their services were no longer needed."

"And you thought they'd just go away, even after one of their family was killed? Who was it? Which one got killed?"

"Freddie."

Mayfield grimaced. "Could be worse, I suppose. Freddie's a distant cousin. At least it wasn't one of the sons."

"I told him no guns," Hyde repeated. "He brought it on himself."

"I don't think old man Lennie is going to see it that way. This is going to cost you more than a couple of quid. This is a bit more than a missing dog."

Hyde stared miserably at his cooling breakfast and attempted to reassess his situation. As Mayfield apparently knew the Vernon family, maybe he could use him to negotiate, because obviously negotiation would be required. He really hated to humiliate himself by even asking questions, but he didn't like the look on Mayfield's face—disdain mixed with fear.

"Well, Sergeant," he said, "as you are so familiar with the criminal element, what's your suggestion for dealing with them?"

Mayfield forked up another sausage and chewed as he spoke. "Have you told them what you're looking for?"

"No, of course not."

Mayfield shrugged. "You may have to."

"Why should I?"

"Because they may settle for a price, but it'll be a big price. They may want a share in the jewels."

"Share in the jewels?" Hyde repeated. "Are you suggesting that I sell them off like a common thief? These are the Crown Jewels of the United Kingdom. They are not for sale."

"Sahib," Kumar said.

Hyde turned on him. "What?"

"They are here."

A shape loomed in the doorway, and a man spoke in a voice so deep and booming that it seemed to have been dragged up from some cavern belowground.

"Where is he?"

Kumar placed his palms together and bowed deeply. "In here, sir, but he is still eating, and—"

His words were cut off as one large man entered the room while two other men pulled the Indian aside and more or less flung him from the room.

The man with the booming voice looked briefly around and then let his eyes alight on Mayfield. "Morning, Harry."

Mayfield, pale but determined, nodded a greeting. "Morning, Mr. Vernon, Mr. Vincent, Mr. Derek."

Hyde realized that he was looking at a family group, father and two sons. Lennie Vernon was built like the side of a barn, with slab shoulders, no neck, and only vestigial hair. His sons were built on the same scale, but they had so far retained their hair.

One of the sons scuttled forward and pulled a chair away from the table, and Lennie Vernon sat, spreading his legs wide to accommodate his belly. The chair creaked ominously as he leaned back and steepled his fingers. He kept his eyes on Mayfield. He still had not even glanced at Hyde. Although he was dressed in a very fine coat with an astrakhan collar, his voice carried echoes of the poorest streets of London.

"So, Harry," he asked, "what are you doing here?"

Hyde bristled. How dare these men come into his house, manhandle his servant, and ignore him? "I am the master of this house," he said indignantly. "You will address your questions to me, not to Sergeant Mayfield, who is merely working for me."

Vernon flicked a dismissive hand at Hyde. "I'm talking to the organ grinder, not the monkey."

It took a moment for Hyde to absorb the insult, and he floundered to his feet, looking for an appropriate response. "I'll have you know that I am not the ... well ... *I'm* the organ grinder; *he's* the monkey. You talk to me."

Vernon spread his hands. They were large, with the bent and distorted finger joints of someone who had once been a bare-knuckle fighter, but his fingernails showed signs of a recent manicure. "Well, Major," he said, "I want to know what went wrong. You said it was a simple job, but you being a new customer and all, I did you a favor and sent a member of my own family, one of my own cousin's kids, and you got him killed."

"He got himself killed," Hyde replied. "I told him no guns."

Vernon continued as though Hyde had not even spoken. "When one of our boys gets killed doing a simple job, then obviously that job ain't so simple." He looked at Mayfield and winked. "Ain't that so, Harry Boy?"

Harry seemed to have set aside any possible loyalty to Hyde

and was staring at Vernon beseechingly, making Hyde realize that he was on his own when it came to negotiating with a scion of the Vernon family. Despite his participation in the first great world war to end all wars, and the subsequent second equally ineffective world war, Hyde had never actually put his courage to the test. He had survived both the trenches and the bomb squad by masterfully leading from behind. Now, without any troops at his command and with no area of his breakfast room that could be described as "behind," he realized how little courage he possessed.

He sank back into his chair and sipped his cold tea as he sought in vain for an appropriate response.

"Well, Harry," Vernon said, "it looks like your boss has lost his tongue."

Mayfield's expression was greedy. "The major's not my boss. Like I've always told you, I'm strictly freelance. Always available for odd jobs or even a long-term—"

Vernon interrupted him by banging on the table and setting the teacups rattling in their saucers. "That's what I don't like about you, Harry. No loyalty. Seems obvious to me you've been working for Major Hyde, and now here you are, licking my boots, looking for crumbs from my table. You ain't getting nothing from me, Harry, except maybe your life if you start talking now."

Mayfield did not even pause for breath. "What do you want to know?"

Hyde was surprised to find that although he could not summon up courage, he could summon outrage. Through the open doorway, he could see into his study, where morning light reflected from the gilt frame surrounding the portrait of George V, king and emperor. He felt an unfamiliar stiffening of his backbone. He considered the array of lethal instruments displayed on the walls of the study. If he could push past Vernon's two sons, he could reach a sword, and then he could ... he could ... What could he really do?

Vernon's voice broke into his disordered thoughts. "So, Major, what do you want with this Paxton fellow?"

"How do you know about him?"

Vernon looked at Mayfield. "I was right the first time, Harry Boy. You're definitely the organ grinder, and he's definitely the monkey." He leaned across the table and spoke to Hyde as though speaking to an idiot. "You told my cousin's boy to go to the

Redbridge Library, find a woman named Valerie Chaplin, and get her to tell him where you could find Jeremy Paxton."

Hyde realized that a cold sweat had broken out on his forehead, and he mopped his face with a linen napkin. "Yes, yes, I did, but he didn't find out."

"On account of him being killed," Vernon said.

"Not by me," Hyde said from behind the napkin.

"No, not by you, by someone from a very secretive branch of the Metropolitan Police, someone who could dispose of the body, bring in a cleaning crew, and get everything shipshape by morning without even a dicky bird being printed in the newspapers, not a single word." He lumbered to his feet and leaned across the table, meeting Hyde eyeball-to-eyeball. "Why are you looking for Paxton?"

Hyde made a final attempt to bluster. "I can't tell you. It's a matter of national security."

Vernon shook his massive head. "Not good enough. The war's over. We won. No more secrets."

He lifted his head and looked at Mayfield. "You gonna tell us, Harry Boy, or will we have to squeeze if from you? You won't have no future in my organization if I have to get rough with you, but if you was to give the information painlessly, well …"

Mayfield gave Hyde a brief apologetic glance before shrugging his shoulders and spreading his hands in defeat. "Jewels," he said.

"What kind of jewels?"

"Crown jewels."

Hyde hoped for a moment that Vernon would ignore Mayfield's answer. How likely was he to believe that a low-level criminal like Mayfield would somehow be involved in the theft of the Crown Jewels of the United Kingdom?

Mayfield was leaning back in his chair, and Hyde tried to read the expression on his face. He had always had trouble thinking on his feet—*That's what sergeants are for*—and Mayfield had certainly presented him with a challenge. He suspected that the Yorkshireman was not playing with a straight bat, and things were not as they seemed. After a moment of frantic thought, he concluded that Mayfield expected him to somehow solve the problem he had created. They were in a tight corner, and Mayfield had said what he needed to say to prevent immediate disaster, but now he had tossed the ball to Hyde.

Hyde wondered what he was supposed to say. Nothing came to mind. This was not the first time he'd experienced this feeling of mental paralysis in the face of extreme danger—and with the two Vernon brothers in the room, he believed he was experiencing extreme danger.

"Not the big ones," Mayfield said.

Not the big ones … Not the big ones. All right, yes, I see what you mean.

He nodded to Vernon. "Well, I suppose as the sergeant has told you so much, there's no harm in filling you in. The fact is, we have discovered, well, not so much the hiding place as the possible hiding place, yes, the possible hiding place of some stones from the royal collection." Hyde knew he was burbling, but he was gaining confidence.

"He said crown jewels," Vernon said truculently.

"I suppose that would be accurate," Hyde said as nonchalantly as he could. "They were once part of one of the crowns, but they're not being used now. The royals always have more stones than they can use, so these are spare, but they're a pretty good size."

Vernon's eyes narrowed. "What did he mean when he said 'not the big ones'?"

"I meant what I said," Mayfield said. "There's big stones in the crown, of course—you know, really big stones—but no one would be fool enough to steal them. They'd be recognized, wouldn't they? On the other hand, a diamond is a diamond, and the royal family has quite a few of them. Just anonymous ones, you know."

"And that's why you're looking for this Paxton fellow?" Vernon asked.

Mayfield rose to his feet, full of casual confidence that Hyde would never be able to emulate. "Here's the truth, Mr. Vernon. It all happened during the war. We were on a squad that was sent to dig a hiding place at Windsor Castle for some of the jewels."

"Minor jewels," Hyde interrupted, beginning to feel a return of confidence. If necessary, he would persuade the American woman to part with some of her diamonds. He understood that she had a good collection of jewelry.

"So we were all doing our patriotic duty," Mayfield said, "except for Paxton. He was a conchie—you know, a conscientious objector, wouldn't pick up a weapon."

"Hey," Vernon snapped, "be careful what you say. Some of my boys signed up as conscientious objectors. Wouldn't have nothing to do with violence or guns."

Hyde could not suppress a snort, and Vernon flicked his head around to look at him. "You doubting my boys' courage?"

"No, no, I wouldn't do that."

One of Vernon's sons fixed Hyde with a slightly amused gaze. "We got courage; we just don't like throwing our lives away. Lots of good opportunities in London during the war for … uh … men of courage."

"So what about this Paxton fellow?" Vernon asked, gesturing to his son to step back.

"He made off with some of the stones," Mayfield said, "and we're in the process of hunting him down. Valerie Chaplin is our best lead. She was his girlfriend. We've made a couple of runs at her, but so far we haven't been able to get her on her own. If Jeremy Paxton has gone to ground with the jewels, we need to find someone who knows where he comes from and where he might be hiding. Valerie Chaplin seems to be the only one who would know that."

Vernon shook his head. "Amateurs," he said scornfully. "No one can disappear completely, unless they're dead, and even then, well, it ain't hard to find where the body's buried. Normally, I'd have nothing to do with the likes of you, but I lost one of my own family in that library. We don't take things like that lying down, and we don't like the fact that the major hasn't been straight with us."

"I have."

"Diamonds," Vernon said. "You didn't say nothing about diamonds." He shrugged. "So now we got that straight, and we're agreed about the diamonds."

Agreed? Hyde thought. *No, we're not agreed. Just wait until you find the stones, and then you'll see. Then …*

Then what? He would need reinforcements. He would have to make a phone call. Hyde did not relish the idea of admitting that things had gone quite spectacularly wrong, but there was nothing else for it: he would have to report the change in circumstances and make a new plan. It would all work out. If Vernon managed to find the stones, he would find himself facing …

Facing what? Hyde thought of all the people who supported

the plan to prevent the coronation—senior army officers, members of Parliament, dukes and earls, high-ranking police officers, all with men under their command, and those were the people Vernon would face. For the moment, Vernon had the upper hand, so let him try to find what Jeremy Paxton had done with that damned biscuit tin. Finders would not necessarily be keepers.

He hid his thoughts behind a smile and a twitch of his mustache.

"We sent a man in to talk to Valerie Chaplin's father," Vernon said. "He's locked up in a loony bin in Epsom, and he coughed up a couple of names."

"Names?"

"Friends of Valerie, friends who might know about her and Jeremy Paxton."

Hyde stared down at the congealing food on his plate, ashamed that he'd been outthought by a Cockney lout. He should have had that idea. He should have realized that there was nothing to be found in Valerie's letters, but girls were always silly, and they could never keep a secret, so naturally, she'd talked to a friend. He lowered his napkin in order to glare at Mayfield before he remembered that all of this had occurred before he'd brought Mayfield on board—and even Mayfield had not thought of doing anything except stealing the letters. It occurred to him that maybe Vernon was the organ grinder, and they were both monkeys.

"We tried another run at the Chaplin girl last night," Vernon said, "but it ended badly." He paused for a moment to examine his manicured fingernails. "Vicars ain't the same as they was in the good old days. We had to go after one of her friends instead." He turned to his sons. "Go and get the girl."

A few minutes later, Vincent and Derek Vernon returned with their captive. She was one of the smallest women Hyde had ever seen, and he had seen service in Africa, where he had actually encountered Pygmies. This woman would fit in perfectly with the tribe he had met in the rain forests of the Congo, although she lacked their dark skin and bright eyes. She also lacked their ready smiles, but that was no surprise, as she was in no condition to smile. The Vernon brothers were literally dragging her, with her feet scraping on the floor like a recalcitrant child or a disobedient dog. Either one of them could have picked her up and thrown her over his shoulder, but they seemed intent on inflicting as much discomfort as possible.

When they set her on her feet, she immediately fell to her knees and raised her eyes to heaven. Hyde expected to hear tearful pleas to the Lord Almighty for rescue, but this woman was not the tearful or pleading type. Her first words took him by surprise.

"May the Lord plague you with diseases until he has destroyed you from the land."

Her eyes, pale and red-rimmed, roved around the room and landed on the massive figure of Lennie Vernon. Her next curse was accompanied by a pointing finger.

"May the Lord strike you with wasting disease, and fever and inflammation."

Vernon glared at his sons. "Just shut her up!"

They responded in unison. "We've tried."

One of them bent over the cursing woman. "Shut up, or we'll gag you."

Her voice was a snarl that drove the two big men away. "Do not touch the Lord's anointed."

Having won herself a reprieve, she turned her attention to Mayfield, who was staring at her in an astonishment that did not seem to include fear.

"The Lord will curse you in the city and curse you in the country. He will curse the crops of your land and the calves of your herds."

Mayfield grinned amiably. "Well, lass, I don't have any crops or calves, or come to that, I don't have any land, so curse away all you like."

Hyde, who did have land, crops, and cattle, tried to catch Lennie Vernon's eye. The woman needed to be silenced before she got around to him. Not that he believed in curses, but he had seen strange things among the Pygmies, and there was always an outside chance that she had Pygmy blood in her and therefore the ability to curse.

She turned her attention to Derek Vernon, who was approaching her with a large handkerchief in his hand. Hyde hoped he would succeed in gagging her before she could turn her curses on him, but he was too late. The woman had spotted him, and her pale eyes bored into him, recognizing his fear. Memory flooded back: the deep green shade beneath the canopy of the Impenetrable Forest, the distant booming of the great apes, the ever-present possibility of venomous snakes, and the small, forest-dwelling people who shot poisoned arrows at his troops and left gruesome talismans beside the paths.

She was looking at him now with complete confidence, and her words were no longer a prayer, just a statement of fact. "You will be cursed when you come in and cursed when you go out, until you are destroyed and come to sudden ruin because of the evil you have done."

He shuddered at the possibility that the madwoman had found him out. There were some who would call his actions over a lifetime in the army evil, but he had always consoled himself with the thought that he had been in service to the king and the empire, and the guilt was not his. Of course, there was the incident in Lucknow, and the problem at Ypres, not to mention the bomb blast at Lambs Farm Road. These thoughts, slithering like snakes into the back of his mind, were suddenly cut off by Derek Vernon's large hand.

"You will become a thing of horror to—"

Derek's handkerchief silenced the curse, and Hyde felt a sudden release from the doubts that had begun to assail him. He heard a contemptuous chuckle from Mayfield and realized that his terror had not gone unnoticed.

Hyde turned on Lennie Vernon, creating courage from embarrassment. "Who the devil is that, and why is she in my house?"

Vernon looked a little pale. Perhaps a couple of the woman's curses had come close to the mark for him also. "That," he said, "is Valerie Chaplin's friend Mary Carpenter. She is going to tell us where Valerie and Paxton used to meet."

Mary made frantic noises behind her gag, but Vernon ignored her. "I sent one of my men into the loony bin where Valerie's father is locked up, and had him ask some questions about his daughter's friends. Turns out she didn't have many, but she had this one. Thick as thieves, or so he said."

Another series of muffled explosions came from behind Mary's gag, but Vernon continued without pause.

"We know that Valerie and Paxton went well beyond exchanging little love notes."

"Do we?" Hyde asked.

"It's hard to get pregnant by writing love letters," Vernon

said.

Hyde could not hide his shocked surprise. "Are you saying Valerie Chaplin had a child?"

Mary Carpenter finally managed to spit out her gag, but she was no longer cursing. "Yes, she did," she said as she rose from the floor and brushed dust from her gray woolen skirt. "She thought it was a secret, but she should have known better. No one can keep secrets from me."

She looked around at the men in the room, and her expression, which had recently been fanatical, was now sly. Hyde had not cared for the fanatical expression, but he found the sly look even more difficult to like or trust.

Mary turned to the two brothers, who still loomed over her. "Where are my glasses?"

Derek reached into his pocket and pulled out a pair of round, owlish spectacles of the kind a child would be given by the National Health Service. When Mary settled them on her nose, Hyde suddenly lost all fear of her. She was just an ordinary, rather small woman. She was not wild and fanatical; her curses had meant nothing. Her hypnotic stare was the result of shortsightedness and nothing else. He'd been a fool to dredge up all those memories of the Congo. She knew nothing about him.

Mary's face settled into a sullen scowl. "She dropped me," she said. "I was her friend, and she dropped me. I was the only one allowed in her house, and then suddenly she took up with April Brady." Her top lip curled. "April didn't know how to behave. She didn't understand about Mr. Chaplin's demons. I had them under control. When I came into the house, I prayed them away, but April didn't know how to do that, and so she couldn't stay."

Hyde was still trying to come to terms with the fact that Jeremy Paxton had fathered a baby. Was it before or after he'd agreed to help with removing the Crown Jewels from their hiding place? Was this the reason for his desertion, if he had deserted—if he was not, in fact, dead?

"Where's the baby now?" he asked.

Mary showed no interest in answering him. Her eyes had once again taken on a glazed look, although this time they were focused on a distant point or perhaps on a memory.

"The sexually immoral," she declared, "will be consigned to

the fiery lake of burning sulfur."

Hyde was surprised to see Mayfield push back his chair and walk over to Mary. His Yorkshire voice was as mild and as matter-of-fact as any dale farmer speaking of crops, but his expression was angry. "That's enough," he said. His eyes flicked to the Vernon family and then back to Mary. "I know what you are."

"I'm a servant of the Lord in the fellowship of the brethren," Mary declared.

Mayfield looked down at her. "You're a nasty, judgmental little woman who has come here to save her own skin by telling tales on her friend—"

"She let me down. She made fun of me."

"Who can blame her?" Mayfield said. "Look at you, lass. You're pathetic. No wonder you had no friends." He leaned closer to her. "Let me explain something to you. These men are serious. They'll kill you as soon as look at you, so stop spouting the Bible at them, and tell them where to find Jeremy Paxton."

Mary, without a Bible verse to back up her statements, seemed to have shrunk. "I don't know where to find him, but I know how to get Valerie to talk."

Vernon's ice-cold smile sent a shiver down Hyde's spine. "So do I," Vernon said. "If I could get my hands on her, she'd be singing like a bird, but she's under guard."

Mary's voice was gaining in confidence. "I know how to get her to leave her house."

Vernon shook his head. "Pull the other one, it's got bells on."

"No, really, I know what to do. Just let me go—"

"We ain't letting you go."

"No, no, I didn't mean that. I meant just let me go there, and I'll make sure she comes out. I know what to do."

Vernon gestured to his sons. "Go with her. Don't let her out of your sight."

When Mary and her escort had left the study, Hyde waited for Vernon to rise from the table and be on his way, but Vernon simply leaned back in his chair and looked around the room with dissatisfaction. "I don't see no television," he said.

"We don't have one."

"Blimey, all this money and no television."

"I don't think it's necessary," Hyde declared. "Staring at the screen weakens the eyesight and softens the spine."

He chose to ignore Mayfield's mocking laugh and kept his eyes on Vernon.

"You got some objection to radio?" Vernon asked.

"No, no objection at all."

"Good. So you'd better go get it and turn it on. The king's funeral will be starting any minute. Wouldn't want to miss that." He was silent for a moment, staring reflectively at the ceiling. "George was a good king," he said at last. "Came down the East End after the bombing. Hope they do him proud."

"What about his daughter?" Hyde asked tentatively. "What do you think about her being queen? Do you think she's too young?"

Vernon lowered his eyes and looked at Hyde in astonishment. "No, I don't. She's queen, and that's all there is to it. You got some better idea?"

"No, no, of course not."

Vernon nodded. "Good." He folded his hands across his belly. "How about a cup of tea while we're waiting?"

"Waiting for what?"

"For the funeral to start."

"You're staying here?"

Vernon nodded. "Oh, yes, mate. I'm staying."

Little Clamping, Kent
Davie

Daylight teased Davie into wakefulness, piercing his eyelids and forcing him to confront the morning and his shivering wretchedness. He had spent the night in a kind of waking dream, aware of Pete's and Colin's voices raised first in bawdy songs and then in arguments. Curled in a corner, he had heard them retching and smelled the sickly sweetness of vomit.

Somehow, despite their noisy belligerence, he had managed to fall into a fitful sleep interrupted by his constant need to cough and the burning pain in his throat whenever he tried to swallow. That pain was not so bad now; his throat had become dry with no saliva. He was sick and he knew it. He was not sure he could stand; he didn't even want to try. When he attempted to move, a heavy weight held him down.

He opened his eyes fully and blinked at the shaft of pale sunlight that crept in through the half-open door of the coal shed. He plucked at the weight that held him down and discovered that he was under a pile of empty coal sacks—well, not really empty. He could feel the weight of coal dust and the lumpiness of coal that had not been shaken out. The weight was not unpleasant; it felt almost like someone was holding him. He was not familiar with that feeling, but sometimes he wrapped his arms around himself just to see what it would feel like. This, in its own strange way, was better than holding himself. This was comfortable.

He shook his head. No, this was not comfortable. This was cold, dirty, and wrong. He had to get up before someone came and found him. He forced himself into a sitting position and looked to see where Pete and Colin were sleeping. Last night they had been drunk, and from what he'd heard, drunks always fell asleep. They must have crawled into a corner somewhere.

The floor of the coal shed was littered with empty potato chip packets, spilled jars that had once contained pickled eggs, and broken bottles. Squinting, he could also make out the places where the boys had vomited, but he could see no sign of the boys themselves. Surely they hadn't … He could hardly think the words. Surely they hadn't left him.

That's what you wanted. You said you would go your own way.
But Pete said I could come.
Only if you could keep up.
I stole food for them.
They don't care.
I have to find my father.
You dreamed it.
No, I had a note.
Where is it now?
I lost it.
Lie down. Go back to sleep.
I'm really sick.
No one cares.

CHAPTER FOURTEEN

Churchgate Close
Redbridge, Surrey
Valerie Chaplin

"Get up, dear. We have a surprise."

Valerie opened her eyes to her familiar bedroom and a dull gray morning light creeping between the curtains. Aunt Olivia bustled across to the window and drew the curtains back to reveal a misty morning that could not be anything but cold. Valerie snuggled back beneath her eiderdown. Last night she had fallen into an emotionally exhausted sleep, her security assured by the presence of Mrs. Gordon, who had remained all night, as Lestock apparently thought Valerie was still in danger.

With Jane Gordon keeping watch over the house, Valerie had slept without dreaming, and that was how she wished to continue: just sleeping, not thinking, not wondering, and not remembering.

Aunt Olivia, dressed in an unusually formal black frock, tugged at the quilt. "We have a surprise."

"I don't want a surprise."

"You'll want this one. Just come and see."

Valerie swung her legs over the side of the bed and reached for her dressing gown. Aunt Olivia shook her head. "No, no, no, dear. You must be properly dressed."

Valerie sighed, well aware that she was reacting like a sullen child but unable at that moment to behave any differently. As the last shreds of peaceful sleep departed, memory swept in to take their place, and after the memory came the questions, and after the questions, the anger directed at Alan Lestock, who, in front of the vicar, had forced from her a secret she had never intended to tell.

She struggled to find a glimmer of hope and saw none, and therefore, no reason to get out of bed.

Aunt Olivia had opened the wardrobe door and was looking through Valerie's meager collection of dresses. She finally selected a black dress with a white lace collar. It was something that Valerie wore only for funerals.

The funeral! Today was the king's funeral. Her spirits lifted slightly, because even a funeral would be a distraction, and that was what she needed. She had slept late; the funeral was probably already underway. She supposed that her aunts, along with Mrs. Gordon, would be listening to the radio.

She looked at Aunt Olivia, who was holding out the black dress and shifting her feet restlessly as if her agitation alone would make Valerie move faster.

"It's radio," Valerie said. "No one will see us."

"But it's not radio. The vicar has rented a television set. It's downstairs. We're going to watch the whole thing."

Valerie, still emerging from sleep, and still battling the demons of memory, nonetheless found a new reason for excitement. *Television!* She'd seen the flickering black-and-white images playing in the window of the Radio Rentals shop in the high street, and like everyone else, she'd paused to watch and wonder.

She could hear the commotion downstairs as she dressed. Furniture was being moved, and unfamiliar masculine voices drifted up the stairs, accompanied by Mrs. Gordon's impatient but very clear instructions. Aunt Gladys was expressing anxiety as to the safety of her Wedgwood knickknacks, and the dog, still without a name, was barking. The excitement was contagious.

Looking over the banister rail, she saw two men in brown warehouse coats, tending to a bulky wooden box that trailed wires across the hallway. The light fixtures in the parlor jangled and fluttered as someone in heavy shoes walked on the roof above. Martin McAlhany appeared to be fighting Mrs. Gordon for control of the proceedings. As McAlhany's voice took on a tone of ever-increasing insistence, Valerie hastily ran a comb through her hair and hurried down the stairs. She had no wish to see a clash between the vicar and Mrs. Gordon, each of them equally alarming in their own way.

Aunt Olivia met her at the foot of the stairs. "It's warming up. Come and sit down. Any minute now."

The parlor was in chaos, with the windows partly open and a wire trailing out through one while a cold, dank wind fluttered the pristine lace curtains. The chairs had been lined up in front of the television, and the screen was glowing a ghostly gray, interrupted every now and then by wavering lines and the shadowy outlines of what could be people moving.

"Any minute now," Aunt Gladys said encouragingly as she indicated that Valerie should sit in the chair next to the vicar, who was being kept in his place by a stern look from Mrs. Gordon.

"They know what they're doing," Mrs. Gordon said, "so let them get on with it."

Before McAlhany, flipping his hair impatiently, could voice his doubts, a voice erupted from the television, and the picture cleared. The aunts both clutched their bosoms in twin gestures of maidenly amazement. Mrs. Gordon took her seat, and the man who had been on the roof slipped in through the window.

"We'll stay and watch," he said, "in case you have any problems."

The mellifluous voice of Richard Dimbleby silenced all other voices in the room. "And here are the four royal dukes, following the coffin. The Dukes of Edinburgh, Windsor, Gloucester, and Kent."

Valerie sat transfixed as the picture finally emerged, sailors pulling the king's coffin on a gun carriage, and immediately behind the carriage, four men. Richard Dimbleby's voice provided the details in hushed, reverent tones, describing the new queen's closest male relatives: the sixteen-year-old Duke of Kent, surely too young to take the place of his dead father, wore formal clothes and a top hat, but the other men were in uniform. The Duke of Edinburgh, husband to the woman who was now queen, wore his naval uniform. The Duke of Gloucester wore the uniform of the Royal Hussars. And the Duke of Windsor—the man who had so briefly been king—also wore a naval uniform.

Valerie leaned forward in her chair, taking in the appearance of the man who had abandoned his post and now, according to Lestock, wanted to take it up again. Slim, gray-haired, and blank-faced, he followed the steady pace of the sailors pulling the gun carriage, looking neither right nor left. Dimbleby made no comment. What could he say? What could anyone say? The man who should have been king was living and breathing, but the man who had picked up his burden was in a flag-draped coffin. Remembering her conversation with Lestock, Valerie wondered how many people watching the television that day, or listening on their radios, or even standing bareheaded in the street, were thinking the same. How many of them really wanted to see the exiled duke reclaim his throne?

The camera moved in to reveal the coffin draped in the Royal Standard and bearing the orb, the scepter, and the Imperial State Crown. Another camera took up the picture, showing the crown in close-up. Even the gray overcast of the British weather could not dull the glitter of the jewels. The crown sparkled with diamonds, rubies, emeralds, and sapphires. Valerie could not begin to imagine the value of the gems on display—not that it mattered, for surely no one would touch them.

Valerie could not say how long she sat staring at the flickering black-and-white images, with the commentator's voice and the sound of martial music as the only background to her thoughts. For once, her aunts were silent and still, and even the vicar seemed to have his random inappropriate urges under control. She could see him from the corner of her eye, with his hands clasped in his lap. How had he ever become a vicar? Had his new calling helped him to overcome his psychiatric diagnosis of intermittent explosive anger disorder? Did his disorder mean that he was truly undeserving of his medals? She thought not. Courage was courage, however it manifested itself.

He was a fascinating contradiction. Last night he had awoken the entire neighborhood with his frenzied bell ringing and his insistence that a satanist was loose in the belfry, and yet this morning, he had displayed incredible kindness by turning up at the house with a television.

The men who had delivered the TV set remained in the background, no doubt happy that they were able to see this event for themselves. Only Mrs. Gordon seemed distracted. No, Valerie thought, not distracted, alert. Jane Gordon was on duty. Even now, with all eyes on the marching soldiers, the two queens draped in black veils, and the clerics in their fine vestments, her eyes flickered from the doors to the windows, and she never once sat back in her seat.

In the end, it was not Mrs. Gordon who sounded the alarm; it was the dog. The pug had been shut away behind the kitchen door, where his excited barking and occasional dyspeptic emissions could be ignored. Valerie had all but forgotten about him until the moment when the cameras were trained on the king's coffin on its way to meet the Royal Train at Paddington station for its journey to Windsor. As the sailors set down their ropes, and the coffin of George VI was lifted from the gun carriage, the dog broke into a bout of frenzied barking.

Mrs. Gordon was on her feet in a moment, and from somewhere in her clothing, she produced a pistol. She motioned for everyone to sit still, but naturally, McAlhany had no intention of being still. He, too, was on his feet, and he reached the kitchen door ahead of her.

Richard Dimbleby continued his calm, respectful commentary as Mrs. Gordon and the vicar tussled for control of the kitchen doorknob and the men from Radio Rentals uttered words that were not normally spoken in polite company. With no frame of reference but the evidence of their own eyes, they had to choose between a mad Scotswoman with a gun and a slightly less mad vicar, and they very unwisely came down on the vicar's side.

Mrs. Gordon had downed one of them with a swift kick and was about to deal with another when the vicar succeeded in turning the doorknob, and the kitchen door swung open to reveal nothing but an empty kitchen.

The dog snuffled and barked at the back door, but whoever or whatever had disturbed him was no longer to be seen. So far as Valerie could tell, the only evidence that anyone had been in the room was a frighteningly familiar blue envelope propped up against the teapot—an envelope that no one else had noticed.

She snatched it up and concealed it behind her back as the combatants sorted themselves out. While Gladys and Olivia twittered in dismay, the Radio Rentals men loudly demanded an explanation for their treatment. Valerie was amused to hear McAlhany distracting everyone by expressing a renewed interest in satanists. His well-timed suggestion gave Jane Gordon time to make the pistol disappear back into the folds of her dress. Only the dog studied the table with knowing eyes, and only Valerie knew the full import of what she had found.

She excused herself from the fray and went upstairs to the privacy of her bedroom. She opened the envelope with trembling fingers and found what she had expected—a sheet of blue Basildon Bond paper and a note written in a familiar round, somewhat childish hand.

London
Alan Lestock

Lestock was out of uniform. He wore his medal ribbons in order to fit in with the other men who marched in the funeral procession. Bareheaded and wearing a dark coat, he was an anonymous figure marching with many others, some of high status, some of great military rank, and some, like Lestock, anonymously keeping a close eye on the security of the jewels atop the coffin.

The procession itself was a mile long, with the coffin pulled on a gun carriage by Royal Navy sailors. As the gun carriage moved out from Westminster Hall, with the band playing the Dead March from Saul, Big Ben tolled fifty-six times—once for each year of the king's life. In Hyde Park and at the Tower of London, the guns also measured out the short life of the man who had never intended to be king.

As the procession passed Marlborough House, Lestock looked up, knowing that the king's mother, Queen Mary, would be looking down, perhaps shedding a tear for the loss of yet another son, perhaps reflecting on the fact that the son who should have been king now bore only the title of duke. Or perhaps—and Lestock did not enjoy this thought—the dowager queen knew something of the plans that were afoot.

Although detachments from all branches of the military lined the route and headed the cortege, Lestock still felt the burden of responsibility as though it were his alone. Let the military prevent any attack on the four field marshals who marched side by side, along with four admirals of the fleet and four marshals of the Royal Air Force, and kings and dignitaries of foreign nations. He was keeping watch for a very different kind of threat.

The cortege maintained its solemn but relentless pace through the streets of the city. Some who walked were of an age where they were surely struggling to keep the pace set by the Earl

Marshal, but he could not imagine that any man would willingly refuse the honor of the day.

Behind the gun carriage, and behind the four royal dukes, came the closed carriage of the new queen, Elizabeth, who rode with her mother, now the Queen Mother, her sister, Princess Margaret, and her aunt Alice, the Princess Royal.

The funeral procession arrived at last at Paddington station, where the Royal Train awaited them. The king was now about to leave London for the last time, on the train that would carry him to Windsor and burial in St. George's Chapel.

Outside the station, the long funeral procession ground to a halt. The sailors set down the white ropes that yoked them to the gun carriage, and gave the king over to the care of the Grenadier Guards, who lifted the coffin to their shoulders and carried it to the train.

The four royal women stepped out of their carriage. Measured against the phalanx of guardsmen in their bearskin caps, the black-veiled women were achingly small and vulnerable. The young queen was a tiny, slim figure dwarfed by the men and women who were now her subjects. She did not have the regal bearing of the king's sister, the Princess Royal, the comfortable plumpness of her mother, Queen Elizabeth, or the sharp alertness of her younger sister, but she carried herself with dignity. Her face, and the faces of the other women, was almost invisible behind a heavy black veil, and what little Lestock could see of it was pale and expressionless. He wondered what it had cost her to endure that endless ride through the grieving city in an ordeal that was not yet over. Ahead lay the short journey to Windsor, yet another solemn procession through the streets of Windsor, and finally the burial in St. George's Chapel, where George VI would lie among the other kings and queens of England.

For Lestock, the journey was over, and other men in dark overcoats would pick up where he had left off. He was anxious to hand off his responsibility and get back to what he thought of as his "real work." The funeral, so far, had been a success, if a funeral could ever be called a success. The great and famous had negotiated the streets of London without incident; the crowds had been mostly silent; the military had been rigidly precise; and even the horses had borne themselves with dignity.

This was all a great accomplishment for a nation that was still bloodied and bruised by the terrible struggle of world war. It was a spectacle for the ages, and a great start for the age of the "New Elizabethans," but Lestock knew that the aura of security was as false as the jewels in the crown that rested on the king's coffin.

At long last, his replacement approached and spoke the code words. Lestock knew the man, but without the completed code, he would not relinquish his post. He could not shake the feeling that traitors were everywhere, even here in the presence of the new queen. He was relieved to see David Smythe standing behind the newcomer while they exchanged the meaningless phrases that belittled the seriousness of their purpose.

"The sun is over the yardarm in Madras."

"But not in Rangoon."

They were ridiculous words, but they relieved him of his responsibility, and now, at last, he was free to think of Valerie Chaplin and her rendezvous with Jeremy Paxton years ago in the New Forest. The area was vast, more than two hundred square miles of woodland and heath crisscrossed by ancient trails and dotted with villages. As clues went, it was a very poor clue indeed, but it was the best lead he had—better than anything handed to him by Scotland Yard.

He knew he would have to go back to Redbridge and force her to reveal additional details. It would mean treading with heavy feet on memories she would sooner forget. He had told her he could provide a name if that was what she wanted. It had been a rash promise and one that he would prefer not to keep. He had the authority to open records and reveal truths, but was it a good idea? If the boy had a happy life with devoted parents, wasn't it better to leave him alone? So far Valerie had refused his offer. He hoped she would be wise enough to continue.

The Royal Train departed in a cloud of steam, and Lestock and Smythe stood on the platform and watched the slow disintegration of the elements of the cortege. The soldiers marched away. The horses, released from rigid restraint, tossed their heads and pranced impatiently. The military bands moved on in silence. He felt that he was witnessing the end of a particularly wild cocktail party— not that he'd been at one of those in a great many years.

"Well," Smythe said at last, "that's that. I have a car standing by. We have to go."

"Where?"

"Redbridge. There's been an incident at the Chaplin house. I'm afraid Mrs. Gordon has let us down, and Valerie Chaplin has disappeared."

CHAPTER FIFTEEN

Churchgate Close
Redbridge, Surrey
Valerie Chaplin

Valerie waited in her bedroom until the chaos abated and she could hear a chorus of voices offering apologies. The Chaplin twins apologized for everything that had happened anywhere in the house. The vicar apologized for becoming overexcited. And the Radio Rentals men apologized for interfering. The excitement was blamed on the dog, who had obviously imagined danger where there was none. Mrs. Gordon stayed out of the discussion. She did not apologize for producing a weapon, and no one thought to apologize for the fact that the back door had been unlocked while everyone was watching television.

No one but Valerie knew that someone had crept into the kitchen and planted the note that was now in her trembling hands. With all eyes on the television as the funeral procession approached Paddington station, she was confident she would not be missed for at least a few minutes while she studied the note.

She recognized the paper, of course. Whoever wrote the notes that had arrived sporadically over the years had always used this same paper. It was pale blue with fine lines and a Basildon Bond watermark, and as usual, the envelope matched. Feeling the quality of the paper, Valerie had always assumed that it was prewar stock. Impoverished Britain had not yet returned to making luxury goods, and this paper was a luxury. It was the kind of paper one gave as a gift to the aunt who had everything. In the happy days before Hitler invaded Poland and war broke out across the world, someone had received a box of fancy stationary as a gift. Instead of using it to write thank-you notes, they had squirreled it away, and when the time came, they had used it, a little at a time, to inflict guilt and misery on Valerie. Why?

This note was not the same as the others. Instead of vague warnings that could well be nothing but malicious lies, this note contained a challenge.

If you want to know about your son, meet me in the graveyard by the shed where the verger keeps the lawnmower. Come now.

She was surprised at her own sense of relief. After years of trying to ignore the notes and suppress her feeling about the baby, she had given up. She was finally going to confront her tormentor. This was not the same as Lestock's offer to reveal her child's identity. This took no thinking about at all. The letter writer had tortured her for years, and the time had come to end the torment.

She had been so young when her son was born—young, innocent, and desperate—and giving the baby up seemed to be the only thing to do. Jeremy Paxton, the love of her life, had disappeared, and she was in no position to care for a child.

She had been slow to realize that the long, idyllic afternoon with Jeremy had led to such a tangible result. Pregnancy was what happened to bawdy women in Hogarth paintings and girls who were "no better than they should be." Pregnancy could not have been happening to Valerie, not after just the one time—well, several times, but all in the course of one afternoon.

When her mother's sharp eyes forced her to admit her pregnancy—to herself as well as her mother—she had been surprised at her mother's resourcefulness and strength. Wasting no time on blame or recriminations, Adeline Chaplin had made all the arrangements, offered all the excuses for Valerie's absence from various events, and eventually accompanied her to the convent.

It was also her mother who had made her see sense.

"We have to take care of this. Stop crying, and take your head out of the clouds. I will arrange for you to go away and give birth, and then we'll never speak of it again."

"But it's Jeremy's child."

"And where is Jeremy? Gone, that's where he is. Run off and left you

holding the baby. I will not have you upsetting your father with this, so no more nonsense about keeping the baby."

The nuns, who had seen this so many times before, had assured her that there was a woman somewhere just waiting to love and care for Jeremy's child in a way that Valerie could not. *"You'll never even have to hold him, and you'll forget about him in no time at all."*

Perhaps they had been right. Perhaps she would have forgotten him if it had not been for the arrival of the blue envelopes. Every anonymous note tore at her heart and reminded her not just of the baby but of Jeremy himself and set her wondering if he had really abandoned her or if something had happened to him.

Now, as the sound of the king's funeral wafted up the stairs, she studied the new note, feeling that she was missing something vital. She applied the skills that made her a good librarian and researcher. The notepaper had remained the same over the years, as though the writer had dedicated this box of expensive stationary to the sole purpose of writing to Valerie. The handwriting was neat and rounded, the letters perfectly formed, as if for a writing exercise in primary school. She was certain that this note was written by a girl or woman, who liked to conform to rules. These two facts were nothing new, but now she had something else to go on.

Meet me in the graveyard by the shed where the verger keeps the lawnmower.

These words were important. Only someone local would know where the verger kept the lawnmower. Only someone who was familiar with the practices of the Church of England would refer to the groundskeeper as a verger. Additionally, this note came from someone who lived nearby, or—and this thought was additionally disturbing—someone who spent time specifically observing Valerie. The thought made Valerie shiver, but it did not put a dent in her resolve. This couldn't go on any longer. She had spent too many years at this person's mercy, always wondering when the next note would come.

She had already decided to go to the rendezvous point, but she wondered if she should take someone with her. The obvious choice would be Mrs. Gordon, whose sole purpose in being at the house was to keep her safe, but if Valerie arrived with such a formidable person in tow, maybe the letter writer would back away from the meeting. This was a now-or-never moment, and she would have to go alone.

The Radio Rentals men were having trouble with the television, and the picture was fading in and out, offering only occasional glimpses of the funeral procession. Richard Dimbleby's voice continued unabated, describing the scene in front of him, but his reverent description was drowned out by the noisy communication between the man on the roof adjusting the aerial, the man with his head out of the window, passing on information, and the man who stooped behind the television, making adjustments to the many wires and valves in its interior. Meantime, the would-be viewers of the funeral kept up a running commentary on what they could and could not see. If ever there was a right moment to slip out of the house unseen, this was it.

Valerie crept down the stairs, took her coat from the hallstand, avoided the kitchen, where the dog was no doubt waiting, and let herself out of the front door. She was not even concerned that opening the door would admit a wave of cold air, as the parlor windows were open, and cold air was already wafting throughout the house.

The street was deserted, with almost every resident inside, listening to their radio or watching their television. The letter writer had chosen her moment wisely when she had written *come now*, and Valerie found herself running to obey the command. She was impatient to finally come face-to-face with her tormentor.

She focused her mind on maintaining a simple anger that would drive out any doubts. She wanted to deliver some kind of justice to the person whose malice had disturbed her for so many years, and she wanted answers. What had she ever done to this person?

She tried to keep any other thoughts at bay. She could not, would not, believe there was any truth in the notes. The harsh things that had been said over the years were simply not true. They were just the wild imaginings of a disturbed mind. No one knew the identity of the boy Valerie had given up. He was not sick; he was not unloved; and he had not been abandoned. The letters were not really about him; they were about her. Someone had hated her for years, and she was about to find out why.

The graveyard was as deserted as the street, and she assumed that Martin McAlhany had learned his lesson and the church doors were locked. The stone shed where the verger kept his equipment was set in a corner of the graveyard, partially sheltered from view by two ancient yew trees as green in the winter as they were in the summer. She slowed to a walk as she approached the building, and she forced herself to be cautious. She assumed that the letter writer was a woman, but what if that was not the case? What if it was a man? What if—and this thought was totally new—what if it was Jeremy?

That thought brought her to a complete halt. It couldn't be. He didn't even know that he had a son. After that one day in the forest, she had never heard from him again. She had waited in vain for another letter, and she had pestered April Brady—*"Have you heard from him?"*

She had tried to go back to the forest, but her mother had been watching. *"If he shows his face around here, I'll have the police on him."* She couldn't risk the police, couldn't risk him being arrested as a deserter. Her father's stories still rang in her ears: deserters shot at dawn.

She glanced nervously around the graveyard, regretting that she had not brought Mrs. Gordon and her pistol. The open door of the shed was an invitation to enter, but she was in a perfect position for an ambush, as she was surrounded by gravestones that could be hiding any number of assailants.

This was ridiculous. She'd come this far, and she was not going to retreat. At the very moment she made up her mind to go forward, a small figure appeared in the doorway of the old stone shed. For a moment, Valerie thought that she was seeing a child, and her heart leaped. Could it be ...? The figure took a step forward into the light, and she saw not a child but a very small woman with mousy-brown hair and spectacles. The passage of years had done nothing to change her; she had not grown taller, and her spectacles were still round and owlish. *Mary Carpenter!*

Puzzle pieces swam crazily in Valerie's mind, assembling and reassembling into a pattern she could not comprehend. Mary had always planned to go overseas to convert the heathens in Africa, China, India, or some other foreign clime, and yet Alan Lestock had found her living in Kent. What had made her change her mind? Yesterday she had been seen in the company of notorious gangsters, the same gangsters who had broken into the library, and now she was hiding in the verger's shed, just as the note had promised. Did this mean that Mary had written the note? Did this mean that Mary had written all the notes?

She backed away as Mary advanced, taunting as she came. "Well, Valerie, what do you say now? You thought you could just drop me, didn't you?"

"Mary?"

"Yes, Mary. That's right, Mary, who was dull and boring and not as exciting as April Brady."

Valerie struggled for words, and her tongue felt thick. "Mary Carpenter?"

"Yes, Mary Good-as-Gold Carpenter. You should have listened to your mother. She understood. She knew that I was good for your father. He needed my prayers, but you didn't want me in the house, did you? You didn't want to be seen as my friend. You wanted April as your friend, and look where that got you—up the spout."

"What?"

"Up the spout. Pregnant. Did you think I wouldn't guess? I was watching. I knew."

Some of the pieces of the puzzle were assembling themselves now. It had been only yesterday that she had told Lestock about Mary and how she had been embarrassed that her mother wanted them to be friends.

"Why don't you invite Mary? Perhaps she could come to tea."

"I hate Mary."

Valerie had not been alone in mocking Mary. She was easily shunned by the girls at school as dull, undersized, judgmental, and prudish. She often responded by accusing her mockers of being demon-possessed, which brought forth gales of laughter from her tormentors. Looking at her now, Valerie could see that nothing had changed in Mary except that an edge of pure hate had been added to her usual sour expression.

If there was truth to Mary's accusation, and if Valerie had reason to feel guilty for her treatment of Mary, now was not the time to pause for reflection. She only wanted to know one thing.

"Were you telling me the truth? All those things you said about my son, are any of them true?"

Before Mary could respond, a deep, masculine voice spoke up from behind her. "You give us Paxton, and your son will come to no harm."

Valerie spun on her heel and caught a glimpse of a large man emerging from behind a gravestone. With a sinking heart, she realized that Mary had set up an ambush and lured her into a position to be captured by the man hidden behind the gravestone, all in order to ask her about Jeremy Paxton. Why? What had Jeremy done?

Before Valerie had a chance to ask herself any more questions, a man dashed past her and hurled himself forward in an explosion of energy. As she watched, the two men went down among the gravestones in a tangle of kicks, punches, and curses.

Valerie, shocked into immobility, recognized that the new arrival was Martin McAlhany, who had obviously released his inhibitions. He was attacking so viciously that she was certain he would emerge the winner. Unfortunately, just as it seemed the fight might be over, two more men emerged from the shed and joined in the melee.

Valerie knew that the best thing she could do now, while no one was looking at her, was to run. If she could get as far as the house, she could find Mrs. Gordon, who would surely bring her pistol and put an end to whatever was going on. Although her mind told her what to do, she couldn't make herself move. She remained rooted to the spot, mesmerized by McAlhany's fierce and frenzied struggle, until she saw something from the corner of her eye. Mary was poised for flight.

Valerie turned her back on the struggling men and tackled Mary before she had taken more than a couple of steps. When Mary fell, Valerie fell on top of her. The young ladies who went to Redbridge Grammar School for Girls were fully capable of whacking each other with hockey sticks and elbowing each other in a game of netball, but they did not normally bite, scratch, or pull hair, all of which were tactics that Mary seemed to have learned since she had left school. In her own way, Mary was just as frenzied as the vicar, and Valerie was shocked to find that she could not escape Mary's fierce, clawlike hands.

When the dust finally settled, Valerie and the vicar were both losers, unable to resist as they were dragged to the road behind the shed and bundled into a large black car.

Valerie was jammed up against McAlhany in the back seat, squeezed in on both sides by large but breathless men. McAlhany had fought like a berserker and inflicted considerable damage, and his assailants were regarding him with grudging respect.

Valerie murmured an apology. "I'm sorry, Martin. I should have told Mrs. Gordon where I was going. This was stupid."

McAlhany's smile was surprisingly cheerful considering the bruised state of his face. "Don't worry," he said. "They don't know that they've awakened the sleeping beast in me. I still have it on a leash, but I can release it at any time."

He flicked his hair back, and she was able to search his face and see the fire smoldering in his gray eyes. *"Once I get started, I can't stop."*

She hoped that was still the case. She didn't need the vicar now; she needed Martin McAlhany, the man who won medals.

**Churchgate Close
Redbridge, Surrey
Alan Lestock**

Lestock had never seen Jane Gordon in such a state of distress. By the time he arrived in Redbridge, the television had been removed from the parlor, and order had been restored to the house, but not by Jane. When Lestock and Smythe let themselves in through the back door, the Chaplin sisters were in the kitchen. Olivia was washing teacups, and Gladys was busy at the stove. From the fact that the dog was seated at her feet, Lestock deduced that Gladys was cooking up yet another potion to settle the dog's upset stomach. He wished she had something she could give *him*, not for his stomach but for the roil of emotions that accompanied both the burial of the king and the disappearance of his one and only witness.

Lestock left Smythe in the kitchen to question the sisters and went quietly into the living room, where Mrs. Gordon was slumped in a chair, methodically running her fingers through her hair until it stood on end and gave the appearance of a tall, crowned fur hat.

She looked up when Lestock entered, and then looked down again. "The locals are searching house to house," she said.

"What about the church? If the vicar's gone from here, perhaps they're both inside."

Mrs. Gordon shook her head. "No, they're not."

"Not even in the bell tower?"

"No." She looked up and made an attempt at her usual fierceness. "Do you think I haven't thought of that?"

"Sorry. Tell me what happened."

She was suddenly on her feet, pacing impatiently. "We thought there was someone in the kitchen, because the wretched dog was barking, but I looked, and ..." She shook her head. "I made a bloody fool of myself and very nearly killed the vicar, but there was no one there."

"How many men were setting up the television?"

"Three." She shook her head again. "I've already thought of that, and no, it wasn't any of them, although I have the locals keeping an eye on them. The truth is, I don't think anyone took her against her will. She did the same thing when I had her at the safe house. She's slippery. I should have known that. I should have remembered."

She slumped down into the chair again and recommenced running her fingers through her hair. "If I can't do better than this, you'd better put me out to pasture."

Lestock closed his eyes, remembering how he had sat in the special commissioner's office and thought exactly the same thing. They had fought a war and won medals they could display and wounds they would show to no one, but what was happening now, this high-level game of kings and queens and stolen jewels, threatened to overwhelm them both.

"Jane," he said softly.

She looked up sharply. "We agreed that I can't be Jane. I have to be—"

"Mrs. Gordon," he said. "We agreed you would be Mrs. Gordon. That was a long time ago, Jane, back when I needed a reminder that you have a husband."

"Are you saying you no longer need a reminder?"

He knew that this was not the right time for this conversation, but there had never been a right time.

"I remember your husband every day," he said softly. "How is he?"

She shook her head, but he refused to be embarrassed by his question. He needed to know if Alec Gordon, confined to a wheelchair, would ever recover from his wounds.

"Declining," she said.

Their eyes met, and he recognized that the spark was still there, waiting to be fanned into a flame. They had faced death together in France, but it was not just the feeling that time was short that had driven them into each other's arms. If they had met anywhere at any time, the fire would have existed, but she had a husband, and Lestock had a moral code that he could not take advantage of another man's war wounds.

They each took a step backward, and he turned his thoughts away from France and away from the man in the wheelchair.

"Mrs. Gordon," he said abruptly, "I need a report. Tell me what I need to know and why you think Valerie left of her own accord."

"I found an envelope in her room."

"What makes you think that it's relevant?"

"It wasn't there this morning."

"And you know that because …?"

"Because I looked. You may have a soft spot for this girl, but I have a clear head about her, and I don't trust her any farther than I can throw her."

Lestock found himself taking a sudden breath. *Jealousy!* He wished he could take the time to reassure her.

"During the preparations for the television viewing," Mrs. Gordon said, "I made several trips upstairs while Valerie was still sleeping—she slept very late this morning. I peeked in, and she was not moving. I can assure you that she did not have a blue envelope anywhere that I could see at that time. I also looked more thoroughly while she was downstairs watching the funeral procession, and there was no blue envelope. That envelope appeared as a direct result of the mysterious incident of the 'dog in the night-time' as Sherlock Holmes would say."

"You can't know that."

"Call it an informed hunch. I would also say that Valerie knew what it was, and there are signs that she ripped it open in haste."

"Anything written on the envelope?"

"Just her name. 'Valerie.' I've called for a handwriting expert. From my own observation, I would say that it's a woman's writing, maybe even a child's."

"So we're guessing that someone, a woman or a child, slipped in the back door while all eyes were on the television and the back door was unlocked with no one on watch but the pug," Lestock said.

Mrs. Gordon frowned. "I have already admitted that I should have been more careful."

He knew that his silence would convey agreement—she should have been more careful. So should he. They were both losing their edge.

In the awkward silence that followed, he heard the back door open and close, and agitated voices drifted in from the kitchen. Smythe put his head around the door.

"Sir?"

Lestock waved him away. "In a minute. I have to deal with this."

Smythe retreated, but the damage was already done. "I am not something you have to deal with," Mrs. Gordon said through clenched teeth. "I know when I'm at fault."

He took a deep breath and tried again. "You're not at fault, Jane. The men from Radio Rentals were in and out all morning. I assume that's why the Chaplin sisters left the back door unlocked. I think that someone was watching the house and waiting for their opportunity."

Mrs. Gordon shook her head. "I don't see the point. They have a letter box in the front door. Why not just put it through the letter box? Why wait for the back door to be open?"

"More dramatic," Lestock said. "Getting the dog to bark, and getting everyone riled up, would throw Valerie off balance. If the letter just slipped through the front door, it wouldn't have the same effect. Someone is trying to frighten her."

"And then there's the vicar," Mrs. Gordon said.

Lestock could not believe he had forgotten about the vicar. Martin McAlhany was a hard man to forget, but for the past few minutes, he had entirely slipped Lestock's mind.

"Do you know for certain that he went with Valerie?"

"No," Mrs. Gordon said angrily, "I don't know. I don't really know anything. He's not here, and he's not at the church or the vicarage, and that's all I know. He slipped away at the same time I discovered that Valerie had gone. They didn't go together, but they could have arranged it in advance."

Lestock tried to silence an unwelcome suspicion. For all his mad impetuousness, he liked McAlhany, but liking had nothing to do with the situation in hand. "McAlhany hired the television set, didn't he?"

"Yes."

"So he knew that the result would be chaos, with men climbing on the roof, windows open, everyone distracted."

Mrs. Gordon looked at him. "Are you suggesting that he's involved?"

Lestock rubbed his temples, wishing that he could massage his brain into making sense of the situation.

"One more thing," Mrs. Gordon said. "I searched Valerie's room, and I found another note. It's written on fancy blue letter paper, Basildon Bond prewar stock. I would say that it matches the envelope I saw this morning, but it wasn't written at the same time. This was written some time ago. It's been folded and refolded over a number of years. It was caught in the back of a drawer. I don't suppose Valerie knew it was there."

"What does it say?"

Mrs. Gordon reached into her pocket and produced a sheet of blue lined paper. "Read it for yourself."

Lestock took the paper, noting that it was indeed marked with permanent fold lines. There was no greeting, no date, no return address, just a stark message written in a careful round hand.

No one wants him. He's too weak. He'll never find a family.

He turned the note over as if he expected to find something more written on the back, but there was nothing beyond the unkind words.

"Presumably, the writer is referring to the baby," Mrs. Gordon said. "It's a spiteful piece of work."

"I wonder if it's true," Lestock said.

"You can find out," Mrs. Gordon challenged. "You can find her child."

Lestock continued to stare at the note. "That's why she went, isn't it? Someone's been tormenting her all these years. She wants the truth."

He could not take his eyes from the note as he imagined the pain it must have caused. "Is it possible that Paxton was writing to her?"

"No. It's a woman," Mrs. Gordon insisted. "We can wait for the experts to confirm, but I'm sure of it. It's someone whose writing has not changed since they were in the lower fourth. No writing development and probably no character development. Look, Alan, I don't care how you feel about her—"

"I don't feel anything about her."

Mrs. Gordon ignored the interruption. "I don't care how you feel about her, or how much you like the crazy vicar, there is more here than meets the eye. There is a deep level of evil behind that note."

"I believe you," Lestock said wearily, "but whether we like it or not, Valerie isn't our first priority. If we can't find her and get her to tell us what she knows, we will have to go on without her and follow whatever leads we have. The Duke of Windsor is here, and before he goes back to France, or America, or whatever fancy house party is next on his list, we have to find out who he's talking to, and what he knows about the missing jewels."

"And that brings us back to Paxton," Mrs. Gordon said. "Everything brings us back to Paxton, and so everything brings us right back to Valerie."

"Who doesn't know anything," Lestock said.

Mrs. Gordon leaned forward in her seat, her expression deadly serious beneath the absurdity of her frazzled hair. "She knows more than we do. You have to find her, Alan."

A sharp rap on the parlor door brought David Smythe into the room with a grin on his face. Lestock looked up, welcoming the distraction. His mind was running in circles, and he needed something to break the circle and set it on another track.

"Tell me you know something," Lestock said.

Smythe nodded. "I know the dog's name."

Lestock spoke without thinking. "Oh, good, now we can get him to come when he's called. Tell me you know something useful."

Smythe was grinning. "Ask me how I know."

Lestock shook his head. "I'm not in the mood to play games."

"It's not a game; it's a clue. Remember, the dog was found tied to the front gate when this house was burgled. Whoever tied the dog to the gate also broke the kitchen window and ransacked the house. The dog is our tie to whoever that was, and now ask me how I know his name."

Lestock sat back in the chair, relieved to find that his brain was working again and no longer running around in circles. "Sorry, Smythe. You're right. Well, get on with it."

"There's a boy in the kitchen. In fact, there are several boys in the kitchen, and they are members of the Dog Spotters Society. They're like trainspotters. They have little *I-Spy* books, and they write down every breed they spot and where they spotted them, and that gives them points. So, this boy, Ranulph Witherspoon, seems to be the leader of the pack, and for the past twenty-four hours, he's been canvassing his fellow dog spotters to see if anyone is missing a pug. They're not a breed you see every day of the week, and apparently, they score high in the *I-Spy Dogs* handbook if you see one, and that is how we now know that the noisy little creature in the kitchen is named Roger."

"What else do we know?" Lestock asked.

"I have people working on what they told me," Smythe said, "but I think you should talk to them yourself. I'll bring them in."

Lestock raised his hand. "No, don't do that. We don't have time to waste."

Smythe, who Lestock had known for a number of years, suddenly shot Lestock a rare disapproving look. "I know the stakes, but I know these boys."

"You know them?" Lestock asked.

"I know boys like them," Smythe said. "They're the misfits, the ones who don't play football or make jokes in class. They're the boys who always finish their homework and win all the prizes on prize day. They have no social skills, but they have this one thing they do better than anyone else: they identify dogs. They've found you the biggest clue you're going to find today. They don't know why you need this information, but they're bursting to give it you, so just let them tell you." He paused and raised his eyebrows quizzically. "How would you like it if your parents had called you Ranulph? Witherspoon is bad enough, but Ranulph is the final straw. Give the boy a break."

Lestock heard Jane Gordon's soft laugh, and he realized that, just for a moment, his mood had lightened. "All right, bring them in, and when we're done, give them a couple of bob and some government ration coupons so they can go down to the sweetshop."

"Will do," Smythe said.

He opened the parlor door and ushered in three half-grown boys, dissimilar in height and coloring, one with hair so blond as to be almost invisible, one who was most probably Anglo-Indian, and one who had the reddish hair of a Viking but not the tall, muscular build.

This rather puny Viking introduced himself as Ranulph Witherspoon, and there seemed to be an element of regret even in his introduction. What the boy needed, Lestock concluded, was a really good nickname, but Smythe was already ahead of him, eschewing the obvious Ralph and calling him Randy.

"Randy here has something to show you," Smythe said.

Randy was smartly dressed in his school blazer and gray flannel uniform shorts, which reached to his knees. Lestock noticed that his knees were clean, an unusual condition for a boy of his age. He produced a small printed *I-Spy* book of the kind that could be bought at any newsagent for sixpence. Randy's book looked well worn and somewhat battered.

"I've never seen a pug," Randy confessed, "but Leonard's seen him."

Leonard was the Anglo-Indian boy, who also carried a copy of *I-Spy Dogs*. He bowed slightly before speaking. "My father drives a bread van and has a long route. Sometimes I go with him during school holidays. I have seen this dog before. I marked him in my handbook on the thirtieth of July last year and earned five points. Would you like to see?"

"No," said Mrs. Gordon. "We don't need to see; we believe you. Just tell us where you saw him."

"Yes, madam. We saw him at a place called Southdown Hall, and he belongs to the gardener. The dog's name is Roger. I do not know the name of the gardener."

Lestock looked at the boy's earnest face. "Are you sure this is the same dog?"

"Pugs are quite rare," Randy said, "and that is why they are worth five points, but Leonard says that this one is easy to recognize because of his … smell."

Lestock found himself smiling. Obviously, word of Roger's stomach problems had spread throughout the dog-spotting community, and he wondered what would happen now that Miss Gladys Chaplin was working so hard to eliminate Roger's most distinctive means of recognition.

Lestock looked up and saw Smythe nodding as he fished in his pocket for coins. "While you've been in here, I've been making inquiries," he said. "Southdown Hall is the home of Major Cardrew Hyde, formerly commanding a squad of non-combatants at Windsor Castle. We were told he'd been questioned and cleared, but I think he needs another visit. I've ordered up two cars from the locals. They'll be here any minute."

Lestock, with his heart skipping a beat, reached into his inside pocket and slid out a pound note to add to Smythe's handful of silver. "Knickerbocker glories all round," he said.

CHAPTER SIXTEEN

Little Clamping, Kent
Davie

Davie tried to move from beneath the pile of coal sacks, but they weighed him down, and the effort was more than he could manage. He lay back again. At least he was warm beneath the coal sacks. Maybe too warm. He shouldn't be so warm in such a cold place. The light he could glimpse through the open door of the shed was now tinged with orange. In a rare moment of clarity, he recognized that the sun was setting. Whatever warmth had built up in the day would soon be gone. He should at least close the door of the shed.

He made another attempt at moving and managed to roll out from beneath the sacks and crawl to the door, but it refused to budge. For a long time, he lay spread-eagled on the floor, breathing in coal dust as he summoned the strength to crawl back to his makeshift bed.

He was angry now with Pete and Colin.

They said they wouldn't wait for you.

They could at least have closed the door instead of leaving me to freeze to death.

You said you were hot.

Well, now I'm cold.

You're going to die.

The certainty of his prediction brought tears to Davie's eyes, and he sniveled and sniffed as he crawled back to the pile of sacks and wormed his way underneath. His head was swimming, and far from being cold, he was once again too hot. He knew he was sick. The symptoms were only too familiar. Usually when he had this kind of sickness, Matron would shake her head angrily, as if somehow he had brought the illness on himself, and reluctantly call the doctor. Davie liked the doctor, who was not afraid to argue with Matron.

"This boy should be in hospital."

Matron would have nothing to do with hospitals.

"I should report you for lack of care."

"Lack of care!" Matron repeated. *"We're the only ones who care. If we don't take care of him here, he'll have to go to a home for feeble-minded children. Just give him the medicine and mind your own business."*

Lying alone in the rapidly gathering twilight, Davie began to weep in earnest. He had been so close to finding his freedom. He had found the blue envelope under his pillow and read it in disbelief. He had a father who wanted to meet him and take him away to a better place. Although his father had managed to smuggle in the note, probably because fathers were known to be very clever, he could not come in person to the charity home, but Davie could come to him. If Davie could escape over the wall, he should make his way to Redbridge, where his father would meet him, but first he should make a telephone call to say that he was coming. In the corner of the envelope, he had found six pennies wrapped in a scrap of paper with a name and telephone number.

Davie blinked back his tears. He had lost the note from his father but not the money and the phone number—they were still in his pocket, where he had put them for safety. He slipped his hand into his pocket and gripped the bulky coins. If he died here in this coal shed, he hoped that someone would open his hand and find the coins and the phone number. He imagined that anonymous someone dialing a phone number and passing on the information.

"The boy's dead, but he tried. He really tried, and he almost made it."

Southdown Hall
Dorking, Surrey
Major Cardrew Hyde

The king's funeral was over, and Vernon departed in yet another large black automobile. Presumably, the driver of the vehicle had brought him news, but Vernon was not willing to share anything beyond a genial smile and a satisfied nod.

"Have they found her? Are they bringing her here?" Hyde asked.

Vernon said nothing to Hyde and only a mild thank-you to Kumar, who had helped him into his coat and was adjusting the astrakhan collar.

Hyde looked at Mayfield in disbelief as Vernon walked to his car. "What now?" he asked.

Mayfield shrugged. "We wait."

"For what?"

"I don't know. Maybe for hell to freeze over."

Hyde, with nothing else to do, settled for taking his impatience out on Kumar, delighting in putting his manservant in the unenviable position of doing everything right and being told that whatever he did was wrong. The major's tea was too strong. The major did not want digestive biscuits; he wanted custard creams, damn it. No, he could not tell the memsahib how many people were expected for dinner, maybe six, maybe none, and where the hell was the rest of the major's brandy?

Mayfield, sitting unperturbed in a chair by the fire, answered the final question. "I drank it."

"Who the hell said you could?"

"It's a cold night."

"Doesn't mean you can drink my brandy."

"I'm sure you have more down in your cellar."

The sheer impertinence of Mayfield's every action brought Hyde's blood close to boiling point. The fact that Mayfield had helped him to break into the Chaplin house did not mean that he, a mere sergeant, could now lounge by Hyde's fire, drink his brandy, and look so insufferably smug.

"The Vernons won't be back," Mayfield said with an undisguised air of *I told you so.* "You should have insisted that I go with them."

And then you wouldn't be back either, Hyde thought, surprised to find that the thought of Mayfield's absence was worse than the thought of his presence.

Mayfield understood the criminal minds of the Vernons, and so far, he had been correct. The sun had almost set, and there had been no sign of the Vernons returning and not even a phone call. Now that he thought about it, Hyde knew he should not be surprised. Why would they come back? They had Valerie Chaplin, and she was the only hope of tracing where Paxton had gone with the jewels. If they could find the jewels without any recourse to Hyde, then that was what they would do.

He shuddered at the thought of those barbarians cutting up and selling the four great historic stones. Thugs like the Vernons would not recognize them for what they were, for they were quite deceptive. The last time Hyde had seen the jewels was when Jeremy Paxton had levered the lid off the biscuit tin he had dug out of its hiding hole. The guttering light of his lantern revealed an old jam jar stuffed with cotton wool. When they unscrewed the lid and unwrapped the stones, it was hard to believe that these colored rocks were, in fact, the great imperial gems—a massive ruby, an even larger diamond, and two enormous sapphires. Of course, they glowed in the faint light, but even faceted glass could glow.

Kumar poked his head tentatively around the door.

"Sahib."

"Has the car arrived?"

"No, sahib."

"Go away. I don't want to be disturbed unless a car arrives."

"Telephone, sahib."

"Who is it?" Hyde asked with rising hope. Mayfield was wrong. Vernon was phoning to say that he had the Chaplin girl.

"It is the angry lady, sahib."

Hyde's heart sank. "I can't …"

"She insists."

Mayfield rose nonchalantly, strolled to the desk, and picked up the telephone receiver. "Major Hyde can't talk to you right now, so you'll have to tell me what you want," he said in his casual, disrespectful Yorkshire voice.

Hyde winced as he heard an explosion of sound from the receiver. Mayfield grinned and held the instrument away from his ear. When the sound died away, he spoke again. "Don't get so het up, lass."

Another explosion of sound. Hyde leaped to his feet and tried to wrest the phone from Mayfield's grasp, but Mayfield kept his distance and interrupted the diatribe with a casual "All right, all right, keep your hair on. I'll tell him."

Mayfield set down the receiver and casually dismissed Kumar, who had been listening open-mouthed, before he turned to Hyde.

"She's in quite a lather," he remarked.

"Of course she is," Hyde barked. "You can't talk to her like that. Do you know who she is?"

Mayfield looked down his rather red nose and winked. "Yes, I know who she is, and I know who she would like to be, but right now she's no one."

"You don't understand."

Mayfield shrugged. "I understand, but I don't care. You see, *sir*, at the moment, you have nothing to offer me. If I play my cards right, I can still get in with the Vernons after they get what they want, but what do you have to offer?"

Hyde struggled to find a response. What did he have to offer beyond a high-flown ideal of patriotism that meant nothing to people like Mayfield?

While Hyde struggled, Mayfield turned a knife in the wound. "She, the woman on the phone who we will not name, says that the duke is coming here, tonight."

Hyde's mind ran in frenzied circles. She'd told him that *someone* would come. He had expected some high-placed confidant of the duke, but not the duke himself. He wasn't ready. What was he going to tell him?

"Did you hear me?" Mayfield asked.

"What?"

"Would you like me to repeat what I said?"

"No, I would not, and don't you repeat it—not to anyone."

"So, what are you going to tell him?"

He's coming here. He's coming here. What am I going to tell him?

"Major?"

"I'm going to tell him that we're very close."

Mayfield grinned innocently. "Someone's very close, but it's not us."

Kumar was at the door again. "Sahib, there's a car outside."

Hyde breathed a great sigh of relief. The Vernons were back. Mayfield had been wrong all along.

He turned impatiently to Kumar. "Don't just stand there. Let them in."

"In here?"

"Yes. Why not?" Perhaps he shouldn't have said that. Perhaps someone was bleeding. He wouldn't put it past the Vernons to make even a woman bleed. He hoped they hadn't made Valerie

Chaplin bleed. She seemed a decent kind of girl, but the other one, the one who looked like a malicious troll, he wouldn't mind if she bled a little.

Kumar gestured to the hunting dogs snoring in front of the fire. "But, sahib, if I bring Roger in, he will disturb your dogs."

"Dogs?" Hyde barked. "Why the devil are you talking about dogs? And who is Roger?"

"The gardener's dog, sahib. They have brought him back."

"Tell them to take him to the gardener. He's nothing to do with me."

He heard Mayfield swear under his breath and turned on him. "What?"

"Is Roger the dog you left tied up at the house where the two old ladies live?"

"What if he is?"

Mayfield shrugged. "I don't think it's the RSPCA that's brought him. I think it's most likely the police."

"Yes, sahib, it is the police. Two cars."

"Police?"

"Yes, sahib. Police. They have done very well to bring Roger home, and the gardener will be very glad. Also, Roger no longer smells."

"Smells? What are you going on about?" Hyde knew that he was attacking Kumar simply for the sake of attacking someone and to divert his own attention from his racing heart. Over the past few hours, he had forgotten about the smelly pug, but now it all came back. He couldn't imagine how the police had managed to trace him to Southdown Hall. They wouldn't take that much trouble for just any lost dog, but Roger had quite literally been tied to a robbery at the home of a woman who was known to be associated with Jeremy Paxton.

He had been so sure he could trust Paxton—the man was a simpleton and a conchie coward. It should have been easy to convince him that he could make his contribution to world peace just by digging up that old biscuit tin.

The squad was on its final days in Windsor, awaiting new orders, when Hyde approached Paxton. The boy had been on guard duty. Ridiculous notion! How can he be on guard duty if he won't carry a weapon? *He'd already spent several days watching the boy and listening without comment as Paxton whined about his principles and his belief that world peace would be achieved if people would just stop killing. Well, of course it would, but that would never happen—people would always kill.*

Paxton doesn't know that.

Paxton's an idiot.

But gullible. Tell him it can happen. Tell him you know how to end the war.

Tell him everything?

No, not everything. Just tell him what he wants to hear.

Hyde knew that he was advocating sedition, maybe even high treason, but he told Paxton nothing but the truth.

"*We're outnumbered. The Germans will be invading any day now, and the Americans won't lift a finger to help us. If they didn't come after Dunkirk, they're not coming now. It's all up to us, and if we have those jewels and the right man, we can strike a bargain with Hitler. We'll have peace. No more killing. We'll all be able to sleep safely in our beds again.*"

It took him several days to convince him, but eventually, Paxton agreed.

"*For the sake of world peace.*"

"*That's right, Paxton. World peace!*"

He could still remember the look in Paxton's eyes when he had opened the tin and seen the stones. The boy had been amazed. How could anyone *not* be amazed by the sheer size of the stones? Hyde had been slow to spot when amazement had turned to something else. He hadn't understood the telltale flicker at the corner of Paxton's eyes, the slight narrowing, the sudden concentrated focus and then ... then the damned sniveling traitor was gone with the tin tucked under his arm.

Hyde was still reliving that moment of utter disbelief when Mayfield pushed back his chair and stared at Kumar with cold concentration. "How many policemen are outside?"

Police! Hyde dragged himself back into the present and the disaster that was unfolding. He glared at Kumar. "How many policemen?"

"Very many."

"Are they covering all the exits?"

Kumar responded with a puzzled, uncomprehending frown.

"Are they at the back door?" Hyde snapped, already planning

his exit.

"They are at all the doors, sahib."

Mayfield rolled his eyes and slowly shook his head. "I'm not going down for this, Major. Bring them in, Kumar, and I'll tell them what they want to know."

Hyde could hardly believe his ears. "You can't give orders to my manservant."

Mayfield actually laughed. "Me ordering Kumar around is the least of your problems. As far as I'm concerned, it's all over, and I'm turning queen's evidence."

Hyde reacted to the sharp sting of the words. It was not just that Mayfield had told him that he would not try to defend himself and instead would give direct evidence to the prosecution, but it was the use once again of the word *queen*. Elizabeth was now the state. King's evidence had been replaced by queen's evidence.

He snarled at Mayfield. "Traitor."

Mayfield raised his eyebrows. "I'm just remembering how many men on my squad died under your command," he said.

"Damned cowards."

"No, they were not the cowards."

Mayfield turned to Kumar. "Bring the police in," he said again. He looked back at Hyde. "Don't forget you're expecting another visitor. How are you going to warn him?"

The duke! Hyde had forgotten about the duke. He was already on his way, and there was no way to warn him. Hyde's mind was still reeling at the possibilities when the study door burst open and admitted two large men and one small dog.

Hyde's dogs, who had no interest in barking at humans, sprang to their feet at the sight of the pug and surrounded him in an inquiring and intrusive pack that threatened to entangle the two newcomers. Hyde toyed with the idea of escape. Southdown Hall was a maze of stairs and passages, and perhaps he could break free and disappear into the night.

Mayfield seemed to read his mind, and he took a firm grasp on Hyde's shoulder, drawing attention to himself by shouting. "This is him. This is the man you want."

Leaving the dogs to their sniffing, the two men advanced on Hyde, who, unable to move, had to fall back on simple belligerence. "Who the devil are you? What do you mean by coming in here?"

The younger of the two men flashed a warrant card. "Alan Lestock, Metropolitan Police."

Hyde knew he was delaying the inevitable, but he could not help blustering. "Metropolitan Police? You're out of your jurisdiction. You have no business here."

The man with the warrant card smiled. "The Metropolitan Police have responsibility for the security of the sovereign." He gestured to his companion. "Smythe and I and a number of uniformed officers are here on the queen's business."

CHAPTER SEVENTEEN

Castrol Service Station
Somewhere in Surrey
Valerie Chaplin

"Now's our chance," McAlhany whispered as the big car pulled into a service station. "Tell them you have to use the ladies' room, and I'll see what I can do out here while you're inside."

When one of the enormous men opened the rear door, Valerie tried to tell him what she wanted. "I need to use the—"

"No, you don't." He clamped a hand around her arm and pulled her shivering into the cold afternoon air. "Inside! Move!"

From the corner of her eye, Valerie could see McAlhany being treated the same way, and before either of them had a chance to make any kind of move, they were shoved into the dank, odorous interior of the building.

Valerie knew immediately that they had been expected. This was not some random petrol station where their kidnappers had stopped to fill the tank. The service bay was deserted, and the man who held Valerie's arm had a key to the manager's office. He unlocked the door and pushed them inside the cramped space, where the pervading odor of gasoline was replaced with the odor of cigarette smoke and sweat.

Valerie tried to speak again. "I need to—"

Her captor gave her the same response. "No, you don't. Just sit. This won't take long."

She sat on an old car seat that was serving as a sofa, and McAlhany sat beside her. Their captors departed, locking the door behind them, leaving only the light that leaked into the room through a glass panel in the door.

"Don't worry. I have an idea," McAlhany said. He patted her knee encouragingly. "Nil desperandum."

Valerie turned to look at him and was not comforted or encouraged. His eyes were smoldering, and his grin was very close to lunatic.

"Did you notice the smell when we came in?" he asked.

Valerie nodded miserably. "I thought I was going to be sick."

"It has that effect at first," McAlhany said. "It's because of the castor oil."

"What?"

"Castrol R. It's an additive for motor oil."

"I don't see—"

"That smell means that there's a racing machine here somewhere, a car or a motorbike, something that will go really fast."

Valerie, deep in a tangled web of emotions, could only offer a "so what" shrug.

McAlhany stood up and flicked his hair out of his eyes. "Not many service stations carry Castrol R. I'm thinking we must be somewhere near a racetrack. It's a clue. It will help identify where we are, so your friend Lestock can come and arrest them all." He walked to the door and peered out through the wire-reinforced windowpane. "There's a big motorbike over there in the corner. They'd never catch me on that."

"What do you mean?"

"If I can get away ..."

"And leave me here?"

McAlhany shook his head and turned away from the window. "No, of course not. Just thinking aloud, but when we get out of here, we'll ..."

Valerie turned on him. "We're never going to get out of here."

"They can't keep us forever."

"No," Valerie said, acknowledging a new truth. "They can't keep us forever, but they can kill us."

McAlhany shook his head. "I'm not going to let that happen."

Valerie was surprised by the ugly sound of her own mocking laughter. "How are you going to stop them?"

"I'll find a way."

"No, you won't." Valerie's laughter turned to a sob that threatened to choke her and then to fierce, raging anger as she forced out unwelcome words. "Mary Carpenter knows about my son."

"About that …"

Valerie hissed at him. "I don't need your spiritual advice. I had an illegitimate child, and that makes me a terrible sinner. The nuns already told me that. I don't need you to tell me again."

"You're not a sinner," McAlhany said. "A baby is not a sin. You did the only thing you could: you gave him life. And I'm sure he's fine and happy."

Valerie would not permit his words to have any meaning or comfort. "You don't know what you're talking about. He's not fine and he's not happy. I always knew there was something wrong. I just wouldn't admit it even to myself."

. She took a breath and allowed a memory to fight its way upward from where she had kept it hidden and unacknowledged.

The labor ward was bleak beneath the harsh white lights, and the nuns wore white aprons and short white veils. There were no bright colors to welcome her baby into the world, no soft voices or gentle hands. The nuns treated her as a gym teacher would treat a girl who refused to climb a rope or fling herself at a vaulting horse. They didn't offer gentle encouragement or speak in soft voices; they bullied and demanded.

"Push."

"Be quiet."

"Don't complain. You did this to yourself."

"Push harder."

And then a small strangled cry, sudden silence, and finally, "It's a boy."

She was older now, and wiser. She had read numerous fictional and factual accounts of childbirth, and she had been to the cinema and watched the filmmaker's idea of how a child should be born. She knew that, in addition to the cruelty and contempt of the nuns, there had been something else amiss when her child was born. For years, despite Mary's letters dripping poisonous doubts into her life, she had refused to ask herself what was meant by that moment of silence after the baby's birth. What had the midwives seen that had momentarily stilled their bullying tongues? They, who delivered illegitimate babies almost daily, were not overcome by the miracle of birth, but something had silenced them. What was it? Now, at last, she accepted the truth.

"I don't know how Mary found out, but she knew. She always knew that there was something wrong."

McAlhany turned from the window and sat down beside her on the sofa. "You should talk to her."

"Why? What's the point? She can't change anything."

"I think she can," McAlhany said. "She's the only friend we have here."

"She's not my friend."

"And," McAlhany continued, undaunted, "we're the only friends she has."

"She doesn't need us."

"Really? What do you think they'll do to her after you tell them what they want to know?"

Valerie drew in a sharp breath. "But she did what they wanted. She set a trap for me, and I walked right in."

"Think about it," McAlhany said. "Right now, these men, whoever they are, believe that you and Mary are enemies, and that works in our favor. They'll probably send her in here to get more information out of you by promising to tell you about your son in return for information about Paxton. I can't tell you what to do about your son, but I think you should tell them about Paxton. He's obviously dead or deserted. You can't hurt him now."

Valerie nodded hesitantly. "I thought he loved me, but I was wrong."

"Not necessarily, but after all this time, telling them what you know won't make any difference to him."

"But I don't know anything. I have no idea what they want or what he's done."

"You know more than you realize. Drop any little hint you can that will keep them interested and give us time to get Mary on our side."

"How am I supposed to do that?" Valerie asked. "You heard her. She hates me. She'll never come over to our side."

McAlhany reached out and took her hand. "She will if you apologize to her."

Valerie tried to pull her hand from his grasp, but he held her firmly. In the dim borrowed light from the office window, she saw that his face was kind.

"Apologize," he said again. "You wronged her."

"I did not."

"You didn't intend to," McAlhany said, "but it is obvious that she was deeply hurt. The memory of what you did to her has eaten away at her and turned her from someone who planned to be a missionary into someone whose only thought is revenge for a hurt inflicted years ago. What will happen if you acknowledge that and tell her that you're sorry?"

"I don't know."

McAlhany continued to hold her hand. "You hold all the cards," he said. "Tell her you were wrong and you regret what you did, and she will lose her whole reason for hating you. All she ever wanted was to be your friend. Give her back that friendship, and the hate will be gone." He released her hand and flicked his hair out of his eyes. "Trust me. I'm a professional."

Valerie leaned back in the lumpy car seat. "And if we become friends, what then?"

McAlhany shrugged. "I don't know, but I'll think of something. Perhaps ..."

Whatever he planned to say next was interrupted by a loud rumbling sound. McAlhany sprang to his feet and rushed to the door, pressing his face against the glass. "They're opening the doors," he said, "and bringing in another car."

Valerie joined him at the door, standing on tiptoe to look into the service bay. The open doors admitted the last of the twilight before it was washed out by the dazzle of headlights from the car that was easing into the service bay. As men ran to open car doors, neon lights flickered on, lighting the polished paintwork of the big black limousine.

"There," McAlhany said, moving his head and pointing, "in the corner, a racing motorbike. They'll never keep up with that."

A passenger emerged from the back seat of the limousine. He was a big, bald-headed man wearing a dark coat adorned with an astrakhan collar. His broad red face wore an expression of grim anticipation. The reality of his presence sent a chill of fear down Valerie's spine, and she was surprised when, out in the service bay, Mary Carpenter darted forward fearlessly and greeted the newcomer in her small, spiteful voice.

"Mr. Vernon, they won't let me talk to her. I can make her tell you. I promise, I can."

Vernon's dismissive voice spoke of a life in London's East End. "All right, girlie, keep your hair on. You'll get your chance."

Valerie and McAlhany stepped back from the door as the big man approached. Instead of opening the door, he pressed his face against the glass and searched the room with small, close-set eyes. McAlhany put out an arm to sweep Valerie behind him and away from those gimlet eyes.

A voice called out. "Mr. Vernon, sir."

The face retreated as a loud argument broke out somewhere behind him, with Mary's voice the loudest and most malevolent. Valerie shivered as she realized that Mary's frustrated hatred was strong enough to overcome any natural fear of the hulking presence of Mr. Vernon.

McAlhany returned to the window, pressing his face against the glass while Valerie stood behind him, finding a surprising level of imagined protection from his presence. He admitted to being a madman, but his madness consisted of a level of reckless courage she had never seen before. She was certain that Lestock was a brave man who faced danger with cold logic, and Mrs. Gordon had her own brand of courage, but logic had no place in McAlhany's courage. She supposed it had also taken a certain amount of a different kind of courage to turn the tables on her and tell her to apologize to Mary. The idea still rankled, although a small part of her brain was beginning to accept the inevitable. Mary was their only hope.

Out in the service bay, Vernon was bringing the argument under control, and individual voices were making themselves heard.

"We don't need the vicar. We should get rid of him now."

Valerie saw that McAlhany had tensed, but he said nothing.

Mary gave a sharp scream of pain as someone else spoke. "We don't need this little bitch. I'll do her in myself."

Vernon's voice was firm and authoritative. "No one's doing anyone in. Not yet. We work with what we have, and then we decide. Put the little woman in with them, and let's see what happens."

Mary gave another sharp scream, and McAlhany withdrew his face from the window as Mary began to babble, making loud promises of success. She would get Valerie to talk; all she had to do was threaten Valerie's child.

Someone else spoke up to assure Mr. Vernon that he could get Valerie to talk and he didn't need "no little troll woman" to do his dirty work for him.

McAlhany stepped back from the door, his face anxious in the flickering neon light. "Are you ready to make a break for it?"

Valerie shook her head. "We don't have a chance."

"They're distracted and arguing with each other. This is our best chance. When they bring Mary in, I'll keep them busy, and you run. The main doors are still open, and it's dark outside."

"No."

"You have to. These people are not going to leave anyone alive."

Valerie battled disbelief. How could this be happening? Jeremy had been a man who would not pick up a weapon. He had been a romantic dreamer with the quiet courage to act on his beliefs even when people called him a coward. What could he possibly have done that would now bring people into her life to kill her? Why were so many people looking for any trace of him, and what did any of this have to do with the coronation?

She knew one thing: she did not want to die without knowing the reason, and she definitely did not want to die if there was a way to live.

She touched McAlhany's arm. "You go."

"Not without you."

"I can't come with you. I'll hold you back. You go and I'll stall them. I'll make them drive me to Minstead. It's a long way and it will give me time to get Mary on my side."

"The only thing Mary wants is an apology."

The words almost stuck in her throat. "If that's what it takes, I'll do it. I'll apologize."

McAlhany glanced out the window. "They're coming." He took her hand for a moment. "I won't let you down. I'll find you."

She felt something that was almost like an electrical charge pass through her hand as she returned his grip.

As the door opened, she felt the moment when Martin McAlhany threw caution to the wind, released her hand, and resurrected the madman who did not know when to stop.

Little Clamping, Kent

Davie

Something skittered in the dark. Rats, Davie thought, but there was no fear in his thought. He was past fear now, and all he had was the cough and the cold and the bleak despair of knowing that he would never meet his father.

There were very few mirrors in the Brethren Charity Home for Boys, but Matron had a mirror in her office, presumably to admire her own reflection. The mirror was visible from the beds in sick bay, and Davie, a frequent visitor to sick bay, had glimpsed his own reflection from time to time. He had no opportunity for lengthy examination, but he had seen enough to know that he had light, almost red hair, freckles, and wide hazel eyes. He kept that image in mind when he thought of his mysterious father. Did he have the same face, or was Davie's face the face of his mother? He had a mother, of course, a woman of loose morals who had carelessly birthed him, and equally carelessly given him away. He had never wanted to meet that awful woman whose sin had condemned him to be a cripple with one leg shorter than the other and weak lungs that caught and magnified every infection that came his way, but he had wanted to know his father.

He was still thinking of his father when the sound of skittering rats gave way to the sound of footsteps. Someone was approaching. Davie lifted his head and saw a shadowy figure in the doorway, blocking the very last of the daylight.

"Davie."

"Pete?"

"Yes, mate. It's Pete."

"You came back," Davie croaked.

"Yeah, well, not really."

A cough clawed its way up out of Davie's lungs and rendered him speechless and breathless. He was aware of Pete squatting beside him.

"Here, mate. I brought you water and a blanket."

"Are we leaving?"

Pete sat back on his heels, and for a long moment, he said nothing.

"Pete, are we leaving?"

"I can't take you. You can't keep up. I warned you. It's every man for himself."

Davie did not have the energy to feel angry, and what was the point? Pete was right. He'd promised to keep up, and he'd failed.

"Where's Colin?"

"Gone."

"You should have gone with him."

"Didn't want to. He's a jerk. I'm better on my own. I'm going to travel all night and try for the ferry tomorrow morning."

Davie acknowledged Pete's plan with a small nod of his head. "Good luck."

Pete moved in the darkness, and Davie felt him shift the weight of the coal sacks and replace them with something soft. "Brought you a blanket," he said. "Some water and some aspirin. It's all I can do for you. I'll try to tell someone where to find you."

Tell someone! Davie saw a glimmer of hope. "Pete, do you know how to make a phone call?"

"Yeah, I know. Don't you?"

"No, but I have a number and money. Can you do it? Can you phone for me?"

Davie fumbled in his pocket for the coins and the slip of paper. "This is a message from my father. Will you phone him and tell him I'm sorry? I wanted to come, but I couldn't."

He coughed again and felt Pete lift his head. Water poured into his mouth. He tried to swallow, but the pain was too intense. He allowed the water to trickle out of his mouth and down his chin.

Pete stood up. "Give me the money and the number. I'll try. No promises, mate."

Davie nodded. He had always wanted to be one of the big boys, and now he had a chance. Now he could be as strong as they were—no crying, no pleading.

"No promises," he agreed, and he lay back beneath the warmth of the blanket and watched as Pete walked away, closing the door behind him.

CHAPTER EIGHTEEN

Castrol Service Station
Somewhere in Surrey
Valerie Chaplin

Martin McAlhany lurked behind the office door and flung himself into action the moment that it opened. He easily barreled past his surprised opponents and went on the attack. Even Mr. Vernon, the man who seemed to be feared by everyone except Mary, could not stand up to McAlhany's charge and was soon flat on his back on the floor. When Vernon went down, all eyes turned to him, and Valerie saw a chance to sneak out of the door and maybe out of the building. She had taken no more than two steps when Mary charged at her and attacked in a welter of scratching, biting, and hair pulling.

Fully occupied in warding off Mary's attack, Valerie had almost no opportunity to see what McAlhany was doing. She knew he planned to take the motorbike, but with so much opposition, that was going to be impossible. From the corner of her eye, she saw him throwing off his opponents and fighting his way toward the open doors and the darkness outside.

She lost sight of him when Mary dove at her and grasped her around the knees, dragging her to the ground. Where had she learned to fight like this? This had not been taught at Redbridge Grammar School for Girls. She was painfully aware that the only way to deal with Mary was to give as good as she got. For the first time in her life, she took hold of another woman's hair with the sole intention of hurting her. Mary's hair was short and wiry and hard to grasp. Struggling on her back with Mary on top of her, she finally managed to grab a handful and tug. Mary responded with a yelp of pain.

You don't like it when I do it to you! She pulled again, shocked by the satisfaction it gave her to hurt the person who had hurt her. Mary rolled away, and Valerie lost her grip on Mary's hair. Still filled with a strange euphoria, she gave Mary no opportunity to get back on her feet but flung herself on top of her so that they were face-to-face, eyeball-to-eyeball.

Gouge her eyes. Valerie had no idea she was capable of such a thought. Her hands were actually twitching with a desire of their own to scratch and claw and inflict pain. *Oh no, dear, don't do that. That's not right.* Who was speaking? Who was stopping her? Was it one of her aunts, or was it her own conscience? She restrained herself from raking her fingernails down Mary's face, but she kept her weight on her while she turned her head to see what had become of the vicar. He was nowhere in sight, but a group of men clustered at the doorway, pointing and arguing. So he had made it out of the door, and he was out there somewhere in the dark. If he had the motorcycle, he would be away by now, but he was on foot. How long would it take them to find him?

Did they need to find him?

No! McAlhany didn't matter to them. Valerie was the one who mattered. Finally she had a part to play in the strange, ongoing nightmare of the past two days. Finally she was the one who could control the actions of others; she was the one who could give McAlhany time to get away.

Feeling Valerie's attention wander, Mary tried to sit up. Valerie slammed her head back to the ground as she shouted and shouted above Mary's screams of protest. "Hey, over here! If you want to know what I know, come over here, all of you!"

Vernon had already recovered from McAlhany's attack and was back on his feet, brushing dust from his expensive overcoat. Valerie caught his eye. This was between her and him and no one else.

"Call your men off, and I'll tell you."

"Everything?"

"As much as I know."

Mary tried to lift her head, and Valerie slammed it down again as she spoke. "Let the vicar go. He knows nothing."

"He knows where we are," Vernon said.

"Then leave. Don't be here. Be somewhere else. I can tell you which way to go."

Vernon's eyes narrowed. "Where?"

"The New Forest."

He took a step toward her. "The New Forest's a big place. Lots of trees."

"Call your men off, and I'll tell you."

Vernon took another step. "I can make you talk."

Valerie discovered an unexpected inner calm even as she crouched over Mary and faced down a man who was threatening to torture her. She thought of Mrs. Gordon and the network of scars that spoke of the unspeakable. *Things went wrong, and I didn't wait for rescue. Made my own way out.* She thought about Martin McAlhany. *"I won't let you down. I'll find you."* She thought ruefully of her own promise. *"I'll get Mary on my side."*

She looked down at Mary's agonized face. Well, that wasn't working out very well.

She rolled away from Mary and stood up. "As you say, the New Forest is a big place, lots of trees. Call your men off. You don't need the vicar to show you the way; you need me, and I'm here."

She felt Mary tugging at her ankles and kicked her hands away. "Get off me."

Vernon barked at Mary. "Keep your hands to yourself, girlie. I don't have no need of you now I've got your friend, so you just stay out of my way, or I might remember you doing all that cursing and weird stuff. My boys don't like that kind of talk; they want you gone."

Mary staggered to her feet. "All right, I'll go."

Vernon caught her arm in one meaty hand. "You ain't going nowhere."

"But you know everything now. Valerie told you."

"Yeah," said Vernon, "we know everything, and so do you." He poked Mary in the chest. "I ain't letting you loose."

He tightened his lips and whistled through his teeth, summoning his men back from outside. "Get the cars ready. We're moving out."

"What about the man who got away?"

"We ain't gonna be here when he gets back. He don't know nothing more than his girlfriend's gonna tell us."

Girlfriend, Valerie thought. How could anyone look at them and think that?

Vernon's men moved obediently into action, and within minutes, Valerie was sharing the back seat of Vernon's limousine with Mary, although *sharing* was not quite the right word for what they were doing. Mary had rolled herself into a fetal ball in the far corner of the wide seat, and Valerie was clinging to the door handle, trying to think of a way to break free.

Vernon climbed into the front seat and closed the glass privacy screen. They could not hear what he was saying to the driver, and he could not hear them. The silence gave Valerie time to move beyond anger and into anxiety. For a few minutes, as McAlhany had made his escape and as she had battled Mary, her mind had been fully consumed and fully in the moment, but now she had time to think of her own situation.

Offering to take Vernon to the New Forest had probably saved McAlhany's life, but she couldn't do anything else for him now. Her only thought was of her son. After years of wondering, she had come to a moment of truth. She had to know where he was. She had to know what Mary knew.

The car pulled smoothly out of the service station and onto the dark road. Valerie looked across the wide expanse of seat and tried to meet Mary's eyes in the darkness, but Mary was just a silent shape without features.

"Mary?"

"What?"

"About my son ..."

"Ha!" Mary's shadowy shape shifted. Valerie assumed that she was looking at her from behind her ugly round glasses. "So now you care?"

"I've always cared, but I couldn't keep him, and they promised he'd have a good home."

Mary's voice was chilling in its triumph. "They lied. He never had a home."

"You can't know that."

Mary laughed. "I may be small, but I'm not stupid. I knew what was going on. After you dropped me—"

"I didn't drop you."

"Yes, you did. Everyone in the school could see what you'd done."

Valerie was silent, remembering how good it had felt to finally be rid of the burden of friendship with Mary Carpenter. Mary had always been a figure of spiteful fun for the other girls, and as her friend, Valerie had been painted with the same brush—Valerie Chaplin, quiet, weird, never allowed to bring friends home, and with a crazy father who should be locked up in an asylum. When Valerie had finally cast off Mary's cloying friendship, she found out what she had been missing. At last she was free to be one of the girls who gossiped and poked fun. She had suddenly become popular, and having a boyfriend was the icing on the cake. Jeremy's letters, so very romantic, had been the price of admission to the very top tier of popularity.

"I knew what was going to happen," Mary said, interrupting Valerie's guilty remembrance. "I heard you all laughing at his filthy letters, but I know where that kind of talk leads. If you'd let him write to you like that, you'd do anything he wanted if he could get his hands on you, and he did, didn't he? You didn't care about the consequences."

Valerie could hardly deny the truth of Mary's words, but Mary lacked understanding. Mary had never been in love, never known what it meant to want something so badly that consequences were unimportant.

"I knew you'd get pregnant," Mary said smugly. "All I had to do was watch you, and all of a sudden, you were missing gym class, and you were getting sick, and then you didn't come to school anymore. Then I knew, but I still kept watching. You went to the nuns, but when your baby was born, he didn't stay with the nuns; he came to the Brethren Charity Home for Boys, didn't he?"

"I don't know."

"But I do. That home is one of the charities run by my church, so I could walk right in and see him. I could see what was wrong with him."

Valerie's heart fluttered. "Is there something wrong with him?"

Mary laughed. "Is there something wrong? Of course there is. That's why he was never adopted. He has one leg shorter than the other, and he will limp for his whole life." She laughed again. "Oh my God, he was a pathetic baby: weak legs, always crying and coughing. Did I tell you he had weak lungs? It was obvious he'd never be healthy. No one wanted him. When he was old enough, he was moved to the Brethren Charity Home for Boys, and he's been there ever since. They're the ones who gave him a name. They called him Davie. Poor Davie, not in a good home. I told you all about it."

"Told me!" Valerie exclaimed so loudly that the sound defeated the privacy glass, and she saw Vernon turn his head. They were both silent for a moment, and Vernon turned away again. "You never told me," Valerie hissed.

"I tried," Mary said. "I sent you notes."

"You tormented me."

Mary laughed. "I suppose I did. It was no more than you deserved. Do you know what it feels like to be betrayed?"

Valerie took a deep breath. How could she possibly do what Martin McAlhany wanted and apologize to this demonic woman? Almost ready to bite off her own tongue, she dredged up conciliatory words.

"I understand why you might think I betrayed you, but I didn't."

"You dropped me."

"I know, and I'm sorry." There, she'd said it. Would it be enough?

"Sorry? You think it's enough just to say you're sorry?"

Apparently, it wasn't enough. Valerie tried again. "My mother really liked you. She was angry with me for … for what I did. You were really helpful with my father."

"He had demons, and I was casting them out."

He didn't have demons; he had shell shock. No, don't say that. Agree with her.

"I didn't understand what you were doing for him."

"Because you're a pagan."

"I'm certainly not as Christian as you are."

"No, you're not."

Valerie let that moment of agreement settle and take hold before she ventured another remark. She was having trouble handling her anger. All these years, her son had been without love or care, and they were years she could never get back for him. Now she had to know where he was; she had to survive and claim him for her own.

"Mary," she said at last, "I'm really sorry about what happened, but can't you see that you're not punishing me, you're punishing my son?"

"I never hurt him," Mary said. "I never even spoke to him. Because I'm a church member, I was allowed to go in and out of the home, and so I'd see what was happening to him. I never hurt him. You did that."

"How?"

"By abandoning him."

"I didn't know."

"Well, now you do."

Valerie took a deep breath. The moment had arrived. "Mary, where is he now?"

"I don't know. He's run away from the home. I don't know where he is."

"When did he run? How long ago?"

"Just a few days," Mary said, almost nonchalantly. "I sent him a note to encourage him."

Blue Basildon Bond notepaper, Valerie thought. *She's been tormenting him, just like she tormented me.* She tried to remain calm. "You encouraged him to run away?"

Mary shifted in the darkness. "It wasn't hard. All the boys want to leave, but most of them have nowhere else to go. If Davie went with some of the other boys, he could be on the ferry to France, because some of them have tried that. On the other hand, he might just be looking for his father, because that's what I told him to do."

Valerie's heart lurched. "You told him to look for Jeremy? How could you do that? No one knows where Jeremy is."

"Then he won't find him, will he?" Mary said.

The dark shape that was all Valerie could see of Mary shifted again as if settling down onto the seat. "Things are not going as I planned, but maybe this is even better. You can't blame me. I gave him a phone number to call."

"You have a phone number for Jeremy?"

"No. I have a phone number for you and your aunts."

Valerie's mind was spinning. "Are you saying that he'll try to come to Redbridge?"

"That really depends on what your aunts say to him on the phone," Mary said. "At the time I wrote the letter, I assumed you would be at home, but now everything has changed. You're here with me and not at home to receive a surprise phone call from your long-lost son."

"But my aunts know nothing about him. I don't know what they'll do if some strange boy phones them."

"Neither do I," Mary said. "We'll have to wait and see, won't we?"

Valerie slid across the seat until she was face-to-face with Mary. The reflection of the dashboard light on Mary's glasses gave her a place to focus. "You're enjoying this, aren't you?" she hissed.

Mary nodded. "Of course I am. I've been planning it for a long time. I couldn't do it until he was big enough and strong enough to try to escape."

"And you were looking forward to shaming me in front of my aunts," Valerie said.

"Oh, not just your aunts. I was looking forward to shaming you in front of everyone you know."

Valerie could hear McAlhany's voice telling her to apologize and get Mary on her side. The stakes were higher than he had ever imagined, but Valerie knew that a simple apology would change nothing. Mary was too far gone in hatred to accept anything but the triumph she had long imagined: Valerie's public disgrace.

She stared into the blank lenses of Mary's glasses. She could not see the eyes behind the lenses, but she could imagine the hatred that had clouded them for so long. Long years had passed since Valerie and Mary had left school, packed away their school uniforms, and taken their places in the adult world, but Mary had occupied all those years in building her hatred for Valerie. Instead of taking up her call to be a missionary, she had stayed close to Redbridge and brooded over her grievances.

Only a form of obsessive madness could account for her actions. She had stalked the halls of the children's home, delighting in the sickness and misery of one small boy. She had set aside a box of notepaper for one single purpose—to torment the boy's mother. Without even knowing their purpose, she had taken up with criminals who wanted to capture Valerie. She had sent a sick child out into the cold to look for a man he would never find. An apology would not end such an obsession—an obsession that was a direct result of Valerie's abandonment.

Hatred may have blinded Mary to what lay ahead, but Valerie

was not so blind. Mary had served her purpose, and Vernon had no need of her. Although she had come with Vernon of her own accord, she was now as trapped as Valerie. Her hatred, born of Valerie's teenage carelessness, was going to get her killed, and Valerie did not want that death on her head.

She peered at Mary's face, forcing herself to see her not as an enemy but as a woman desperately in need of understanding. The thought did not come easily, and Valerie had to fight against her own rage at what had been done to her and her son. She told herself that it was not all Mary's fault. Others had been involved. Even her own mother had ... She cut off that avenue of thought. That was for later.

Setting all other thoughts aside, she pounded on the privacy glass, and Vernon slid back the screen. As they passed beneath a single streetlight, she caught a glimpse of his face. There was nothing reassuring about his frown or his small dark eyes, but she forced herself to speak to him. She would have to risk Mary's life to save it.

"Let Mary go."

"What?"

"Let her go."

He tried to close the glass, but Valerie caught hold of it and leaned as far forward as she could, so that her face was very close to his. The driver shifted uncomfortably, and the car swerved.

"Let her go," Valerie said again.

Vernon struggled with the screen, but Valerie now had her arm in the gap, and the driver fought her off distractedly while the car swerved, skidded, and finally halted.

"What the hell?" Vernon said.

"Let her go, and I'll tell you things you don't know."

"You'll tell me anyway," Vernon said grimly. "We can make you talk."

"It'll be quicker if you do it my way," Valerie argued. "If you hurt my friend, you'll find it very hard to get me to talk, and you're in a hurry, aren't you? You don't know where the vicar's gone, and you don't know if he knows anything. Maybe he's already talking to the police. Maybe they're already on their way. Let my friend go, and I'll sing like a bird."

"You want me to let her go?" Vernon asked.

"Yes."

"Right here?"

The headlights of the limousine picked out a narrow road with hedges on either side, glistening with frost. Beyond the hedge, the world lay in darkness, with not a house in sight. It was a bleak spot, but it had not been long since they'd passed a streetlight. Valerie hoped that Mary had seen that light and would walk in the right direction. Or maybe she wouldn't. Maybe she would discover how it was to be cold and lost and unloved.

Valerie nodded. "Right here," she said.

The driver climbed out, opened the passenger door, and hauled Mary out. Valerie sat back in her seat. She was not sure if they were even. She was not sure they would ever be even, but she had done what she could.

CHAPTER NINETEEN

Southdown Hall
Dorking, Surrey
Alan Lestock

Lestock sent the Indian manservant to return Roger the dog to the gardener, and put the uniformed officers on duty at the exits of the building and along the driveway.

The major's wife was not so easily dismissed. She was a big woman, with silver hair and an impressive bosom that allowed her to produce an equally impressive amount of sound, most of which was addressed to her husband.

"What's all this disturbance? Why are the police here?"

Lestock suspected that Major Hyde had not shared the details of his activities with his wife, but she would have to know some of his opinions—he seemed like a man who would share his opinion freely. Although Mrs. Hyde appeared to be genuinely shocked, Lestock noted that her eyes strayed to the framed picture of the Duke of Windsor and then back to her husband.

"Cardrew," she said slowly, "what have you done?"

"I have attempted to right an ancient wrong," Hyde said pompously.

Mrs. Hyde continued to stare at the picture of the Duke of Windsor. "How ancient?"

"You know what I mean," Hyde said huffily.

"I think I do," Mrs. Hyde said in a horrified whisper. "Have you done something to the queen?"

"No, of course not. It's just a small matter with the Crown Jewels."

"A small matter!" Mrs. Hyde repeated. "A small matter with the Crown Jewels? Have you lost your mind?"

"No, I have not," Hyde insisted. "I know exactly what I'm

doing."

Mrs. Hyde narrowed her eyes and hissed at her husband. "Be very careful, Cardrew. Better to be a lunatic than a traitor."

Hyde shook his head. "I sometimes think I'm the only sane person left in this country. It's sheer madness to think of putting that chit of a girl and her foreign husband on the throne of Britain."

Mrs. Hyde glowered at him. "Don't be absurd. Of course she should be our queen. Why shouldn't a woman sit on the throne? And age has nothing to do with it. Victoria was eighteen when she was crowned, and she had a German husband. Britain did very well under her reign. You're talking nonsense. I don't know what's come over you."

She turned to Lestock. "What has he done? Just tell me."

Lestock shook his head. "I'm sorry, madam, but I'm not at liberty to share that information. Mr. Smythe will escort you from the room."

"I will not be escorted from a room in my own house," Mrs. Hyde declared.

Hyde glared at his wife. "Just go! Leave! I'm not ashamed of what I've done."

Lestock waited until Smythe had ushered Mrs. Hyde forcefully from the room before he faced Hyde. "Where are the stones?"

"Stones? What stones?"

"The four big ones that belong in the Imperial State Crown?"

Hyde glared at him. "Hell if I know."

"You'll have to do better than that."

Hyde curled his lip slightly as he gave a reluctant account of the first time he'd seen the stones. "Morhouse, the royal librarian, wrapped them in cotton wool, put them inside a jar, and put the whole thing in a Bath Oliver biscuit tin, which he buried separately just outside the sallyport on the south of the castle." He shook his head angrily. "I don't know why I'm telling you this. You already know the facts. Mayfield's told you everything."

Lestock shook his head. "Not everything. Mayfield wasn't with you when you dug them up. Did you take them out of the tin?"

"No. I removed the lid to ensure that they were still in there, and then I replaced the lid, and I gave the tin to Paxton to hold."

Lestock turned to Mayfield. "What about you? What do you

know?"

"Not much," Mayfield said nonchalantly. "Like I told you, I had nothing to do with the major taking the stones. That was between him and Paxton. Paxton told me what the major planned, but I don't know anything else." He looked at Hyde. "I don't know what the major did to Paxton, but the boy hasn't been seen since. Makes you wonder, doesn't it?"

"I didn't do anything to him," Hyde blustered. "The damned coward stole the stones and deserted."

Lestock decided to ignore Hyde for the time being. Hyde had his own way of looking at things and his own idea of who was to blame, but Mayfield was practically chomping at the bit to tell his side of the story.

"So, Sergeant Mayfield, why are you here now? How did you know about this?"

"Word on the street," Mayfield said. "I heard someone had put out a contract to find a woman named Valerie Chaplin and a man named Jeremy Paxton, and I put two and two together. I knew Paxton had a girlfriend—he'd shown me some of her letters, and things were hot and heavy between them. So I heard these two names, and I thought about the king being dead, and it all clicked, and I thought to myself that they'd soon be needing the crown. I asked a few questions here and there, and then I went looking for Valerie Chaplin. When I got to her house, I found the major up a ladder, doing his own dirty work."

"I wasn't the one who broke the window," Hyde said petulantly.

Smythe, who had returned to the room and closed the door, grinned at Hyde. "A broken window is the least of your problems," he said.

Lestock began to feel overwhelmed by the weight of his new discoveries. He seemed to be holding the loose ends of too many strings tied to too many important items. The four historic stones were tied to one string. The fate of Jeremy Paxton was tied to another. And the involvement of the Vernon crime family was a string he had only just discovered. The string for which he felt personally responsible was the string that led to Valerie Chaplin, and he was impatient to pull on that string before it was too late and something happened to her.

Mayfield interrupted his thoughts. "There's a man on his way here now," he said, "who might tell you everything you want to know."

Hyde took an angry step forward. "No!"

"You can't stop him," Mayfield taunted.

"Stop who?" Lestock asked.

"The Duke of Windsor," Mayfield said.

Lestock added another string to the tangle he was holding. This string was not just another simple string; it was a thick purple imperial cord, and it could not be ignored.

Smythe was first to speak, placing a meaty hand on Mayfield's shoulder. "You sure about that, mate?"

Mayfield nodded. "Queen's evidence," he said. "I'm telling you everything I know—that's the agreement—and I know the duke is on his way here now."

Lestock blanked out Major Hyde's imaginative cursing of Mayfield and concentrated on his memory of the man he'd seen so recently walking in solemn procession behind the king's bier. Lestock had been young and just starting his career when Edward VIII had shocked the world by abdicating his throne before he was even crowned. He remembered the cynical laughter of the hard-bitten men he worked with, men who had guarded Edward as Prince of Wales.

"Thank God he's gone. Nothing but a playboy; never done a hard day's work in his life, and as for her ..."

What they said about Wallis Simpson had shocked Lestock's young ears, and it had been some years before he had even understood the vices they were attributing to the American divorcée. He wondered what they would say about Edward now. Had fifteen years in exile changed him at all?

If the former king was truly on his way here to Southdown Hall, then Lestock would have to assume that confirming that fact and allowing him to enter the building would lead to repercussions far beyond anything Lestock could even imagine. He reconsidered the strings in his hand. For the time being, he would have to release all the others and deal with just this one. It was one thing to privately suspect the duke of treason, but quite another to prove it publicly.

Leaving Smythe to control the chaos in the study, he strode out of the room and spoke to the uniformed officer standing guard at the door.

"Do you have men out on the road?"

"Yes, sir."

"Get them out of sight. There's a car coming. Let it come, but don't engage."

He received a salute in return and then went in search of a telephone. He hoped he would have time to do what needed to be done.

The kitchen was in semidarkness, but he found a wall-mounted telephone and placed a call to Special Commissioner Sir Walter Perrin.

Perrin was adamant. "No, absolutely not. Do not engage with him. Just get the car turned around. Tell the driver that there's a fire. Tell him the whole damned place has burned down, but make sure he turns around. There will be no confrontation. Do you understand?"

Lestock, with his mind on an alternative course of action, spoke softly and reasonably. "Yes, sir. I understand. Turn him around and get him out of the way. What do you suggest I do about Hyde?"

"Hyde," Perrin practically spat the name. "I would never have believed it. The man's military record is not exactly stellar, but he was always loyal. Are you sure it's really him? Could this Mayfield fellow be lying?"

"No, sir. I don't think he is."

"Then you'd best take Hyde into custody. Get the blighter under lock and key. Keep him incommunicado, and we'll decide what to charge him with." Perrin paused for a moment and then spoke tentatively. "Any possibility we can get him to cough up something new about the stones? Hyde is the only witness you haven't managed to kill or knock unconscious; maybe this one can be persuaded to talk."

Lestock ignored the gibe and the hint that Perrin would be willing to use any means necessary to get information from Hyde. "I don't think he has anything new to offer."

"Someone has to know something," Perrin said. "The only clue you have so far is that Paxton met his girlfriend somewhere in the New Forest."

"Minstead," Lestock said. "She met him in Minstead."

"Minstead," Perrin repeated. "I'll see what I can find out. I've heard things about that area."

"What kind of things?" Lestock asked.

"Nothing good," Perrin said darkly.

Lestock had camped in the New Forest as a boy and had happy memories of vast open spaces and deeply shadowed groves. At night, with the campfire crackling and the forest dark and unknowable all around them, he had felt its ancient mystery, but in daylight it was a place of wonder. So far as he could see, their biggest problem was the size of the forest, not whatever problem seemed to be occupying Perrin's mind.

"Sir?" he queried.

Perrin sighed wearily. "There are some unsavory characters in the forest, and we don't do much in the way of policing outside the villages," he said. "The forest has its own laws."

Lestock frowned. "Nowhere is outside the law."

"It's outside our law," Perrin said. "They have their own court, their own version of magistrates, and laws going back to William the Conqueror. You can't just walk in there and throw your weight around."

"Then what do you suggest I do?" Lestock growled. "I've told you where I think he is, and now you tell me I can't go in and find him."

"You can go in," Perrin said, "but you'll need a guide. I know someone who is an agister."

"And what the devil is an agister?" Lestock said, no longer caring to keep his tone respectful.

"I suppose you could call him a warden," Perrin said. "He represents the law. I'll get hold of him and ring you back. You're going to need a guide. I'll tell him to meet you at Minstead. Meantime, tell me about the other man, the one who's turned queen's evidence."

"He knows a little about Paxton. It seems they were friendly. I'll keep questioning him."

"You'll have to let Smythe do the questioning. You have something else to do, and you'd better get on it. If the duke is truly about to arrive, you will have to take care of it yourself. Turn a blind eye to who he is, and don't even talk to him; just turn him around and get him out of there. Pray God he's not being followed by a press car."

"Sir," Lestock said, managing to prevent the special commissioner from ending the call.

"What is it?"

"The man who fell from the belfry. Is he talking?"

"Yes, he's talking, but nothing useful. He's a member of Lennie Vernon's gang but low down the chain of command. He doesn't know why he was chasing that poor woman. Have you talked to her? Does she have anything to add?"

Lestock thought of the tangled strings he was holding, and Valerie's place somewhere in that tangle. "She's missing, sir. Valerie Chaplin is missing. We can only assume that the Vernon gang has her."

"Then find her," Perrin snapped. "Obviously, she knows something. Why are you wasting time? Get on with it."

Lestock replaced the receiver with extreme care and restraint. *Why are you wasting time? Get on with it.* Early retirement was looking more and more appealing: a place in the country, a dog … He shut off this idle speculation and went outside to disobey a direct order.

He did not have long to wait before he spotted headlights approaching along the winding road that led past Southdown Hall. He had placed himself in a position where the hall itself was hidden by a curve in the road and a coppice. Wearing a borrowed helmet—it was a long time since he'd had one of his own—and a borrowed coat, and carrying a police-issue flashlight, he stepped out from the hedgerow and placed himself in the center of the road.

The limousine, a Bentley, skidded to a halt as he waved the light. He approached the driver's side and shone the light in the window to reveal a man in a chauffeur's cap. He moved the beam until it picked up a group of men in the two back seat.s As he shone the light on them, they turned their heads away, holding up hands to shield their eyes from the dazzle, or maybe to prevent Lestock from seeing their faces. He was in no doubt as to who they were, and how very much the newspapers would like to get a photograph of these five men together on a country road in the dark of night.

The driver wound down the window and barked out a question. "What's this all about? Why have we been stopped?"

"For your own safety, sir," Lestock said. "Are you on your way to Southdown Hall?"

"What business is that of yours?"

"Not my business at all," Lestock said affably, approaching even closer to the window, knowing that his own features were hidden behind the glare of the flashlight. He shone the light around the interior of the vehicle one more time before he spoke. "If any of these gentlemen plan to visit Major Hyde, well ..." He paused. He had their attention now.

"Well, what?"

The question came from the back seats. Four of the men were looking at him, but the fifth man kept his eyes lowered. Lestock could fill in the missing features from memory. He knew that the duke's eyes were pale and heavy-lidded and he was clean-shaven. His features, although delicate, bore a strong resemblance to those of his late brother. His silver-gray hair was a little longer than fashionable and fell into a wave across his forehead.

Lestock now shone the light intrusively. Let them think he was just an insolent local bobby too big for his boots. How was he to know that one of the passengers was a royal duke and a former king? If they overreacted, they would give themselves away. He realized that he had found a small way to jerk the chain of the man who would steal the throne.

"What's this all about?" the driver asked again.

"Robbery, up at the hall," Lestock said, keeping his eyes on the duke. "Valuable items, so I'm told, mostly jewelry and loose stones. They say the thief's been caught red-handed. My colleagues are up there making the arrest, and you gentlemen wouldn't want to get caught up in that, would you?"

The men in the back shifted uncomfortably, but the man they were protecting lifted his head. Lestock caught a glimpse of light, slightly bulbous eyes, and a mouth twisted into a sullen droop of disappointment before he lifted his chin and made an impatient, haughty gesture. No words were needed; the duke knew what was being said.

Castrol Service Station
Somewhere in Surrey
The Reverend Martin McAlhany

The first wave of euphoria was retreating, taking with it the separation of mind from body that prevented McAlhany from feeling pain as it was being inflicted. The pain he was now feeling would not have mattered at all if he had succeeded in what he tried to do, but he had failed, and he was left standing outside the locked doors of the petrol station, wondering how to get inside.

He was not the unthinking, irrational man he used to be. It helped to have the psychiatrist's diagnosis and to know that he was not a madman doomed to fight at the drop of a hat. The personal enemy he held within himself had a name—intermittent explosive anger disorder—and calling that enemy by its name allowed him to start controlling it. Even at the height of this most recent conflict, while he was kicking and punching his way to freedom, he had not lost control of himself. Tonight he had harnessed the power of his disorder, but at the same time, he had kept his focus on the motorcycle.

Unfortunately, the past six years since he had left the army had weakened him physically, and he had soon realized that taking the motorcycle was not going to be possible. Was the key in the ignition? Was there petrol in the tank? Would the engine even start? He knew that he could still summon the sheer lunatic will to fight with no end in sight, but therapy had given him the common sense to see that fighting was not his only option. If he could not fight his way to the motorcycle, he would have to run, and so he turned his back on the fight and ran out through the doors, across the lit forecourt, and into the darkness beyond.

As he crouched in a ditch and watched the activity at the service station, he hoped that Valerie would understand his choice. He did not want her to think him a coward. He had promised to save her, and he would, but he would need time to catch his breath and come up with a far better plan.

He had expected to be followed, but a piercing whistle from the garage drew Vernon's followers back inside. Within minutes, a limousine pulled out onto the road and sped away into the darkness. Moments later, the other limousine pulled out. With the lights in the forecourt extinguished and the doors closed, McAlhany was suddenly alone in the dark.

He walked back across the road and tried the doors and windows of the service station. The moon offered him only intermittent assistance, occasionally emerging from behind the clouds and giving him enough light to see sturdy locks and barred windows, and then retreating and plunging him back into darkness. In one brief moment of illumination, he discovered a door held closed by a padlock. The padlock was sturdy, but it was his only hope. He groped in the darkness for a rock, and finally his fingers closed over something that was not a rock, something better, a heavy metal rod.

He was not sure what he held, but it had weight, and that was all that mattered. He waited for the moon to reappear, and as its light caught the gleam of the padlock, he took aim, striking the lock again and again and continuing to strike blindly as the moon went behind a cloud.

He was not sure which would be first to surrender, the padlock or the door itself. It made no difference. One way or another, he was going to find a way into the building. Alone in the darkness, he rained blows on the door until he heard the wood beginning to splinter.

He was somewhere else now. He was not the Reverend Martin McAlhany, vicar of Redbridge Parish Church. He was Captain "Mad Mac" McAlhany, two days out from the Normandy landings and pinned down by German gunfire in the village of Villers-Bocage. His men needed to find cover, and a locked door stood between his unit and the temporary safety of a stone farmhouse. Why had the farmer locked the door? Was he a fool? Didn't he know what was going to happen to his house, his farm, and his village? The battle was not over; it had hardly begun. Mad Mac welcomed his misplaced rage at the hapless French farmer who had locked his door. He translated the rage into a frenzy of kicks and curses and remained utterly oblivious of enemy gunfire as he battered down the farmer's door and led his men to a defensible position.

When he had used his army-issue boots to kick down the Frenchman's door, McAlhany had felt no pain, and his actions had won him a medal. Now, as he used his soft leather dress shoes to batter the door of an English service station, he thought that he had probably won himself a broken toe. Without the anesthesia of rage, his foot throbbed, and he winced as he stepped through the broken doorframe.

He turned on the lights in the service bay. No point in sneaking around now—he'd already kicked and cursed loudly enough to awaken the dead, and no one had come to investigate. The motorcycle was a Norton, with glossy black paint and shining chromium accessories. The keys hung temptingly on the wall, and McAlhany was already buttoning his jacket and looking for a crash helmet when he saw what lay on the ground beside the motorcycle—the engine! Whoever was repairing this motorcycle was not finished. Tools were spread around as if the mechanic had departed in a hurry. Maybe he had. Maybe the arrival of the Vernon gang had sent him skittering for cover. For the time being, the Norton was going nowhere.

McAlhany looked around for another vehicle, but the service bay was empty. Just like the motorcycle, he was going nowhere. The residual buzz of his previous violent outburst impelled him into the manager's office, looking for a telephone, but once he had snatched up the receiver, his manic energy deserted him, leaving him momentarily unable to make a decision. He had a phone, but who should he call? He cursed under his breath. Apparently, this, too, was the result of his six years of therapy. He no longer had the ability to fight to the bitter end while barking orders and making life-and-death decisions. His undoubtedly broken toe throbbed, his heart pounded, and his whole body yearned to be on the move, and yet all he could do was stand.

"Number, please."

He stared at the telephone receiver, hearing the operator's voice as if from a great distance. What was he doing? Who did he intend to call? He set the receiver back on its cradle. He had to think. He had to tell someone what was happening.

He had left the Chaplins' house without saying a word to anyone. The sisters would know by now that he and Valerie were both missing, but they would not know why. No one else knew what had happened in the graveyard; no one else knew about Mary Carpenter. No one else knew that Valerie was on a one-way ride into the New Forest.

He summoned up a picture of Lestock's grim face. Without a doubt, he was the man who should decide what happened next. All McAlhany had to do was reach him. He stared at the telephone. It would be a simple matter to ring 999 and alert the police, but if they came, what would they do? He imagined the arrival of a squad car, the discovery of a shattered door, and the evidence that McAlhany himself had done the shattering. Identifying himself as a vicar would probably help the situation, but he had run from the Chaplins' home without his wallet, and he had been running ever since. He had no proof of anything.

He needed to speak to Lestock personally, but he had no idea how to reach him. He and his partner had not been watching the funeral at the Chaplin house; security had been in the hands of the mysterious Mrs. Gordon. He imagined she was kicking herself now. She had managed to produce a gun and terrify the television-installation crew, but she had not managed to keep Valerie from slipping out of the house. He gave himself a quick pat on the back. She had not seen Valerie leave, but he had.

He withdrew his self-congratulations. If Mrs. Gordon had been in the graveyard, perhaps Valerie would never have been kidnapped. Mrs. Gordon's gun could have solved the problem, or maybe it could have started a firefight.

Could have ... should have ... It didn't matter now. What mattered was the fact that his brain was working again, and he had moved beyond paralysis.

By now Mrs. Gordon would have called Lestock and admitted that she had failed to guard Valerie and Valerie had disappeared. He had seen the way Lestock looked at Valerie. It was obvious that, in his cold, businesslike way, he felt responsible for her. He had knowingly pushed her into an impossible position, and this was the inevitable result. Whatever special commission he held and whatever his superiors ordered, if Lestock had any honor at all or any recognition of guilt, he would surely set everything aside and look for the woman he had dragged unwillingly into his shadowy underworld.

Of course, Lestock didn't know where to look, and McAlhany did, but they couldn't both be heroes. McAlhany did not want glory, but he did want to keep his word. He had glory and he had enough medals. All he wanted now was to keep his word to Valerie. *"I won't let you down. I'll find you."*

He picked up the telephone receiver and requested directory assistance. He imagined that the Chaplin sisters would be relieved to hear his voice. The operator supplied the number and inquired whether she should ring through. McAlhany said that she should and then waited, tapping his foot impatiently, as a series of clicks told him that the operator was trying to make the connection.

He pictured the people assembled in the parlor at Churchgate Close. He had to assume that at least one of Lestock's operatives was still at the house, if not Lestock himself. Smythe seemed like a competent fellow, and Mrs. Gordon was nothing short of alarming.

He toyed with the idea of giving them incomplete information. If he told them about Minstead, they would go to Minstead and no doubt bypass the petrol station where he would be waiting impatiently for them to pick him up and make him part of the action. He wanted to be there when Lestock and a squad of police officers took down Vernon, and he wanted to see Valerie's face when she realized that he had kept his word.

The operator was on the line again. "I'm sorry, sir. The number is engaged."

Engaged! Who the hell were they talking to? Didn't they realize …? No, of course they didn't.

He remained calm. How long could a phone call last? He would try again in a minute.

CHAPTER TWENTY

Churchgate Close
Redbridge, Surrey
Olivia Chaplin

Olivia had never minded sharing a face with her twin. It didn't matter that her appearance was not unique, that someone else in the world had her eyes, her hair, even her rather stubborn chin. She and her twin shared the same taste in clothes, and the same lack of a husband, but they did not share the same personality. Gladys was practical, all money and common sense, but Olivia was softhearted.

It was softhearted Olivia who was attempting to make sense of the phone call she had received. She thought the voice belonged to an uneducated young man, maybe even a boy. He sounded nervous.

"Davie's ill. He can't come."

Olivia spoke clearly and politely in her very best telephone voice. "I beg your pardon. Would you mind repeating that?"

"He's ill. You have to tell his father."

"To whom am I speaking?"

"Me? I'm Pete, but I ain't gonna hang around. Tell him to come. Davie's real bad."

"I'm sorry, young man. I don't know anyone called Davie."

Now the caller was irritated. "The message ain't for you, lady. You have to give it to Davie's father."

"How did you get this number?"

"Davie got it. His dad gave it to him, and money for the telephone. Look, lady, I have to go. Just tell Davie's dad. I got him a blanket and some Aspro, but he's really ill and he's cold. He's in a coal shed, and that ain't the right place for him."

If the voice had belonged to an older man, Olivia would not have hesitated to hang up. She was not very familiar with drunks, but she assumed that being drunk would result in the kind of conversation she was currently having. However, given that the caller sounded so young, and so very upset, she decided to keep listening. Perhaps something would make sense eventually.

"Is Davie a friend of yours?"

"Well, no, we ain't exactly friends, but I sort of promised he could come if he could keep up, but he can't, on account of his leg."

Olivia was aware of Gladys standing beside her and listening curiously. She placed her hand over the mouthpiece.

"It's a boy who wants us to pass on a message."

"What sort of message?"

"Something about his father." Olivia shook her head. "No, that's wrong. Something about another boy's father. He says the other boy is really ill and he's in a coal shed."

"Hang up," Gladys said. "It's just children playing around."

Olivia shook her head and kept a firm grasp of the receiver. "I don't think so. He sounds very sincere." She returned her attention to the telephone. "Young man," she said, "are you sure you have the right number?"

The caller was becoming impatient. "It's the number what's wrote on the paper Davie gave me. He says it's his dad's number."

"Well," Olivia asked, "do you know his father's name?"

"No, lady. Most of us don't got no fathers."

Olivia set aside the interesting concept that the boy was one of a group of boys who had no fathers, and addressed the caller firmly. "If you don't know his name, I'm afraid I can't help you."

"Just hang on a minute," the boy said. "I got something … hold on."

In the ensuing silence, Gladys made another impatient attempt to wrest the phone from Olivia's hand, but Olivia actually slapped her hand away, something she had not done since they were small children. She had a *feeling* about this phone call. She could not describe or explain the feeling, but in a world that had suddenly descended into chaos, she felt that she had found something to hold on to. Valerie was missing; the vicar was missing; policemen were tramping all over her house; Mrs. Gordon had actually produced a gun; and Olivia and Gladys were being told nothing. Well, if she could just get the young man on the phone to speak coherently, she, too, would become a person who knew something that no one else knew.

"Just give me the phone," Gladys said through clenched teeth. "I'll send him on his way."

The boy was back. "Jeremy," he said.

Olivia's heart stood still for a moment. "Jeremy," she repeated.

"Yeah. I don't got the letter what Davie had from his dad, 'cause he lost his pack, you know, when we climbed out the window, but he got this number and some pennies, and the number says Jeremy—ask for Jeremy. Sorry, lady, I forgot about that. Look, I gotta go. I can't stay here no more. You gotta come for him."

"Where is he?"

"In the coal shed."

"And where is the blasted coal shed?" Olivia asked in exasperated impatience.

Gladys gasped. "Olivia, language!"

Olivia ignored her as she listened to the boy's voice.

"Lower Clamping. There's a cottage just outside the village. It's been bombed, and it don't look like no one lives there. He's round the back in the coal shed. Tell his dad to come by himself. Don't you go calling the police. Davie don't want no police. They'll take him back to the home, and Matron will beat the living daylights out of him. His dad has to come for him."

Olivia straightened her shoulders. "His dad is not here at the present, but I will take care of this. I will come."

The phone beeped in her ear. The boy had already hung up.

Gladys was looking at her sister in stunned disbelief. "You struck me!"

"Not hard," Olivia said impatiently.

"You swore."

"Saying 'blasted' is not really swearing," Olivia said. "Even Mother said it sometimes."

Gladys shook her head. "I don't know what's come over you. Who was that on the phone?"

"A boy named Pete who wants us to come and get his friend Davie, who is very ill and is in a coal shed in Lower Clamping," Olivia said succinctly. "And we are not to call the police."

"Why not?"

"Because the boy's father is called Jeremy."

Gladys narrowed her eyes. "Does that name mean something to you?"

"That was the name of the soldier that Valerie was writing to during the war. Her mother told us about him. Don't you remember?"

Gladys's look softened. "Oh, Livvie, I'm sorry."

Olivia shook her head and fiercely repressed the memory of a day so very long ago when she had opened an envelope edged in black and knew that her life had changed forever. "This is nothing to do with Albert," she said. "Albert is in the past, but Jeremy—"

"It's not the same Jeremy."

"It could be," Olivia said, "but even if it isn't, we should do something. There's a very sick boy somewhere who needs our help."

"We should tell Mrs. Gordon."

Olivia considered the suggestion. She was not clear as to Mrs. Gordon's role in the chaos that reigned in their house. Perhaps she was a police officer, or perhaps she was some kind of special agent. No one had explained to Olivia or to Gladys exactly what was happening. The past seventy-two hours had been a whirlwind of mysterious dogs, guns, police guards, and secret meetings with Valerie behind closed doors. Now Valerie was missing—they hadn't been able to keep that a secret—and so was the vicar, and they were left with only Mrs. Gordon prowling restlessly around the house.

The phone rang again. Gladys pushed past Olivia. "This time I'll talk to him," she said. "I'll get to the bottom of this."

"I already know everything I need to know," Olivia said. "I'm going to fetch the road atlas and find out how far it is to Lower Clamping, and you're not going to stop me."

Gladys ignored her and picked up the receiver. "Who is this?" she demanded.

Olivia heard the rumble of a masculine voice and Gladys's surprised response. "Oh, vicar, we were worried about you."

The voice rumbled impatiently, and Gladys set the receiver aside and called out for Mrs. Gordon.

Within moments, Mrs. Gordon had picked up the phone, listened to the masculine voice, and then turned and dismissed Olivia and Gladys from their own living room, asking them to wait in the kitchen while she made some important phone calls.

Still thinking of the harsh words she'd spoken to Gladys, Olivia followed her sister to the kitchen and waited while Gladys closed the kitchen door. She was surprised to see that her sister was still really angry.

"I've had enough of this," Gladys said.

"I'm sorry," Olivia said. "I shouldn't have sworn."

Gladys's lips were set in a straight, angry line. "I'm not angry with you, Olivia. I'm angry with all these people coming in and out of our house as though they owned the place. I'm tired of making cups of tea for people who don't even say thank you and who shut us out of our own parlor. And ..."

Olivia held her breath as she saw Gladys struggling to control herself. "And what?" she asked.

"And they took the dog. Didn't even give me a chance to say goodbye. I was going to send the recipe with him for the broth and instruct them to tell the owner not to give him any more whale meat."

Olivia could see tears forming in her sister's eyes. Gladys's voice was rough with suppressed sobs. "What's happening, Livvie? Where's Valerie?"

"I don't know."

Gladys leaned back against the kitchen counter, carelessly rattling the pile of unwashed teacups. "Valerie's mother talked about Jeremy," she said.

Olivia nodded. "Yes, she did, but only for a little while. She seemed proud that Valerie had a boyfriend, and she said he was very polite, but I'm not sure she ever met him."

Gladys's eyes hardened. "And then she stopped talking about him, and for a while we didn't see Valerie. I sometimes wondered ... well, you know what I mean, but I didn't want to say anything. I didn't want to suggest that Valerie was not a nice girl."

Olivia felt a flush rising in her cheeks. She and Gladys had always been close, but there had been a period when Albert had come between them. It hadn't lasted. It couldn't. The war in the trenches had stolen the future from a generation of young women; Olivia was just one of a number.

"Nice girls make mistakes," Olivia said.

Gladys looked at the closed door. "She can't shut me out of

my own parlor. I won't have it. I'm going to get the map."

When they entered the parlor, Mrs. Gordon was just replacing the telephone receiver. She seemed excited.

"Good news," she said. "We've heard from the vicar, and we know where Valerie is."

Olivia and Gladys spoke in unison. "Where?"

"I'm not at liberty to say."

"Then what are you at liberty to say?" Gladys said sharply, and Olivia felt proud of her sister. Mrs. Gordon was a formidable woman, and Olivia would have hesitated to challenge her.

Gladys was standing on tiptoe, making herself as tall as possible. "Are you at liberty to say what has happened to the dog?"

"The dog?" Mrs. Gordon was puzzled and impatient. "Why are you asking me about the dog?"

"Because I'm trying to find a question, any question, that you would be willing to answer," Gladys said. "I know you won't tell me where Valerie is, so at least tell me where the dog is."

Mrs. Gordon shook her head. "I don't know precisely. He's been returned to his owner, and you have no need to worry about him."

"And Valerie? Should we worry about Valerie?"

Mrs. Gordon walked past Gladys and took her coat from the hallstand. As she shrugged it on, she looked down at Gladys and smiled. Olivia studied the suddenly smiling face and saw that beneath the professional exterior, Mrs. Gordon was not an unkind person. With so many questions unanswered, the smile was out of place, but it was intended to be comforting.

Olivia took Gladys's arm. "I don't think Mrs. Gordon can tell us anything else," she said, "because she doesn't know anything else."

Mrs. Gordon fumbled with the buttons on her coat, seemingly unsettled by Olivia's understanding.

"You could at least refrain from lying to us," Gladys said, still full of her newly acquired belligerence.

Mrs. Gordon nodded. "I will do that," she said.

Olivia waited, but Mrs. Gordon had nothing else to say. Her silence spoke for itself. Any reassurance would be a lie, and she had agreed not to lie. Silence was the only alternative.

Mrs. Gordon paused with her hand on the front-door knob. "I'm sorry," she said at last. "I'm leaving, but you will be quite safe.

The pursuit has moved on."

She let herself out, and Olivia waited until she had closed the door before she spoke.

"I'm going to get the road atlas."

"And I," said Gladys, "am going to get the car keys."

They looked at each other, suddenly aware of the enormity of what they planned to do and where they planned to go.

Castrol Service Station
Somewhere in Surrey
The Reverend Martin McAlhany

McAlhany carefully replaced the telephone receiver. The operator had managed to put him through to the Chaplin house on his second attempt, and he had spoken to an impatient Jane Gordon.

"What happened? Where is Valerie?"

"The Vernons have her, and they're on their way to Minstead, in the New—"

"I know where Minstead is."

"There's a woman named Mary Carpenter, who—"

"Yes, we know about her. Thank you, vicar. We'll keep you informed."

"I want to come with you."

Perhaps he could have reasoned with Lestock if he had been there, but there was no reasoning with Mrs. Gordon, who dismissed him with just a few words.

"I'm sorry, but that's not possible. We'll take it from here."

He should have slammed the receiver down hard then and there, just to let her know what he thought of her patronizing attitude. Didn't she know who he was? He wasn't just the vicar of Redbridge; he was Mad Mac, a man who had won medals for sheer lunatic bravery. He was a man to take with you, not a man to leave behind with patronizing words of thanks and a pat on the head.

He struggled to calm himself. He wanted to break something—a window, a desk, a chair, anything—but why? How would that help? His heart was racing, and he wanted to dash outside and start running. Running where?

He knew he was in danger of losing his six-year mental battle for self-control, and he could not let that happen; there was too much at stake. He lowered himself onto the old car-seat sofa and willed himself into stillness. *Think!*

After a few moments, he rose and walked out into the service bay. He stood for a moment and studied the motorcycle he had planned to steal. What was happening here? Was the mechanic taking the motorcycle apart, or was he reassembling it? He knew only one way to find out. He took a work light from a hook on the wall and knelt down beside the engine. He had no idea how he was going to do this, but somehow or other, he was going to put the Norton back together again.

Before he could even pick up a tool, a voice hissed at him from under the workbench. "Hey, you, leave that alone!"

McAlhany shone the beam of the work light into the darkness beneath the bench. It picked up the glitter of frightened eyes in a pale face.

"Come out," he said. "I'm not going to hurt you. I'm a vicar."

"No, you blooming well ain't."

McAlhany understood that the man hiding beneath the bench might well be confused by his appearance and his recent behavior, but he had little time to argue. "I'm the vicar of Redbridge," he said. "Who are you?"

"You ain't no vicar. You kicked down the door, and you fought the Vernons. I saw you. You're a blooming madman."

McAlhany sat back on his heels. "How long have you been under there?"

"I made myself scarce soon as the Vernons arrived. I saw them bring you in. What you done? What those two women done?"

"I don't have time to go into all that," McAlhany said. "Am I to assume that you're the mechanic who's been working on this bike?"

"So what if I am?"

"Will it run?"

The figure under the bench snorted. "Not like that it won't."

"Can you make it run?"

The voice was dubious but also prideful, offering a long-drawn-out "Yeah?"

"Then you'd better get started," McAlhany said. "I don't have long."

He had a feeling about the man under the bench. He'd

hidden but he hadn't run. If he was just one of Vernon's thugs, he wouldn't have needed to hide. Therefore, McAlhany assumed that he was not a thug but a professional mechanic, someone who'd been hired to fix the motorcycle.

He turned the beam of the work light onto the array of tools and selected a spanner at random. "I suppose I'll have to do it myself," he said, making a deliberately clumsy attempt to fit the random spanner over an equally random nut.

The figure under the bench scuttled forward into the light. "Don't bloody do that. Leave it alone."

McAlhany studied his new companion: young and pale, with lank hair shadowing a pinched face. He wore greasy blue overalls adorned with a Castrol R patch above one breast pocket, and his name embroidered above the other pocket.

"Well, Raymond," said McAlhany, reading the name aloud, "are you going to help me with this, or are you going to watch me strip threads and wreck the timing and probably leave a tool or two in the crankcase?"

The thought of what damage McAlhany could do sent Raymond into a fit of stuttering. "N-n-no, d-don't do that."

McAlhany set the spanner down and waited for Raymond to go from terrified to indignant. Now he spoke without a stutter. "Don't you know what that is?"

"It's the transport I need to get out of here," McAlhany said.

"It's a Norton Manx," Raymond said. "Don't you understand?"

"Enlighten me."

"It's a 1949 Daytona Racer; you can't just attack it with a spanner. It's a delicate piece of machinery."

"Is it yours?"

"No, of course not. That belongs to Mr. Derek."

"Mr. Derek?"

"Derek Vernon. If anything happened to that bike, he'd have my guts for garters."

McAlhany nodded his agreement. "I suppose he would," he said, "if he lived to find out."

Raymond's eyes widened. "You gonna do something to him?"

McAlhany avoided a direct answer. "You saw what I can do,"

he said.

"But you said you're a vicar."

"Yes, I am."

"But ..."

"But nothing, Raymond. You get this bike fixed up, and I'll give you my word that Mr. Derek Vernon will not trouble you again."

"You gonna kill him?" Raymond asked with a certain amount of relish.

McAlhany avoided a direct answer, just as he avoided thinking about the possibility that he would not catch up with the Vernons before they reached Minstead. "Can you do it?" he asked.

"Yeah, I can do it. I was almost finished when you came busting in here. I can do it, but you have to do something for me."

"What?"

"Give me a lift out of here. I ain't gonna be here when they come back."

"They ain't coming back," McAlhany said, ungrammatically but succinctly. "Now get on with it."

CHAPTER TWENTY ONE

February 16, 1952
Minstead
New Forest
Valerie Chaplin

Tentative fingers of dawn light were dappling the paths of the ancient forest and striking diamond sparks from the frozen undergrowth. Valerie, alone and silent in the rear seat of Lennie Vernon's limousine, studied the forest that bounded the road between Lymington and Minstead and remembered her previous visit to the ancient woodland in July of 1942.

On that day, nature itself had seemed to defy the dreary news from across the Channel, by putting on a display of its best possible weather. The fields had been green with crops; flowers had bloomed in the hedgerows; the sky had been an unrelenting bright blue; and the heat on the crammed bus had been almost unbearable. If it had not been for the thought of finally seeing Jeremy, Valerie would have given up on that journey and gone home. In retrospect, it would have been a wise decision, but she had not been wise then, just young and in love.

The atmosphere in the lumbering bus had not been just a stifling mix of unwashed bodies and exhaust fumes; it had also carried the unmistakable scent of a fear that Valerie understood. Young and excited as she was, she was not unaware of what was happening in her world. The Battle of Britain was being fought in the skies above her home. Young children were being evacuated from London. And last night she had sat by the radio with her parents to hear Churchill's words of defiance, vowing that Britain would fight on alone, "be the ordeal sharp or long, or both, we shall seek no terms, we shall tolerate no parley; we may show mercy—we shall ask for none."

Now, ten years later, passing through the forest with the desolation of winter all around her, Valerie wondered where she had found the courage to make that long trip to Minstead to see a man she hardly knew. She realized how shallow-minded she'd been. With Britain facing almost certain extinction at the hands of the all-conquering German Reich, she had not even considered Jeremy's pacifism as anything other than noble. As other young men had gone off to fight, she had stubbornly clung to an unreasonable admiration for his determination not to fight.

She was older now, and possibly wiser. She wondered if she had really loved Jeremy, or simply loved the idea of him, soulful and high-minded. What would have happened when the war was over? Would she have been content to raise children with such a dreamer? She remembered the soldiers who had taunted him at the bus stop and the casual way he had admitted to being a deserter. She had been full of sympathy then, but she was not sure what she felt now.

Her cheeks were still stinging from where Mary had raked her with her fingernails, and her head and hands smarted from their mutual hair pulling and slapping. She was glad she'd done the right thing—not exactly in the way Martin McAlhany had suggested, but she'd done it. Mary might well be cold and bruised and alone at the side of the road, but at least she wasn't in Lennie Vernon's car, on her way to whatever awful thing was going to happen next.

Vernon's limousine pulled in behind another black limousine already parked beside the Minstead village green. A half-dozen ponies were cropping the grass of the village green, but only a few of the cottages showed lights in their windows. The men of Minstead were foresters and graziers, not farmers. She assumed they had no need to rise early to milk the cows or whatever else it was that farmers did in the predawn hours. Even the presence of two large, luxurious limousines did not bring the villagers to their front doors or cause curtains to twitch in upstairs bedrooms.

The driver turned on the vehicle's interior lights, bathing Valerie in an orange glow, and Lennie Vernon slid back the privacy screen. He regarded her with hard, suspicious eyes.

"We did what you wanted. Your little friend's gone, but we can always find her again. It's up to you. Tell us where Paxton lives."

"I don't think he lives anywhere anymore. I think he's dead."

"Yeah, well," said Vernon, "we're not asking you what you think. We're asking you where he lives."

"I don't know. I really don't."

Vernon, his eyes suddenly blazing, reached a massive hand through the gap in the screen and caught the front of Valerie's coat.

"No more games. Where is he?"

Valerie gestured with her head toward the opposite side of the village green, where trees crowded in behind the few cottages and the forest stretched away into darkness. "There's a path through the forest."

Vernon released the front of her coat. "Get out. Show us. Start walking."

"I don't know—"

"Out! Now!"

Valerie looked through the window and saw two men climbing from the other limousine and walking purposefully toward her. She heard the click as the driver released the door lock, and she shivered as a blast of cold morning air invaded the warmth of the limousine. She stepped out onto the frost-glazed grass and noted that the air was clear. The last time she was here, the air had been thick with smoke, but the war was now over, and charcoal was no longer in demand. She wondered if the charcoal burners were still in the forest and how they were managing to live.

She waited while Vernon buttoned his overcoat. For the first time since the afternoon of the day before, she considered what she was wearing. She was still wearing the formal black dress she'd worn for the TV viewing of the king's funeral. She was also still wearing her house slippers, but at least she had her coat.

Vernon turned to the two men who had exited the other car and who bore a strong resemblance to him. "Derek, Vincent, go knock on doors. Get us a guide."

One of his sons laughed. "Come on, Dad. It ain't the bleeding jungle."

Vernon glared at him. "You think you're clever?" he asked.

"Well, no, Dad, but me and Vinnie, we don't need no guide to go into the forest. It's just trees."

"And what do you know about trees?" Vernon asked. He reached out and slapped his son's cheek, sending his offspring reeling backward. "Go get us a guide, and be nice. Don't draw no attention to yourselves."

Valerie considered that the presence of two shiny black limousines had probably already drawn attention, but she waited, shivering in the cold, while Vernon's sons went door to door.

Very few people opened their doors, and those who did just shook their heads. The chauffeur, who was built on roughly the same scale as Vernon and his sons, approached with a broad grin on his face. "You want me to try, boss? They're asking too nicely."

"No," Vernon responded, "I don't want you to bleeding well try. You ain't got no finesse. There's guns in this forest."

"Just a few hunting rifles."

"Hunting rifle can kill you," Vernon said. "We don't want to make no fuss, not if there's any chance we're outgunned." He jabbed a finger into Valerie's chest. "You, girlie, can show us the way."

"I'm not sure I remember. It was summer when I came before."

Vernon jabbed her again. "Get walking."

She took several hesitant steps onto the village green, a sea of wet grass and animal droppings, and felt muddy water squelching through her flimsy slippers. The wild ponies looked up as she passed them, and then skittered away uneasily at the arrival of the two Vernon brothers, who were accompanied by a teenage boy shivering in a thin windbreaker.

"My dad says it'll be another five quid if you keep me out here more than an hour," the boy said in a warning tone.

"Five quid for what?" Vernon asked.

"Five quid for showing us the path," said one of his sons. "We gave his father five quid already."

"Blooming heck," Vernon said. "Five quid for walking into the trees. What's in there? Bloody cannibals?"

"Forest folk," said the boy darkly.

"Forest folk," Vernon repeated mockingly. "Well, get on with it. Let's go see these forest folk."

The boy set off across the village green, trailed by the Vernon brothers and their father. Valerie hung back, momentarily forgotten, or so she assumed. She was wrong, of course. Vernon had not forgotten her.

He turned his head and gestured to her. "You, get up front where I can see you. Walk with the boy, and be quick about it. I'm bloody freezing out here." He stomped his feet and looked down at the mud squelching around his highly polished shoes. "These damned jewels better be worth it."

Jewels! Valerie stopped in her tracks and was rewarded by a shove from behind. She turned her head to see that the chauffeur was bringing up the rear.

She allowed him to prod her forward until she was walking beside the shivering boy. They entered the forest, but she barely noticed her surroundings with her mind preoccupied with what she had just heard. *Jewels!* This whole thing, this manhunt that had overturned her life, was because of some jewels. She tried to make the connection. Lestock was not a detective looking for stolen jewels; he was as special officer assigned to protect the queen and the coronation.

God in heaven! She was not someone who took the Lord's name in vain, but this was different. It was time to bring out the strongest words she knew. *God in heaven! This is about the queen's jewels.* The deaths, the kidnapping, the abuse of her father, even Jeremy's desertion and disappearance, they were all somehow connected to the queen's jewels—the Crown Jewels. Lestock was looking for the Crown Jewels. A flush of anger dispelled the morning chill. Why hadn't he told her? Didn't she deserve to know what was at stake?

"Miss! Excuse me, miss."

Valerie did not know how long the local boy had been whispering to her. She dragged her mind back from the startling information about the jewels and saw that they were deep in the forest now, with the trail narrowing in front of them.

"Are we going the right way?" she asked.

"It don't matter," the boy said. "We're being followed. I can hear them in the trees."

"What do you mean?"

"We're in the burners' territory, and they're following us."

"I don't hear anyone."

The boy glanced over his shoulder. "The men with you are making too much noise. Why are they out here dressed like that?"

"They're from London," Valerie said. "That's the way they dress."

"What about you?" the boy asked. "Why are you all dressed up?"

Valerie was well aware that her black dress and her house slippers were not ideal clothing for the forest. Of course, the last time she had come along this path, her clothes had been equally unsuitable. She had never been able to remove the charcoal smudges from her best summer dress—or from her soul.

"I was dressed for the king's funeral," she said.

The boy threw her a sharp glance. "Did you go?"

"Saw it on television."

"Television," the boy said with a note of longing in his voice. "I've heard about that."

She glanced sideways at him and noted that he was shivering and had wrapped his arms around himself. "Don't you have a proper coat?"

"Didn't have time to put it on," the boy replied. "They gave my dad five quid, and he said to hurry. He said I wouldn't be out here long enough to get cold. I don't know what the forest folk are waiting for. They don't like people in their territory. I don't know why they haven't shown themselves."

"Are they dangerous?"

The boy shrugged. "Not to me they ain't. We understand each other. I don't think they'd hurt you, miss. They don't usually mess with women. They might hurt the big blokes you're with."

Valerie's spirits lifted at the prospect. "That would be all right with me," she said.

"You been kidnapped?" the boy asked wonderingly.

"Yes," said Valerie, "I have."

"Blooming heck! I thought so. Don't you worry, miss. I'll tell the forest folk when they come."

Valerie shuddered as her foot sank into an icy puddle. She was ready to deploy one of her very few curse words when she heard a loud crash behind her. The trio of Vernons turned the air blue with their cursing and put to shame any words that Valerie had ever even heard.

She turned her head and saw the three Vernon men trapped under a net and the chauffeur sprawled on the ground. If the morning had not been so cold, and if her need to escape had not been so urgent, she could almost have enjoyed imagining herself in Sherwood Forest. She half expected Robin Hood to swing down from the trees with a feather in his cap and a merry jest on his lips.

"That's me off," said the boy. "Hope you get on all right."

"Wait," Valerie said, trying to catch his arm, but he was already gone, sprinting along the path toward civilization. In his place, a half-dozen men swarmed down from the trees. They were not wearing green, and there was nothing merry about them. They were all slightly built and wearing layers of ragged clothes. Although their faces were relatively clean, she knew who they were. The last time she'd seen them, they had been loading sacks of charcoal onto the Minstead bus.

For the moment, at least, no one was looking at her. This was her chance to escape and make her way back to the village. All she needed was a telephone. She had a story to tell. Lestock wanted her to be silent, but he had done nothing to deserve her silence. She'd been used; even her son had been used, and all for the sake of a few jewels. This was not about the safety of the queen, or about some nefarious plan by the Duke of Windsor; this was about jewels, and jewels meant only one thing—money. This, she thought, was about money and nothing else.

She stood still for a few seconds, so filled with righteous indignation that she could not even decide on a direction. Despite the heavy net entangling them, the Vernon men were putting up a violent struggle and blocking the path behind her. She would have to go around. She struck off into the forest, slipping and sliding on the ice-slicked winter leaves and grasping at bushes and small trees to keep herself upright while thorns and twiglets snagged her clothes. Eventually, she found a narrow path and moved a little faster. The path would surely lead her back to the village. What was the point of a path if it went nowhere?

Daylight was now filtering through the trees, and the way was clear ahead. The path sloped downward to a narrow stream flowing between high banks. She gasped at the sudden stab of memory. She could almost see him.

He jumped down into the stream and stooped to rinse his hands before he caught her around the waist and lifted her across the water.

Tears came now, threatening to blind her. She lifted her eyes and saw where a long-ago fire had consumed his hut. After so many years of silence, did she want to know? She slithered down the bank and stood with her feet in the icy water, wondering if she should climb out and find her answers.

Castrol Service Station
Somewhere in Surrey
The Reverend Martin McAlhany

Raymond stepped back and wiped his hands on a shop rag. "Give it a try," he said.

McAlhany straddled the Norton and rocked it forward off its stand, adjusting his legs to take the weight of the machine. For the first time, he noticed that beyond the shattered side door, night had given way to faint morning sunlight. He'd been fretting for the past two hours, wondering what was happening to Valerie, while Raymond worked with methodical patience to repair the Norton. Raymond was unmovable. He would not be hurried.

"If you want it to run, you better leave me alone to get on with it. I take my time, but I do it right."

Now that he was at last able to try the motorcycle, McAlhany wondered how he would manage to get it started. A shaft of pain shot up his leg as he set his right foot on the kick-starter, to remind him of the storm of anger that had allowed him to batter his way into the garage. *This*, he thought, *is going to hurt*. He had most definitely broken a bone in his foot, maybe more than one. Ignoring the pain, he put his weight on the starter and kicked. The Norton's engine stuttered, caught its rhythm for a moment, and then spluttered, coughed, and fell silent. McAlhany kicked again and again, each kick resulting in shafts of pain. The engine spluttered and died several more times before Raymond forcibly grabbed McAlhany's arm.

"You've flooded it. Get off. I'll have to adjust the carb."

McAlhany was reluctant to stop, but he couldn't ignore the strong odor of petrol that now surrounded the Norton. He rocked the bike back onto its stand and limped away while Raymond went back to work.

Raymond was a tidy mechanic. McAlhany had watched him impatiently for two hours, resenting the mechanic's meticulous care of his tools and the time he took to restore each tool to his toolbox when he was finished with it. He guessed that the tools were Raymond's personal possessions, and he had no intention of leaving them behind for the Vernons to find.

Although his mind was set on reaching Minstead and finding Valerie, he knew he would have to keep his word to Raymond. He couldn't leave him here to face the wrath of the Vernons, should they ever return. He hoped that this wouldn't be the case. He'd warned Mrs. Gordon and told her where the Vernons were taking Valerie, so surely someone, most probably Lestock, was already on their trail.

He had to assume that eventually the Vernons would be arrested. He didn't know the full extent of their crimes, but at the very least, they could be charged with assault for their attack on Valerie in the graveyard. McAlhany made a mental reservation on whether they could also be charged for assaulting him—he knew he was the one who had thrown the first punch.

None of this would play well with his bishop, but perhaps the bishop would never hear about it. He remembered Lestock's dire warning that he would be bound by the Official Secrets Act, and wondered if the case would ever get to open court. Perhaps the Vernons would be tried in some secret arena—a modern-day Star Chamber. What about Raymond, who only wanted to mend a motorcycle? Was he now entangled in the conspiracy that had somehow taken over the lives of Valerie and her aunts?

Raymond sat back on his heels and flapped his shop rag to dispel the petrol fumes. "Give it a minute, and then we'll try again."

McAlhany nodded. He didn't want to give it a minute. He didn't want to give it ten seconds, but he managed to harness his impatience, just as he had managed to harness his unreasoning anger. The pain in his foot was a reminder that anger had consequences.

Waiting was hard, and McAlhany filled the time by opening the main door of the service bay and checking on the forecourt and the road outside, although he did not expect to find any sign of the Vernons. They would not be back for hours, if at all. The road was deserted of traffic, and he glimpsed a signpost in the distance.

While Raymond had been working on the bike, McAlhany had studied a map, trying to find the best route to Minstead. He thought he could do the journey in under two hours, but his promise to Raymond weighed on his conscience. If he was not a man of his word, he was nothing. He had promised to take Raymond home, and that was what he would do.

Leaving the main doors open, he returned to Raymond, who was closing his toolbox.

"Where do you live, Raymond?"

"Redbridge. Do you know it?"

Redbridge! Half an hour in the wrong direction. Perhaps he could negotiate and take Raymond to the nearest train station. Perhaps Raymond would prefer a train ride over a bone-chilling ride on the Norton.

A female voice interrupted his speculation. "Well, look at this. You didn't get far. Valerie thought you were going to be her hero, and here you are, hiding out all comfortable and cozy."

McAlhany knew the voice. Mary Carpenter was the last person on earth he wanted to see, but there she was. She stepped carefully through the splintered remains of the side door and stood with her hands on her hips, her face sour with disapproval.

Raymond looked up at her and seemed to draw the most obvious conclusion: this small, unprepossessing woman was no threat and was probably in need of help. Mary was looking especially vulnerable with her hair standing on end and her lips blue with cold. McAlhany noticed that she still bore the marks of combat where Valerie's fingernails had raked down her cheeks. He felt no sympathy. Mary had started the fight, and she'd certainly given as good as she'd received in the way of damage.

Raymond abandoned his toolbox and approached Mary as a passerby might approach a stray kitten—a kitten whose claws could do no harm. Although Mary had been in the garage earlier in the night, it seemed that Raymond didn't recognize her. McAlhany suspected that Raymond had been hiding under the bench long before Mary had arrived, probably with his eyes closed.

"What's the matter, miss?" Raymond asked. "Has something happened to you?"

"Oh, yes," Mary said vehemently, "something's happened to me." She kept her eyes on McAlhany, not even looking at Raymond. "I've been thrown out of a car in the middle of the road, and I've walked for miles in the dark."

"Oh dear," Raymond said.

"Oh dear?" Mary repeated. "Is that all you can say?"

. "My friend here thinks you have something to complain about," McAlhany said, " but I don't. I think you're damned lucky to be alive. How did you get away?"

"I told you," Mary said truculently, "I didn't get away. I was thrown out. Dumped by the side of the road because your precious Valerie didn't want me in the car any longer. She said she could manage without me. She'd tell them whatever they needed, and she didn't care what they did to me."

McAlhany eyed her suspiciously. "Are you sure those were her exact words?"

"Of course they were. She said to get rid of me, and they threw me out. I'm lucky I didn't die of cold. It will serve her right if her wretched child—"

Mary stopped abruptly.

"If her wretched child does what?" McAlhany asked.

"You don't need to know about that," Mary replied.

"Oh, yes, I do. I know about her baby, Mary."

"He's not a baby; he's a boy of ten."

"What have you done to him?"

"She knows," Mary said. "I told her what I've done, but she's in the car with the Vernons. She can't do anything about it."

"Tell me. Let me do something."

"Why should I?"

McAlhany felt the familiar buzz of rising temper. *Not now. Please, not now!*

"You can try the bike again now," Raymond said.

His interruption gave McAlhany an opportunity to compose himself and suppress his anger.

"See if it will start," Raymond urged.

McAlhany turned from Mary and once again straddled the bike. He was about to try the kick-starter when Raymond spoke softly in his ear. "What are you going to do about that woman? There's something wrong with her, isn't there?"

"You could say that."

"But we can't leave her here," Raymond insisted. "She should be in a hospital."

"She should be in a lunatic asylum," McAlhany said.

"Poor boy," Mary taunted from across the service bay. "Poor little boy. Such a cold night, and no one knows where he is, except maybe …" She paused, her head on one side in a jarring attempt at cuteness. "Maybe … I don't know … maybe Valerie's old aunts. Maybe they know where he is."

McAlhany kept his voice even. "Why would they know,

Mary?"

"Because maybe he telephoned them. If he knows how to use a telephone, and if he's not too sick or too cold to even try. It's a cold night, vicar. I should know. I was thrown out and left to die."

"You were thrown out to save your life," McAlhany said, with sudden understanding of what Valerie must have done. "What happens next is up to you. Tell me what you know about Valerie's son, and I'll help you get away from here."

"Help me?" Mary said. "You can't even help yourself, stuck here and doing nothing to save your precious Valerie." She smiled maliciously. "Her men always let her down, don't they? First her demon-possessed father, then Paxton, who was nothing but a coward, and then you. You don't get to be a hero, and I don't need rescuing. Go ahead. Ride off on your stupid motorcycle. You won't be in time."

Lestock is on his way. He'll be in time. McAlhany was tempted to say the words aloud, but he chose to be silent.

Raymond hovered, holding two crash helmets. "What should we do with her?" he asked.

Mary turned from McAlhany and stood on tiptoe to challenge Raymond. "Do with me?" she repeated. "What should you do with me? You're not doing anything with me. Don't even touch me."

Raymond lifted his hands in surrender, handed a crash helmet to McAlhany, and picked up his toolbox. "She's mad," he said. "We should tell the police."

"They know where to find her," McAlhany said.

He straddled the Norton and kicked it into life. The engine roared as he twisted the throttle, and then settled down into a steady, throaty purr. Raymond climbed on behind him, holding the toolbox. McAlhany hooked his foot under the gear lever, gritting his teeth against the stab of pain. He let out the clutch and barely controlled the power of the engine as he maneuvered across the floor of the service bay and out onto the forecourt.

The motorcycle was a racing machine, but its controls were no different from those of any other motorcycle he'd ridden, which was a blessed relief. Although he had to hook his throbbing foot under the gear lever to achieve first gear, after that, shifting through the gears meant pressing down—one up, three down, standard for any British motorcycle and far less painful.

After only a few minutes on the road, he found his hands and feet going numb. The helmet provided him with a face shield, but the motorcycle had not even a vestige of a windshield, and his hand received the full force of the icy wind.

He could barely maintain his grip on the handlebars or twist the clutch and throttle as his damaged foot worked the gear changes intended to take them smoothly around the curves in the country road. With each juddering gear change and wobbly corner, he felt Raymond tighten his grip, leaning in to help with balance and so pressing the sharp corners of the toolbox into the small of his back.

He concentrated on speed. Slowing down would barely reduce the icy blast of their passage through the frosty morning, but speed would bring them sooner to Raymond's house, where he would have to borrow gloves and a coat. He could not imagine riding to Minstead this way, but he was damned well going to try.

It was absurd, of course, to think that he could make any difference to what was happening in the forest. Hours had passed since the Vernons had driven Valerie away. She would be there by now, and he could only hope that Lestock was close behind. It was irrational to think that he could make any difference.

He clung to the handlebars, looking for that edge of anger that would make him forget his broken foot and his frustrated desire to be a hero. The anger didn't come, and he realized that without a focus, it couldn't come. There was no problem out here on this bleak, cold morning that could be solved by attacking anyone or anything with his fists, and each painful gear change reminded him that anger was the way to pain.

They were approaching Redbridge now, and the world was coming to life around them. People waited for an early-morning bus. A cyclist emerged from a side street and narrowly missed colliding with them. A newsagent arranged the morning papers on the rack outside his store, and at the side of the road, two women—

McAlhany stood on the brake, sending the Norton into a dramatic skid, which Raymond greeted with an equally dramatic yell of surprise. McAlhany himself was not surprised. Perhaps Mary's words about the two old aunts had been circling in his mind, and that was why he knew them immediately.

Olivia and Gladys Chaplin, in their tweed coats and matching hats, stood at the side of the road beside a prewar Hillman car that had steam erupting from every orifice of its pale blue bonnet. McAlhany pulled off the crash helmet, and as his white hair fell across his eyes, they recognized him immediately. For once, they did not twitter or wring their hands, and their language, although still twinned, was not fractured.

"We had a phone call."

"Olivia answered, and there was someone who told her about a boy who was really ill."

"In a coal shed, behind a bombed-out house in Lower Clamping."

He heard Raymond's incredulous whisper. "A boy in a coal shed. What the heck?"

McAlhany ignored him and concentrated on the slowly emerging information. Miss Olivia had received a phone call from someone who wanted her to know that a boy called Davie was very ill and he was in a coal shed in the village of Lower Clamping.

"We have a map," Miss Gladys said, thrusting the neatly folded paper toward him, "and it's not far. We thought we'd go. We don't usually drive except to visit our brother, but we think this is important."

Raymond was whispering again. "Come on, vicar. It's bloody freezing out here. Tell them to call the police."

Miss Olivia pushed past her sister. "We can't do that." She looked at McAlhany and lowered her voice. "It's about Valerie. We think she's involved."

McAlhany frowned. The sisters had not been in the room when Lestock had forced Valerie to admit to giving birth to a baby. Nothing he had seen or heard in the house had given him the impression that the two maiden ladies knew anything about Valerie's fall from grace. He corrected himself. Maybe they wouldn't see it as a fall from grace. Maybe someone should have consulted them when Valerie was pregnant, instead of leaving it to Valerie's mother to have the baby whisked away with no word spoken.

While he was busy jumping to conclusions, he missed the next part of the explanation, but he did hear one of the sisters say the name Jeremy.

"Jeremy," he repeated.

"Yes, that was the name of a young man she knew during the war," Miss Olivia said. "It may be just a coincidence, but I don't think so." She looked at her sister and then looked back at McAlhany. "We think that … oh dear … it seems wrong to …"

"Just tell him," Miss Gladys said, "or I will."

"You do it, dear."

"We wonder if this boy, the one we're talking about, could possibly be something to do with Valerie, if Valerie maybe …"

"She did," McAlhany said, unwilling to waste time waiting for Miss Gladys to find a polite way to suggest her niece had given birth to what he thought of as a "war baby."

"There's a war on."

"Life is so short, and we may die tomorrow."

"I may never see you again."

"We can marry on my next leave."

"Your niece has a ten-year-old son," he said, "and I have reason to believe that he's in danger." He turned to Raymond. "Get your tools. Find out what the hell's wrong with that car, and get us moving."

As Raymond, complaining about being cold and wanting to go home, lifted the bonnet of the Hillman, McAlhany looked up into the winter-blue sky and nodded his approval. The plan was complicated and had been long in the making, but he was part of it. He was in the right place at the right time, and he now knew everything. He knew why Raymond had carried the toolbox even though it had dug into his back and made the bike hard to balance. He knew why Mary had said more than she'd intended. He knew why it had taken so long to repair the Norton, why he had promised Raymond a ride home, and why he had not gone immediately to Minstead. He didn't know why he'd broken his foot and why it still hurt like the devil, but that was a small matter. The big matter was solved. He had a boy to save.

CHAPTER TWENTY TWO

New Forest
Alan Lestock

Lestock had driven at unreasonable and illegal speed, but the sun was well up when he arrived in Minstead. The people of Minstead were also up and about, wrapped in winter coats. Their breath condensed in the chill air as they crowded around a boy in a windbreaker who spoke agitatedly and waved his arms extravagantly.

Lestock could see why the villagers were out of their houses and why the wild ponies had retreated to the edge of the forest. The village green was crowded with vehicles, and the morning air crackled with energy. Two black limousines, the type of vehicles that would never normally be seen in Minstead, stood at the edge of the road, along with a half-dozen police cars, a couple of horse boxes, two Land Rovers, and several men on horseback.

He was shocked to see a Wolseley similar to the one he himself was driving parked alongside the other vehicles. Jane Gordon was here already. What had she done to secure the safety of the Chaplin sisters before she had left them alone? Lestock was in no position to give her orders, but he was not sure she'd made a wise choice. Hyde was in custody, but the Vernons were still on the loose. Until they were rounded up, Valerie's aunts were still vulnerable. And what about Valerie herself? What was happening to her?

He slotted the Wolseley into the remaining space, and he and Smythe climbed out. Mrs. Gordon strode toward them, grim-faced. "We've lost her."

Lestock's heart sank, but Mrs. Gordon shook her head. "She's not dead. That's not what I meant. She's given us the slip."

Lestock frowned. "Why?"

Mrs. Gordon sounded irritated. "I don't know, Alan. It seems that's what she does. This is the third time she's taken off on her own, despite every warning we've given her."

"How did it happen?"

Mrs. Gordon gestured to a tweed-suited man riding a splendid black horse. "You'd better talk to the agister."

"The what?"

"Agister. I've never heard the word before, but it's a word they use in the New Forest. He's something between a magistrate and a warden, and he's the law around here. It's all quite medieval. The police are here for window dressing, but he's the only one who knows what goes on in the forest. He's going to take you in to look for her."

Lestock looked at the dense forest that crowded the edge of the village green. Winter had stripped the tall oaks of their leaves, and their limbs were skeletal against the pale, cold sky, but still the forest held its secrets and presented an impenetrable barrier.

The agister trotted up, dismounted from his horse, and offered Lestock a handshake. "Jonty Marshall," he said, "and I assume you are the man we've been waiting for."

Lestock returned the handshake. "Alan Lestock, Metropolitan Police."

Marshall, a confident man with the ruddy complexion of someone who spent a good deal of time outdoors, nodded and winked. "If you were truly from the Met, I wouldn't let you into my forest, Mr. Lestock. I have spoken to your agent Mrs. Gordon, and she has filled me in on a need-to-know basis. It seems there's a great deal I *don't* need to know."

Lestock nodded. "I'm afraid so."

While Marshall handed the reins of his horse to a waiting groom, Lestock took a moment to consider the response he needed to make to Jonty Marshall. He wanted the man to take him into "his" forest, where no other law enforcement officers were permitted, but he could not tell him why. On the other hand, he had no control over what they would find, and whatever they found, Marshall would see it and be forced to interpret it in his own way.

Marshall's accent was pure boarding-school English without a hint of the local Hampshire burr. He rode a handsome and obviously expensive horse, and he held an ancient position of privilege that no doubt went along with aristocratic roots. These factors, taken together, made Lestock hesitate to share details. What was Marshall's opinion of the young queen? Could he be someone who had joined in the conspiracy to return Edward, Duke of Windsor, to the throne? The uncertainty made it impossible for Lestock to trust him, and yet trust was all he had.

Lestock realized that he was glimpsing a possibly catastrophic future where rivalry for the throne would tear British life apart and set brother against brother. It would have to be stopped, and he would be the person to stop it, right here and right now. He would begin by going into the forest with Jonty Marshall and hoping to come out alive.

He gestured for Smythe to follow as they walked toward a barely discernible track marking the entrance to Marshall's New Forest kingdom.

Marshall spoke as they walked, pitching his voice loudly enough for Smythe to hear him. Lestock listened for any tone of deceit but found nothing. He trusted Smythe to do the same. They had worked together long enough that he had no need to give instructions. Smythe knew what to do. Also, Smythe had his Browning and would know when to use it.

"It's been years since I've been along this path," Marshall said. "We leave these people alone, and they leave us alone. They were here first. I have a medieval title and ancient rights, but they have history." He shrugged. "I call it history, but it's not even that; it's prehistory. There have been charcoal burners in this forest since the Stone Age. I would bet that if there was a way of measuring these things, you'd find that the people who live here now are descended from the people who were here before the Romans. All they've ever asked is a place to make charcoal, and that's all we've ever given them. I don't come in here and interfere with them. They keep their own laws." He sighed. "Today is different. They've invited us in. Seems they've inherited one of our problems." He looked at Lestock. "I should say that they've inherited one of *your* problems."

He stopped walking and stood still for a moment, giving Lestock a chance to hear voices up ahead. The voices grew louder as they continued down the path and emerged into a place where the underbrush had been cleared and a small collection of neat mud-and-wattle huts and Gypsy-like caravans clustered together beneath a canopy of ancient oaks.

Lestock grinned to see that Lennie Vernon, his two sons, and a man who was probably his driver were being held prisoner by a tribe of ragged men and women. The Londoners, whose threats and curses had echoed through the forest, now fell silent as Lestock approached.

Lestock allowed Smythe's gasp of surprise to speak for both of them. "Cor blimey! Well, they've taken care of that, haven't they?"

Lestock nodded. "I think they have. I don't think we'll be needing the Browning."

"Shame," said Smythe. "I would really like to …"

Lestock turned away from Smythe and spoke to Marshall. "I assume you won't be inviting the local police to come in here, so my associate will need help from these people in bringing their captives to the village. They are known criminals."

Marshall nodded briefly. "Understood."

"Will you ask them what happened to the girl who was with them?"

"You can ask them yourself. They're not savages. They speak English. They can even read and write."

Lestock muttered his apology and raised his voice. "Does anyone know what happened to the girl who was with them?"

A small man with unkempt silver hair stepped forward. "She went into the forest."

"Alone? You let her go alone?"

"Wasn't up to us." The man spoke with a gentle Hampshire burr to his voice, but even the soft West Country cadence couldn't hide his annoyance. "We don't tell people where to go. She weren't going to harm anything."

"Didn't you think something might harm her?"

"No bears in the forest, not these days, and no wolves neither. She'll be all right."

Lestock looked past the charcoal burner into the depths of the forest and considered the acres of woodland and heath that lay beyond what he could see. If Valerie was not found by nightfall, she'd be lost in there forever.

"We'll have to go after her," Lestock said. He turned to Marshall. "I'm sorry, but this means bringing in a search party."

Marshall looked at the local man. "What do you say, Ned? Will you allow a search party?"

Ned shook his head. "No need for that. We know where she is. Some of the women have followed her. She's at Jeremy's old hut, what's left of it."

Jeremy's old hut! The words came with a jolt, casting aside the strange magic of the forest and settling Lestock back into reality. This was it. This was the place he'd been seeking. Suddenly the elusive Jeremy Paxton was a reality.

"Take me there," he said urgently.

Marshall raised his eyebrows. "There's no one there. The lad's been gone for years."

"Gone where?"

"No one knows. They didn't ask questions."

Lestock challenged the agister's bland response. "I don't care what laws you work under or how ancient they are. People can't just go into the forest and never come out again. Surely it was up to you to find out."

"I was otherwise occupied," Marshall said, "in North Africa with Montgomery. My predecessor told me the man was a deserter. He assumed that he'd escaped through the forest and made himself scarce. The charcoal burners didn't know anything, and no one came asking for him, so it seemed best to just leave it alone. That's what he told me. It's old history now."

"Not anymore," Lestock said. "I need someone to take me to this hut."

"I'll go," Ned said. "Follow me. Are you coming, Mr. Marshall, sir?"

"Wouldn't miss it for the world," Marshall said.

Ned led them on a narrow, winding forest track that was little more than a deer path. After only a few hundred yards, Lestock caught glimpses of movement in the underbrush and saw a group of women straggling across the path. One of the women put her finger to her lips as she approached.

She spoke softly. "Why have you brought outsiders here?"

"We need to see Jeremy Paxton's hut," Lestock said firmly. "I'm on government business." He reached into his pocket for his warrant card and then thought better of it as the woman scowled at him.

"We don't have any truck with government business, and keep your voice down. There's grief here."

Ned gestured to Marshall. "Leave it be, Anna. Agister says he can come."

"Well, if he don't care about a grieving woman, then I suppose he may as well go ahead. We thought it would be kind to leave her alone for a while."

"I need to see the hut," Lestock insisted.

"It'll still be there when the woman has finished grieving," Anna insisted.

Lestock, with his mind on the possibility that he was one step closer to finding the missing jewels, dismissed Anna with a wave of his hand. "Let me through."

The women stood aside, and Lestock hurried past them, following the path downhill. His feet skidded on the frost-slicked leaves, and he stumbled as the path dropped away, revealing a fast-flowing stream, and on the opposite bank, the burned remains of a hut. Valerie Chaplin stood amid the desolation, holding something in her hand.

Lestock's heart skipped a beat as he waded into the icy water.

Little Clamping, Kent
Davie

He had ceased to be cold. He had not the strength to cough or to toss and turn for comfort on the hard, unforgiving cement floor. The weak body that he had inhabited for the past ten years was no longer a burden to him. His thoughts were separated now from the boy who lay in a cold coal shed. He was aware only of fingers clutching at the soft blanket that had become his only reality. While he held the blanket, he held the words that Pete had spoken. *"Give me the money and the number. I'll try. No promises, mate."*

No promises. That was the rule, wasn't it? No one had ever promised him a better future, not even Pete. He had no one but himself to blame for where he was now. He had believed the note and chased the dream, and this was where it ended. The soft blanket was a final mercy, but that was all it was. He knew that no one would ever come for him.

He let the blanket slip from his grasp. He would not be

missed, and drawing painful, shallow breaths in order to stay alive was no longer necessary.

Voices whispered around him. They had come for him, but what were they? He knew the alternatives: demons or angels. The voices were soft and reassuring. *Angels!* He breathed a sigh of relief. Breathed? He was still breathing! How could they come while he was still breathing? Did that mean he was still alive? He tried to look. His eyelids fluttered reluctantly, giving him a glimpse of white hair, three white-haired beings, two women and a man, but if he was not dead, these could not be angels.

The man lifted him; the women led him out into the daylight. He felt the cold morning air, saw the light of the sun. He twisted his head to look back at where he had been. The coal shed was empty. This was not a dream. His spirit had not left his body. As the white-haired man held him close to his chest, he felt the strong beat of the man's heart and felt his own heart flutter and skip and then settle into a steady rhythm.

The white-haired man spoke. "He's alive!"

New Forest
Valerie Chaplin

She watched Alan Lestock as he waded across the stream. He was smiling the first genuine, unrestrained smile she had seen from him. It transformed his face, offering a glimpse of who he might have been in some other place at some other time. It was a good face, but not the face she had hoped for; it was not the face of Martin McAlhany. She added that disappointment to her confusion of feelings. He had promised to come for her, but instead, she was faced with a smiling, apparently happy Alan Lestock.

As Lestock crossed the stream and scrambled up the bank, she realized that he was not expressing joyous relief at finding her alive. His eyes were focused on what she held in her hand, an old yellow biscuit tin, scorched by the fire that had destroyed Jeremy's hut.

He held out his hand, and she saw that it trembled. His words were a desperate stuttering confusion of questions and demands. "Where did you …? Where was …? Have you opened …? Give it to me!"

She was in no doubt of the urgency of his final command. She hesitated for only a moment, wondering why he would want this battered old object she had found in the ashes, but her hesitation was met with a repeated command.

"Give it to me!"

She handed it to him, and he took it with something approaching reverence, his fingers brushing at the smudged lid until a few faint words emerged: *Bath Oliver Biscuits.*

"Have you opened it?" he asked.

She shook her head. Why would she have opened it? What could possibly be inside except for stale biscuits? She had found it by raking her feet, in their cold, wet slippers, through the ashes in search of something more important. Alone in the hut where she had last seen Jeremy, she had looked for only one thing—bones. Her mind recoiled at the idea of uncovering a burned body, but it was necessary, and it would not be the first that she had seen. On the day that her home on Lambs Farm Road had exploded, the very same day that she had first seen Jeremy Paxton, she had also seen burned bodies in all their horror.

She was prepared to face the horror if it meant she would finally know what had happened to her lover. If he had died here in a fire, she would understand his silence, and she could forgive him for everything that had happened since. However, she had found no bones, only shotgun pellets, a few shards of metal from domestic objects, and the tin that Lestock was now attempting to open.

"Damn." The joy had gone from his face, replaced with frustration. The heat of the fire had apparently welded the lid to the tin. Lestock's fingers scrabbled unsuccessfully at the lid, and then he turned to kicking through the ashes.

Valerie tried to get his attention. "Alan, I have to know what's happening. Mary told me that my son is in danger."

He picked something from the ashes, looked at it for a moment, and then pocketed it. "I don't know anything about that," he said abstractedly.

She was angry now. "I have to get back home. What if he calls? Alan, listen to me."

He pocketed several more items before he found a shard of metal and tried to insert it under the rim of the lid. He did not even look up when he spoke. "Go back the way you came. Smythe is there, and Mrs. Gordon. They may know something."

Valerie tried to stamp her foot, a pointless exercise in wet slippers on soft ashes, and resorted instead to taking hold of the tin. "Alan, listen to me. I need answers."

He snatched the tin back. "And I need to know what's in here," he said.

She stepped back, recognizing that at this moment, Alan Lestock was devoid of any humane feeling. He was unable to act on anything she said or respond to any need other than his need to open the biscuit tin.

Lennie Vernon's words echoed in her ears. *These damned jewels better be worth it.*" So this was it. This was all about jewels, inanimate objects that were worth nothing when set against the price of a human life.

Lestock set the tin on the ground and squatted beside it, working at the rim with the metal shard he'd found. Valerie stepped away. She would have to find her own way out of the forest. Whatever was in that tin would not answer the question that had begun to haunt her—what had happened to Jeremy?

In the meantime, she had other questions that could be answered but not, apparently, by Lestock. She would do this on her own. She would find Martin McAlhany and Mary Carpenter, and she would find her son.

As she approached the stream and prepared to cross, she saw figures running in her direction and recognized Jane Gordon and David Smythe. They were smiling, just as Lestock had been smiling, but she had learned not to trust those smiles. Lestock and his associates apparently saved their smiles for inanimate objects, such as jewels and biscuit tins, and not for their confused victims who so badly needed a kind word.

Mrs. Gordon called from the opposite bank. "Stay there, Valerie. We'll come to you."

She was still smiling, and her eyes were focused on Valerie and not on Lestock or the burned hut. Even Smythe's face was wreathed in smiles. He crossed the stream ahead of Mrs. Gordon and lifted Valerie off her feet in a bear hug.

She pounded on his chest in confusion and heard Mrs. Gordon actually laughing as she ordered Smythe to "put the poor girl down."

"Valerie," Smythe said. "I know this has been hard, and I'm sorry. Lestock couldn't tell you everything."

"He didn't tell me about the jewels," Valerie said.

Smythe raised his eyebrows. "But you know about them?"

"I do now."

"Forget about them," Smythe said. "They're not important."

"He thinks they are."

Mrs. Gordon leaned down and looked Valerie in the eye. "The jewels are vitally important to the nation, but not to you, not now. What you need to know right now is that your son has been found."

"My son?"

"Davie," Mrs. Gordon said.

"Davie," Valerie repeated. It was the first time she had ever used his name.

"Where is he?"

"He's safe. He's in the hospital. He was found by your aunts and your friend the vicar."

Valerie's world collapsed for a moment. Her aunts knew about the boy, Davie. Her aunts knew the secret she had kept for all these years. Almost as soon as her world collapsed, it expanded. The secret was no more. Davie could come home. They could be a family. The love that Gladys had lavished on the pug, she could lavish it on that poor boy. She pictured the boy, with Jeremy's eyes and hair, sleeping in the spare room, under the eaves, walking to school, maybe dog-spotting with Ranulph Witherspoon, going to Sunday school and learning from Martin McAlhany.

She was surprised how very well Martin fitted into her picture of the future. Perhaps Martin and Davie could help each other. Perhaps Martin could ...

Lestock's voice interrupted her reverie. He was holding the tin. The lid was off. "Come! Come now!"

They gathered around him as he lifted out the contents of the tin. The jar inside was cracked, the cotton wool slightly singed, but the lid of the jar was easily removed. The four great jewels tumbled out, and the air grew still, as if the forest held its breath.

Valerie could only stare. She had never seen gems of such size. "What are they?"

Lestock took a deep breath before he spoke. "They are the

jewels of the Imperial State Crown. The queen's future is secure .

He separated the jewels one at a time, and Valerie's resentment of them and the way she had been used fell away. The stones, finally released into the light, seemed to speak for themselves and tell their own history, speaking of the world of the past that had created the world of the here and now.

The Black Prince's Ruby rode on King Henry V's helmet at the battle of Agincourt.

St. Edward's Sapphire went into the grave with a king and emerged on the finger of a saint.

The Stuart Sapphire had been possessed by a king whose head was separated from his body at the will of the people and had returned to adorn the head of his son.

The Cullinan Diamond had been torn from the red earth of Africa and proclaimed the largest diamond ever found, so large that it had been fractured so that it could shine in both the scepter and the crown.

Lestock replaced the lid on the biscuit tin and tucked it casually under his arm. The forest seemed to breathe again, and Lestock smiled, a real human smile.

He looked at Valerie. "I'm sorry for the problems we created for you. You can go home now."

Valerie wanted to be angry, but the anger was not there. She knew that Lestock had used her. She had been a cog in the great wheel that had turned for centuries, setting monarchs on thrones and placing crowns on their heads. Her ride on the wheel had brought her something better than a throne; it had brought a boy named Davie. How could she be angry?

Lestock was speaking again, telling her to go with Mrs. Gordon. He pulled something from his pocket and showed it to Smythe, and Smythe nodded.

"You go on ahead," Lestock said. "Smythe and I have something we need to do. Go home, Valerie, and one day soon, I will come to you and tell you what happened here. I will find Jeremy Paxton for you."

EPILOGUE

March 10, 1952

Alan Lestock stood on the front doorstep of the Chaplin house in Churchgate Close. Beside him, a pot of daffodils and primroses welcomed the spring sunshine. New life flourished around him, in the budding trees, the hopeful dandelion buds, and the chirping birds. He wondered if he had the right to come to this house and tell a story of death. Perhaps it would be kinder to leave well alone and let Valerie Chaplin and her son continue to enjoy their new life. On the other hand, he had made a promise. He said he would find Jeremy Paxton, and that was what he had done.

The Chaplin twins opened the door to him, dressed in flowered aprons, smiling their twin smiles, and speaking their fractured twin language.

"Valerie is in the kitchen—"

"—with Davie."

"He's doing so well. You would hardly know how—"

"—very ill he was."

"The vicar is with him. He comes—"

"—every day."

Miss Gladys—Lestock had learned to tell them apart—offered a coy smile and managed to speak an entire sentence without interruption.

"The vicar is very attached to Valerie. We think that one day they might make a lovely couple."

Lestock suppressed the sadness that tried to creep up on him and spoil the moment. In a house in Scotland, an irascible, ungrateful man in a wheelchair still clung to life, and Jane Gordon still kept her distance. Lestock knew what the waiting had done to him. With each day that passed, he became colder, increasingly focused—a man married to his work. Today, however, he was not Alan Lestock, sworn agent of the monarch; he was just Alan, a friend who had come to tell Valerie a truth she needed to hear.

He entered the house and was ushered into the parlor to sit and wait on one of the spindly armchairs. Miss Olivia entered with a tea tray, and Martin McAlhany entered behind her. He seemed very much at home in a pullover, undoubtedly knitted by one of the Chaplin sisters, and with his hair combed back from his face, revealing eyes that were clear and showed no sign of the smoldering fire he was learning to control.

The two men shook hands before Valerie came into the room, carrying a plate of small iced cakes. She set the plate down, and Lestock impulsively, and to his own surprise, greeted her with a kiss on the cheek. It was all he could do by way of an apology. He knew she had suffered at his hands, but he believed the ends justified the means. The Duke of Windsor had returned to France; Major Hyde was set for trial at the Old Bailey; the jewels had been returned to the royal jewelers; and the new queen was earning the trust of her people. Only one loose end remained, and he was here to take care of that.

Valerie sat on the sofa beside the vicar, and Lestock noticed that she reached for McAlhany's hand. Or perhaps it was the other way around. The details made no difference except to tell him that they would draw strength from each other to bear the burden of his news.

Martin McAlhany, a man who had been born to lead, was first to speak. "Well, what did you find? What happened to Paxton?"

Lestock cleared his throat and looked at Valerie. "When we found Paxton's hut, I asked you to go on ahead with Jane Gordon while Smythe and I stayed behind."

Valerie nodded. "That was when you promised you would tell me what happened to Jeremy. Obviously, you had seen something."

"Shotgun pellets," Lestock said. "When I raked through the ashes, I found pellets. I showed them to Smythe, and we both came to the same conclusion."

McAlhany frowned. "Murder?"

"Yes, it was murder."

"Not the weapon I would choose," McAlhany said. "Damned

difficult to get a clean kill shot."

"Everything changes if you are not alone," Lestock said. "It didn't take long to put it together."

Smythe pulled a penknife from his pocket, and Lestock followed him outside, carrying the handful of shotgun pellets. Together they surveyed the trees that crowded in around the hut and identified three trees that stood together but separate from the others. Smythe opened the penknife, studied the trees for a moment, and then began to dig in the bark. He centered his activities at about chest height on the two outside trees of the group, and soon he had acquired an additional handful of pellets.

He put the penknife back in his pocket and walked back into the undergrowth. He emerged with a length of rotted rope and held it up for Lestock's inspection.

"They shot him inside the hut and then brought him out here to finish what they'd started," Smythe said.

"Tied him to a tree," Lestock said, "and used their shotguns."

McAlhany's voice cut through Lestock's careful recitation.

"Firing squad."

Lestock nodded, glad that he would not have to continue.

Valerie looked at him with wide, puzzled eyes. "I don't understand."

"Someone's idea of justice for a deserter," McAlhany said. "Am I right?"

"A squad of local boys were home on leave on the day you went to Minstead to meet Jeremy," Lestock said.

"I saw them," Valerie said softly. "They were jeering at him. They knew he didn't belong there. I thought it was because they knew he was a non-combatant."

"Non-combatants were given uniforms for just that reason," Lestock said. "It was better to be in that uniform than in no uniform. They saw a healthy young man coming out of the forest with the charcoal burners and obviously trying to disguise himself."

"You can't know that," Valerie said.

"I can," Lestock said. "I've spoken to them. In fact, I've arrested them."

Valerie's eyes widened. "They've confessed?"

"They have now." Lestock met McAlhany's eyes. A look passed between them, and Lestock understood that the vicar was well aware of what it had taken to get a confession from a group of men who thought they had escaped scot-free.

"What will happen to them?"

"I don't have an answer for that," Lestock said. "Maybe military justice—they were in the army at the time—or maybe civilian justice. I can only assure you that they will receive justice."

Valerie was silent for a while, and Lestock allowed her that long moment to come to terms with what she now knew and to ask the most obvious question. He was not surprised when McAlhany asked the question for her. He imagined that would be the pattern for the two of them in the years ahead. McAlhany would do whatever he could to protect her until she learned not to be a victim, and until he learned that he did not always have to be her hero.

"When did he die?" McAlhany asked. "When did this mob carry out their so-called justice?"

"Immediately after Valerie left on the bus," Lestock replied. He looked at Valerie. "I can't tell you what Jeremy intended to do with the jewels, but I choose to believe he had only good intentions. He saved them from falling into the hands of a man who intended to betray Britain to Hitler. I think that is all we need to know, and all we ever need to say. As for you and as for the baby, he didn't desert you. He never knew. By the time you reached home, he was already dead."

He took a deep breath before he spoke again. He knew that his heart had grown hard over the years, and he probed for a soft place that would allow him to speak—not for the sake of Valerie, but for the sake of her son.

"Tell your boy he can be proud of his father. His unwillingness to kill did not mean he was a coward. Resisting the urge to conform took more courage than the killing itself. He didn't die as a deserter; he died as a hero."

He hesitated again and opened his heart a little more. "Some of us will never be able to speak of what we've done in service to the Crown. We will have medals we can't display, and wounds we'll never show. Jeremy Paxton is one of us now."

Author's Notes

Although Coronation is a work of fiction, not everything in this story is fictional. Here are a few facts.

The Imperial State Crown is crown is worn as the monarch leaves the Abbey on the day of the coronation and annually at the opening of parliament. In addition to a number of smaller gems and a great many diamonds, it contains four historic jewels.

The Black Prince's Ruby is, in fact not a ruby, but an irregular red spinel weighting 170 carats. It is one of the oldest treasures of the Crown Jewels. The stone is believed to have originated in the Badakhstan mines in present day Afghanistan. It came into the possession of the Black Prince, the son of Edward III of England in 1366. In 1415, Henry V wore the stone on his helmet at the Battle of Agincourt and Richard III supposedly wore it at the Battle of Bosworth. It is mentioned as being set in the crown of Henry VIII and it formed the centerpiece of the crown of Queen Victoria in 1838

St. Edward's Sapphire has the longest known history of any stone in the Crown Jewels. It is a rose cut sapphire that was thought to have been in the coronation ring of Edward the Confessor who was crowned in 1042 (a thousand years before the events of "Coronation".) The sapphire was buried with Edward at Westminster Abbey in 1066 just before the arrival of William the Conqueror. When the religiously devout King Edward was declared a saint and reinterred in 1163, the stone was taken from his finger and restored to a position among the crown jewels .

The English Civil War and the execution of King Charles I, brought about the destruction of many of the most ancient treasures of the royal regalia. The Black Prince's Ruby survived as did St. Edward's Sapphire. The Stuart Sapphire, weighing in at 105 carats, was part of the ancient Crown Jewels, or Honours, of Scotland. It did not form part of the United Kingdom's crown jewels until after the restoration when King Charles II came to the throne. It is now set in the back of the Imperial State Crown.

The Cullinan Diamond is a comparatively modern addition to the jewels. It was found in 1905 at the Premier Mine in Transvaal, South Africa and given the name of the owner of the mine, Thomas Cullinan. The rough diamond weighed 3106 carats and it remains the largest diamond ever found. It was presented to Edward VII as a gift on his sixtieth birthday. The size of the stone made it impractical for almost any purpose and it was fractured into nine pieces. The two major stones, the Cullinan I and II form part of the Imperial State Crown and the Scepter.

The Bath Oliver Biscuit Tin is not fictional. In the early days of the war when invasion by Hitler was considered a very real possibility, some of the crown jewels were hidden in a specially dug bunker just outside a sally port at Windsor Castle. The Assistant Royal Librarian used a screwdriver to remove the major jewels of the Imperial State Crown. They were wrapped in cotton wool, placed inside a glass jar, and sealed into a yellow Bath Oliver biscuit tin. **So far as I know**, they were retrieved at the end of the war but maybe not...

Here are a few additional facts for you to enjoy:

In 1936 Winston Churchill, who was not prime minister at the time, strongly opposed the abdication of King Edward VIII. He believed that Edward should have been allowed to marry Wallis Simpson and should have remained king.

Historical photos record a meeting in 1937 between Edward, now Duke of Windsor and Adolf Hitler at Wolfsgarten. Records continue to emerge revealing numerous contacts between representatives of the Duke and Duchess of Windsor and representatives of the Third Reich.

Prince Phillip, born a prince of Denmark and Greece came from a royal family that no longer held any actual power. He was distantly related to Elizabeth and to many of the crowned heads of Europe through Queen Victoria, and had four sisters who married German aristocrats. He was thought by some to be too German to become Elizabeth's prince consort. He served in the British Royal Navy and over a lifetime of service proved his loyalty to his wife and to his adopted country.

Queen Elizabeth II reigned for seventy years and died on September 8, 2022.

If you enjoyed Coronation please visit Eileen's web page www.eileenenwrighthodgetts.com to find additional books and to sign up for Eileen's newsletter.

Made in the USA
Monee, IL
29 August 2023

41815984R00144